THE
LAST
ONE
TO

FALL

**Books by Gabriella Lepore
available from Inkyard Press**

The Last One to Fall
This Is Why We Lie

Gabriella Lepore

THE
LAST
ONE
TO

FALL

ISBN-13: 978-1-335-91586-3

The Last One to Fall

Recycling programs
for this product may
not exist in your area.

For questions and comments about the quality of this book, please contact us at
CustomerService@Harlequin.com.

Inkyard Press
22 Adelaide St. West, 41st Floor
Toronto, Ontario M5H 4E3, Canada
www.InkyardPress.com

Printed in U.S.A.

For James and our wonderful adventures in life!

JESSE:
Come to Cray's Warehouse tonight.

SAVANA:
What? Why?

JESSE:
Just come. I need your help.

SAVANA

Friday, November 4

I pace across the paved square with my arms wrapped around myself. A cold wind is rolling in from the ocean and whipping at my hair.

The marina is bathed in moonlight, and streetlamps line the water's edge, bending long shadows through the quay. Wooden moorings rise from the ocean, with small yachts and fishing boats attached and moving with the tide. Everything is quiet, apart from the sloshing of water and clinking of buoys. It's too quiet. Too dark.

I shouldn't be here.

Ahead, Cray's Warehouse is tucked away from the rest of the dock. It stands stoically in a sliver of pale white. The boarded-up windows and graffitied walls give away its years of abandonment. Cray's used to be the place where all the boating equipment was stored, but an oil fire nearly burned the whole building to the ground a couple of years ago. Since then, it's been deserted.

A bunch of my senior classmates claimed it as a party spot over the summer break, and for a hot minute, it was *the* place to be. But that was back when the nights were balmy and dusky pink well into the evening. Winter is creeping closer now, and no one wants to brave the cold bite of the ocean air.

I keep walking toward the warehouse, constantly scanning the darkest corners of the marina for Jesse Melo. I don't know why he texted me, I don't know why he needs my help, and I don't know why I care.

The sudden sound of shattering glass ruptures the night and stops me in my tracks. My eyes dart to the warehouse just as a silhouette falls from a window a few stories up, arms slicing and clawing through the air.

An exhale escapes me. On instinct, I squeeze my eyes shut.

But I still hear the thump.

AUDIO FILE_MP3

Title: Case_HPD0149_911 Call

OPERATOR: 911. What's your emergency?

CALLER: I need an ambulance. My friend has fallen from a window.

OPERATOR: Okay, stay calm. Are they conscious?

CALLER: No. The window was high. Four floors up or something.

OPERATOR: What's the location? I'll send it to Dispatch right away.

CALLER: Cray's Warehouse. At the port.

OPERATOR: Okay. Stay on the line, please, miss. Try to take slow breaths.

CALLER: Yes, ma'am. I'm trying.

OPERATOR: Can I take your name?

CALLER: Savana Caruso.

OPERATOR: Thank you, Savana. Just keep taking those slow breaths. Help is on its way.

SAVANA

Saturday, November 5

A draft is leaking beneath the police station door. It feels arctic in here.

I shift in my hard seat and gaze around the sparse waiting room. The walls are painted white, with only a few posters promoting anti-crime ad campaigns and one corkboard cluttered with flyers. I've never been in this room before. The realization makes my stomach knot.

Mom reaches out and touches my hand, and I flinch.

"Is there anything you need, Savana?" she says. "Some water, or something to eat?"

I clench my chattering teeth and shake my head. "I'm fine, thanks."

She gives me a sympathetic smile, then turns toward the reception desk. "Excuse me." Her voice cuts through the stillness.

The guy at the desk looks up. His face is distorted behind the glass partition that separates him from the rest of the room. From us.

"How much longer are we going to be here?" Mom asks. "My daughter hasn't slept all night. She's traumatized, and I need to take her home."

I can see it brewing. She's gearing up for full-on mama-bear mode, ready to grab her purse and bust us out of here. There are dark circles beneath her eyes from her own lack of sleep, and her golden-brown curls—a shade lighter than mine—look out of control.

I don't think either of us has stopped reeling since my panicked call from the marina last night.

"Mom," I whisper, tugging at her woolen sleeve, "it's fine. I'm fine. They just need to ask me a couple of questions. I don't mind waiting."

I'm lying. Nothing about this is *fine*. It's the opposite of fine.

I ball my hands so tightly that my nails dig into my palms. Then I do my best to forget that I saw somebody die last night.

And I do my best to pretend that it has nothing to do with me.

PART ONE
Before

SAVANA

Saturday, July 30

There's a *tap-tap* on the door that leads outside from my ground-floor bedroom.

"Just a second!" I call, digging through a pile of clothes in search of my phone.

My room is a wood-floored sunroom just off the kitchen and living area. French doors open out onto the back deck, framing a clear view of the ocean. When Mom and I first moved here, it took me forever to convince her to let me claim this room—especially because it has a separate entrance from the veranda, leading out to the rugged stretch of coastline backing the house. But all the months of bargaining and negotiating paid off.

I pull back the long white drapes and twist the lock.

Corinne Danes presses her face to the door while she waits, drumming her fingers on the pane. Her glossy black hair is pulled into a high ponytail, and her silver hoop earrings clink against the glass.

I open the door, and she marches in.

"Okay," she breathes, clasping her hands together, "here's the cover story. I told my parents I'd be helping you with your project at your place." She makes air quotes around the words *your place.* "My mom's giving me until eleven thirty, half an hour past curfew."

I nod along with her. "An extension, good work. And not a total lie. You are kind of helping me."

"Exactly," Corinne says, raising an index finger. "Which gives me precisely three hours and twenty-two minutes to get to Cray's, party, and get home."

I quirk an eyebrow. "Party?"

She waves her hand. "Research. Same thing."

Word of the party at the abandoned warehouse in the port spread through our grade like wildfire. Under normal circumstances, an illegal party organized by Raf Lombardi would be a flat-out no from me, but tonight I'm on a mission to observe social hierarchies and the perceptions of personas for an investigative-journalism scholarship I'm applying to; and if that means I've got to join the high school masses by mindlessly partying at a prohibited warehouse, then so be it. Plus, Corinne's been on my case for months about the fact that I almost never go out, so of course she pounced on an opportunity to drag me out of my comfort zone. Senior year, and all that.

"All right, move it, lady," she says, snapping her fingers. "Time is precious."

"Okay. I'm ready." I steal one last glance at the mirror. It took a couple of online tutorials, but I think I've done a reasonably good job at covering my freckles with makeup and defrizzing my unruly light brown hair. I comb my fingers through the strands one last time before Corinne swings the door open and ushers me out into the balmy night.

The gentle *shush* of the ocean accompanies our footsteps as we skirt around my house to the driveway. My ancient lime-green Bug is parked out front, blushed by the streetlamps lining the pavement.

I slide into the driver's side, and Corinne takes her spot in the passenger seat.

"What's your curfew?" she asks, clicking her seat belt into place.

"My mom's working tonight. She gets home at around midnight."

Mom works shifts downtown at Miller's Diner, which I guess saves me having to construct elaborate sneak-out plans. Not that I didn't tell her about tonight, because I did. Okay, so I may have omitted a few minor details, like where the party would be exactly. The port is hardly the most wholesome place for her seventeen-year-old daughter to spend an evening, so I decided to forgo that information. But I told her I'd be at a party with Corinne, that I'd have my cell switched on and fully charged, and that I'd be home before her shift ended—to which she nodded distractedly and told me to have fun.

While Corinne skips through tracks on my playlist, I cruise along the quiet streets of Havelock, following the road that hugs the coastline. The promenade is decorated with string lights, and the salty evening breeze streams through the open windows and ripples my hair. Within minutes we're close enough to hear the clunk of moored boats and slap of water hitting the sheer seawall in the port. Anyone who might work here during the day has moved on now. The port's too dark and desolate for people to bother hanging around after sunset. Unless they have reason to.

I pull into the marina parking lot. There are already way more cars here than there usually are at this time of night.

"I can't believe those guys have actually pulled this off," Corinne comments as I steer into a free space and cut the engine.

Those guys being Raf Lombardi, Jesse Melo, Owen Keaton, Freddie Bass, and Tara Kowalski.

Jesse and Raf have been a duo since middle school, but this new fivesome only formed a couple of months back. As far as I can remember, Freddie and Owen started hanging out with Jesse and Raf sometime during sophomore year, when Owen's older brother started dating Raf's sister. Flash forward to this year, when Tara set her sights on Raf, and *bam*, their troop of five was formed. They claimed a cafeteria table, cut classes together, and made sure that the entire school knew that they were the elites. I've been around on several occasions where Tara has casually relayed stories of wild parties and misadventures to the girls in our grade who so desperately want to be part of her newly formed squad. In response to their requests for an invite, Tara tilts her chin and says, "Maybe," and, "Let me talk to the guys," but the way she smiles apologetically makes me think that she has zero intention of recruiting any new member to her crew.

Jesse Melo is the exception—from my standpoint, at least. He and his family live in the house next door to ours, and over the four years that I've been in the neighborhood, Jesse and I have whiled away many hours hanging out on our stoops, working our way through pints of ice cream, and talking about anything that comes to mind. Somewhere between middle school and now, Jesse went from being *that boy from school* to being my friend. My friend, who I also happen to have the tiniest crush on.

"Okay, let's do this." In the low-lit car, Corinne rests her hand on the internal door handle and turns toward me. "We're going to get busted, for sure," she says. But she still pulls the handle and steps out of the Bug.

I follow her lead. "All in the name of research," I whisper, closing the driver's-side door with a soft thump.

She smooths her fingers over her sleek ponytail, flattening any strands that have been stirred by the ocean breeze. "Yeah," she says. "That, and the fact that if we don't show, we'll probably be the only people in our grade to miss this." She grins at me, her perfectly straight teeth gleaming in the moonlight. "What does it feel like to be one of the sheep for once, Savana?"

I crinkle my nose. "Research."

She nudges me with her elbow. "Sheep. But I'm into it."

She threads her arm through mine and our shoes tap on beat as we stride covertly toward the warehouse, moths flying toward the flame. Through pools of lamplight, we navigate a path to the entrance of the boarded-up building.

After a cursory backward glance, I tug on the solid iron door, and it scrapes the concrete morosely. Suddenly, I can hear voices, music, laughter. Ghostly echoes inside the dim cavernous building. There are people everywhere and the air already smells like smoke and beer. In the dull light, I notice some familiar faces and some people I'd swear I've never seen before.

A flicker of a smile passes over Corinne's scarlet-glossed lips. "No turning back now."

I heave a sigh in response.

"I can't believe Raf has pulled this off," she says again as we venture deeper into the chasm, weaving our way through the crowd. "He should be the subject of your project." Her voice is stolen by the tremors of the sound system.

I frown at her. "What do you mean?"

She plays with the end of her ponytail. "Raf. He's basically the worst person ever, but everyone still kisses his ass. I mean, look at this." She gestures around the packed warehouse. "When Raf says there's a party, there's a party. If that isn't social deception at its finest, I don't know what is."

Corinne's arm slips from mine as she skips toward some of the drama-club crowd. I follow closely behind, chewing over her observation.

We close in on the drama group, and Corinne grabs hold of one of the guys' hands—Brett—and squeals with excitement. A few of the others swarm together to chatter, and one of the girls squeezes my arm. I notch up my smile to match their enthusiasm, but from where I'm standing, their voices are lost in the thump of the speakers. Bassy music bounces off the walls with that "hall of mirrors" trickery, everywhere and nowhere, always hiding its true origins.

My gaze travels across the cavernous ground floor.

And I see them.

Jesse, Raf, Owen, Freddie, and Tara. They're gathered around a metal fire drum, sitting on stacked crates and plywood, and all throttling beer bottles. Raf's obnoxiously muscular and sunburned arm is slung over Tara's bronzed shoulders, pinning down her long blond hair. Freddie is next to them, tall and lean, with flawless brown skin and a quick smile that inevitably makes girls and guys fall in love with him. On the other side of the fire drum, Jesse's broad shoulders are hunched and his ball cap is pulled low, and Owen's wide smile seems fixed in place, his bright white teeth in stark contrast to his deep tan, as he listens intently to the conversation among the group.

Somehow, their voices seem louder than everyone else's—or maybe it's just to me.

I watch them for a moment longer, noticing the way Owen is peeling the label on his beer bottle, his thumb constantly moving. The way Raf's arm is hooked around Tara, weighing down on her slim shoulders. Or how Freddie's eyes keep going to Jesse, as though they're having their own silent conversation that no one else can hear.

All of a sudden, Raf's stare lands on me, and I flinch. Maybe it's because his chiseled face looks hollow and eerie in the low light. Or maybe it's just the awareness that he doesn't like me and I don't like him.

I turn away, shifting my attention back to Corinne and the others.

"Who even knew there was a way to unlock this place," Corinne says above the music. Her eyes sparkle as she looks between Brett and me. "This space would be perfect for a production, right?"

"Totally," Brett agrees.

A hand brushes my back, and I stiffen.

"Sorry." A boy from my math class sidles past me as he makes his way across the dimly lit room.

On reflex, my attention wanders back to Raf and the others. They're laughing now, and whatever tension there might have been seems to have eased. But I can't shake the feeling that lingers in the pit of my stomach. The feeling that something bad is about to go down.

Jesse's gaze strays across the room and settles on me. His lips twitch with a small smile.

I summon a smile back, then break eye contact and pretend to be engrossed in whatever it is that Brett is saying.

I've wanted to study journalism since as far back as I can remember. For my project I had this idea to look at how people's behaviors and images change in social settings. So as Corinne and I blend with our friends, I grab my drink and I watch people. I watch how my classmates pose for pictures, taking and retaking the photo until they find the perfect angle. I watch how people swarm together, mostly staying in their familiar circles, but occasionally daring to stray farther afield. Everyone's different tonight—me included. We're on new ground, freed from the confines of school, and the energy is super high.

It's kind of fun, actually. I'm starting to think I should do this more often, even if my voice is shot from yelling over the noise.

By eleven thirty, groups have started to leave, but the warehouse is still alive with muffled sounds, echoing voices, and bleary-eyed faces.

Corinne and I slip out through the iron door and begin across the marina, stepping quickly. When we reach the parking lot, though, I stop in my tracks. A beastly 4x4 is parked in front of my car, blocking me in.

"Perfect," I say, gesturing to the chrome Jeep. "That's Raf's car."

Corinne groans. "Why would he park like that? Wasn't he already here when we arrived? He must have moved it."

"Yeah," I mutter. "Probably deliberately, knowing Raf." Corinne rolls her eyes, and I hand her my keys. "Wait here," I tell her. "I'll be right back."

The Bug unlocks with a cheery beep and Corinne slides into the passenger seat as I head back to the warehouse.

Inside, the music has softened and mellowed. It isn't hard to find Raf. The five have been based in their chosen spot for most of the evening, closing everyone else out. At least, that's how it's seemed from the outside.

I take a deep breath and make my way over to them.

Jesse looks at me, and he smiles. He tilts the peak of his ball cap up, trapping locks of dark brown hair beneath it.

"Hey, Savana," he says. "What's up?" His voice always sounds a little husky, like he's just woken up or something.

"Hey." Raf, too, fixes his stare on me, although his isn't quite so welcoming. Nothing about Raf is particularly welcoming, in my opinion. He and Jesse are around the same height, six foot something and broad shouldered, but where Jesse looks lean and athletic, Raf's entire image screams gym junkie. His arms are bulging beneath his fitted T-shirt, and the collar looks strained around his neck. An unlit cigarette is balanced between his lips, and he slowly moves it up and down as he watches me approach.

Creep.

"Raf." I stand before him and level his stare. "Could you move your car, please? You're blocking me in."

The cigarette moves up and down again. "Can't," he says through the corner of his mouth. "I've been drinking. I'm intoxicated." I hear the slur in his voice, and I see the smirk on his face.

Freddie and Owen swap a glance, and Tara side-eyes me as she slides onto Raf's lap. The move is a clear marking of territory, as if she genuinely thinks I'm here to steal him. I'd laugh if I wasn't so insulted. Raf and Tara have only been dating for a couple of months, and already Tara's Instagram is flooded with pictures of the two of them together, limbs and lips merged into one four-legged, four-armed entity.

"Fine," I say, holding Raf's stare. "If you give me your keys, I'll move it for you. There are plenty of free spaces."

He shakes his head. "No. Sorry. I don't let other people drive my car." He takes a lighter from his pocket and sparks up the cigarette. The end glows hot, and he exhales a stream of smoke in my direction.

"Raf," Jesse mutters. "Don't do that."

I wave the smoke away. "You're such an asshole."

Raf grins.

Around him, the others have fallen quiet. Tara watches me from her spot on his lap, ice-blond hair tumbling over her bare shoulder; Owen looks down at his sneakers; and Freddie taps his thumb against his teeth, like he's anxiously waiting for whatever will come next.

Then Jesse springs to his feet and snatches the keys that are half hanging from Raf's pocket.

There's a beat of silence, just a split second, and I'm sure I see Raf's jaw tense. "Oh, come on, man," he says to Jesse, barking out a laugh. "I was going to do it." He glances at me with an easy smile, like this was all in good fun. "I was just playing with you, Savana. You know I love ya, girl."

Raf is still calling after me as Jesse and I pace across the warehouse toward the exit.

"Sorry about that," Jesse says, keeping his voice low as we weave a path through the last of the partygoers. He stuffs his hands into his jacket pockets and stoops over a little, almost as if he's trying to shrink a foot to get down to my height. "Raf has a strange sense of humor."

I laugh quietly. "Yeah, he's hilarious."

Jesse catches my gaze and grins. "He's not so bad once you get to know him."

I bite my tongue and say nothing. I have no interest in getting to know Raf Lombardi. I'm pretty sure I've already got him figured out.

Jesse heaves open the iron door, and we duck out into the quiet port.

"I didn't expect to see you tonight, Savana." Out here his voice sounds clearer, with only the slosh of water lapping at the seawall and chains and buoys clunking with the tide. "I haven't seen you around in a while," he adds, his tone softening a little. "How've you been?"

I frown back at him. "I saw you in your driveway earlier."

"Yeah. But I meant…" A shadow of a smile crosses his face. "We haven't talked in a while, that's all. Hey, did your dad come to visit you last weekend?" he asks. "I noticed his Pacer parked outside your house."

I force a smile. "Mmm-hmm."

Mom and I only moved to the neighborhood after the divorce was finalized, so Jesse doesn't know my dad personally. But he knows my dad's classic car, and he and his sophomore brother, Cody, often stray from their side of the fence to inspect it.

"How did it go this time?" he asks.

"Oh, you know. Mostly awkward, with Mom, Dad, and I all sitting around the kitchen island talking about the weather and pretending that our new normal is perfectly normal." I shake off the memory of my parents having way-too-polite conversations about the snowfall in Glenview, Dad's new home some hundred miles north of Havelock, where he lives with his girlfriend, Natasha.

"I'm sorry," Jesse says as we stroll across the marina, stepping in and out of lamplight. "That sucks."

I shrug. "It's okay. I guess the awkwardness is so predictable that it basically *is* normal now."

He snorts. "Yeah."

We reach the parking lot and head toward the Bug. Corinne waves to us from the passenger seat as Jesse unlocks Raf's Jeep. He stops for a moment, with his hand resting on the Jeep's door frame. "Let me know if you want to hang out sometime," he says.

I pause for a second, caught off guard by the notion. We hang out occasionally, sure, but only if we happen to be in the same place at the same time. We've never actually *planned* to hang out.

He grins in a kind of cute way that crinkles a couple of the sun-blushed freckles on his tanned nose. His warm brown eyes stay on mine while he waits for a response.

I find my voice. "Okay. See you, Jesse."

"See you, Savana." He gets into Raf's Jeep, and with the door still swaying open, he steers it into an empty space.

I join Corinne in the Bug and start the engine. The rumble sounds too loud for the clandestine night.

As soon as we see Jesse jogging back toward the warehouse, Corinne extends her fingers wide. "I'm sorry, what?" She blinks at me. "Do my ears deceive me, or did Jesse Melo just ask you out?"

Heat rises to my cheeks. "Yeah, but just as friends."

Her artfully shaped eyebrows shoot up. "Oh-kay." She draws out the word. "Friends? Is that what we're calling it?"

"Yeah. We're friends." Still, my heart gives a little skip at the thought that maybe, *maybe*, there was more to his comment.

Corinne's focus stays on me as I drive out onto the street. "I don't know what to think about this," she says, drumming her finger on her lips. "Personally, I don't think you should get too involved with anyone who's that close to Raf Lombardi. Red flag. Just saying."

"I hear you," I murmur.

But I don't feel the same.

JESSE

Sunday, July 31

Long after everyone else has gone home, we stay.

Just the five of us.

I figure that's something we all have in common, that none of us ever want to go home. So we find things to do, we find places to hide, and we don't ask why.

One by one, though, they start to fall away. First Tara, then Freddie, and finally Owen, until it's just Raf and me left.

Just like it always is, the two of us still going until the bitter end.

High up in Cray's Warehouse, we jimmy open a window and sit on the ledge. Greeted by the chilled morning air, we look out over the water as the sun rises.

My eyes are foggy, maybe because there's something disorienting about being awake at this time, having survived the night to watch the new sun rise. To watch the golden glow spread across the horizon and bleed color into the darkness, reminding us that we should have left hours ago.

I'm about three hours past caring.

"Dare you to jump," Raf says, chewing on the end of a toothpick.

I breathe out a laugh.

We're shoulder to shoulder, our legs suspended over the concrete ground below.

It's a long way down.

"We're going to have a good year, me and you," he says.

"Yeah," I answer.

"We gotta apply for colleges near Havelock." His words sound thick and heavy, and he claps my shoulder. "Close to my dad, you know? With my sister away and my mom playing house with whatever-his-name-is, we need to stick around for my dad."

"Mike has got my folks," I say. "They'll look out for him." Raf's parents split last year, and my parents have made it clear whose side they're on. We have Mike over for dinner a couple of times a month, and he usually chills at our place to watch Sunday-night football. Raf still sees his mom every other weekend, but she's moved across town to live with her new boyfriend. Raf can't stand the guy, so he bails more than he shows.

"College near Havelock, though, right?" he presses.

"I don't know." I stare out at the horizon and the sun rays lancing across the gray water. "I've got to get away from this place, man. Otherwise, I'll end up like my dad." I cringe as the words leave my lips. I didn't mean for that sentence to come out in the way that it did. But the sentiment, yeah, I meant it.

Raf doesn't respond, but he looks at me in a way that makes me know that he gets it. My dad had a lot going for him at my age—top athlete, high GPA, everyone's buddy. And then it all disappeared, his passion, his goals, the stability of a steady job. It all ended up somewhere at the bottom of a whiskey bottle.

"You'll never be like that," Raf says. "We're going to make it, me and you. Don't I always tell you that?"

We've talked about this stuff since we were kids. Wasted hours imagining the lives we wanted that neither of us ever had. Dreaming about getting football scholarships and making it big.

"What?" he says. "You don't think so? What's the matter with you, J? We're the shit, me and you." He glances at me and grins. Then he sways, losing his center of gravity.

I grip his shirt and pull him upright. "Whoa." I choke out a laugh. "You almost fell."

He laughs, too.

Because we're not afraid of falling.

We're not afraid of anything.

From: Allison Duncan
To: Detective Harrison Bridge
Subject: Ref Case HPD0149

Saturday, November 5

Dear Mr. Bridge,

Please find attached the transcript of the 911 call related to the homicide case HPD0149. We have now clarified the names and addresses of all who were present at the former Cray's storage warehouse in Havelock Port last night, Friday, November 4. Security footage from the surrounding area is being subpoenaed to identify if there were any others present and unaccounted for.

Note that the emergency services call was made by a minor, Savana Caruso, whose parent, Ms. Donna Caruso, also attended the scene shortly after.

The following names have been checked and verified and are all known to be senior students at Havelock High School. Full names, including the deceased, are listed alphabetically below.

Freddie Bass
Savana Caruso
Owen Keaton
Tara Kowalski
Rafael Lombardi
Jesse Melo

Regards,
Allison Duncan
Administrative assistant at Havelock Police Department

SAVANA

Sunday, July 31

Havelock is small, and it's pretty hard to walk through town without bumping into someone you know. Particularly on a weekend, when all there is to do is hang out at the same collection of places—beach, diner, waterfront, mall, repeat. So it's never surprising to run into someone from school at Miller's Diner, where my mom works. Miller's is kind of kitsch, with rows of booth tables and Art Deco flooring. They're renowned for their hot wings and unlimited re-fills, and there are a couple of pool tables and arcade games in the back room.

I'm meeting Corinne for a debrief on last night. I'm pretty sure that in the three hours we were at Cray's, she managed to arrange a date with a girl from a neighboring school who'd heard about the warehouse party from her friend's cousin's best friend or something.

As I round the street corner, I notice Raf and Owen leaning against Miller's brick exterior. Owen's sandy-colored hair is darkened with gel and holding fast in the ocean breeze. His mouth is turned downward as he mutters to Raf. Their voices are lowered in private conversation, but they're right in front of the entrance, so I have no choice but to pass them.

Raf notices me over Owen's shoulder and suddenly plasters on a smile. But it's a crocodile smile, and it doesn't reach his eyes.

"Hello." Raf draws out the word, placing too much emphasis on the second syllable. His gaze moves over me in a way that makes me instantly uncomfortable.

I wrap my arms around myself.

Owen jumps and spins around. "Oh," he says, flushing red. "Hi, Savana. I didn't see you there." He glances at Raf and the muscles in his jaw bulge. He shakes his head, just the smallest movement directed only at Raf, but I see it. "We were just talking about last night at Cray's. Good party, huh?"

Raf's eyes come back to me. "You can thank me, if you want."

"Mmm-hmm," I say. I try to sidestep them, but Raf steps out, too, blocking my path. Then he laughs as if it was a coincidence. An accident.

Every time I step one way, he mirrors it, then he barks out more hollow, false laughter. Owen stands to one side, staring down at the pavement. He's blushing right to the tips of his ears.

I try to catch his gaze. *Come on,* I think. *Back me up here.* Owen's better than this; I know he is. Or at least he was before Raf got his claws into him. He was the guy who always had a goofy smile on his face or a joke to tell. The guy who loped through the school corridors like an overgrown puppy, held open doors, and let people cut in the lunch line ahead of him. He's not *this*.

But his focus stays trained on the pavement.

"What's up!" The sound of Freddie's voice makes us all turn.

Freddie and Tara are strolling along the sidewalk across the street, heading our way. Freddie's smiling casually, with a football tucked under his lean arm. Oblivious to the tension, he tosses the ball to Owen, and it lands in his hands with a smack.

Tara's eyes glide over me as she crosses the street toward us—toward Raf, anyway. I catch a rush of her smoky perfume as she positions herself between us.

"Hey, babe," she says to Raf, snaking her arm around his waist. Her long lashes sweep downward and her gaze slides over me again.

With Raf distracted, I take my opportunity and duck past them into Miller's. The door slams shut behind me, and I let out a shaky breath.

I grit my teeth and resist the urge to glance back, even though I can hear Raf's muffled laughter outside. He's laughing extra loudly, extra obnoxiously. He wants me to look back; it's all part of the game.

I hate that I let him get to me like this and that my hands are trembling because of him.

I hate that he's so entitled, enabled, and everyone just stands by and lets him throw his weight around. This is exactly what Corinne was talking about last night. Raf treats everybody like garbage, and yet people still want to be his friend. Even Jesse.

But I get the feeling Raf likes pushing buttons, with me, with anyone, because he gets a kick out of it and no one challenges him.

Whatever. I'm done with this. I'm done with him.

RAF:
Where you at? We're all at Miller's waiting for you.

JESSE:
I'm not coming. Got stuff to do.

RAF:
What? You better be lying.

JESSE:
I'm not.

RAF:
Nah. You better show up.

JESSE

Sunday, July 31

My sneakers hit the ground hard, sinking into the soft sand and disturbing the grains. My breath is coming out fast. Music eclipses everything. Loud thumping music that shakes my eardrums. The sun beats down on my back, and a bead of sweat rolls over my temple.

I don't know what time I got home from Cray's last night, but the sun was already up. My eyes still feel heavy, and my limbs feel like they're on fire. I can't slack off anymore, though, not with our fundraiser football game coming up next week. The charity games always get a huge turnout, and everyone's going to be watching. I can't screw this up.

I aim for one of the small fenced decks that back the whitewashed houses with their weather-beaten saltbox roofs. I keep running, dodging the driftwood that's been washed up by last night's tide.

A planked walkway snakes along the backs of the properties that fringe the bay, and my house is just ahead. I slow my pace and scrub my hands through my damp hair.

My eyes stray to Savana's house as I reach the walkway. She isn't out on their deck today, but I always look for her when I pass, just in case.

My breathing starts to steady, and I slip my headphones down around my neck. Suddenly, I'm back in the world again and the pulsing music is just a faint murmur around the edges. I can hear the ocean slapping against the shore now. A warm breeze is whistling over the water, and there are gulls crying above me.

I jog the last few yards to my house and vault the back railing.

The deck leads straight into our kitchen. It's always dark in here; I don't know why. The walls are beige, and there's an oak table in the middle with a raw bulb hanging above it, but the room never feels light. Nothing about this house feels light.

There are a couple of photos tacked to the refrigerator door, and they stare back at me like they're goading me. There's one of my brother, Cody, and me playing at a water park back when we were kids; there are a couple of family shots, all four of our grins equally strained; and there's my parents' high school prom picture, with Dad in his plastic crown and Mom wearing a puffy-looking dress and rocking the kind of smile I've never seen on her in my lifetime. I don't feel sentimental when I look at these photos. I don't feel anything.

I toss my headphones onto the kitchen counter and grab a bottle of water from the fridge. That's when I see it on the ledge. A Post-it note, half-hidden beneath the fruit bowl. It's just a name written on neon yellow paper, *Stephen Massets*, with a phone number scribbled beneath it. The handwriting is sloppy, like someone had to jot it down fast, no time to even punch the digits into their phone. It's Mom's handwriting.

Stephen Massets. I know that name.

"I need a favor."

Cody's voice makes me flinch. I push the note under the fruit bowl before turning to face him. "What kind of favor?"

"So here's the deal." His coppery hair has grown out over the past few months, and some longer strands stray onto his forehead. He shakes them away. "I did some stuff, and I don't want Mom and Dad to find out."

His shoulders are hunched. I swear, if he stood up straighter, he'd be as tall as me now. Sixteen and way more solid-looking than he was last year. He's still wiry, though. That's a trait inherited from Mom's side of the gene pool, along with his blue eyes and lopsided smile. I've got Dad's broad build and hard-to-read brown eyes that make us look guilty before we've even done anything.

I unscrew the cap on my water and take a swig.

He carries on. "I need you to tell Mom that I was hanging out with you last weekend." More hair falls onto his brow, and he shakes it away again.

I lift an eyebrow and take another swig from my bottle. "What'd you do?"

He's twitchy, but he holds my stare. "Nothing big, just stuff. But Mom and Dad are asking questions, and I don't need them on my case. So if they ask, can you tell them I was with you?"

"I was at Raf's place last weekend. Mom knows."

"All right, so I was with you and Raf."

I squint one eye. "Where were you really?"

"Hanging out with you and Raf."

We're still for a second, locked. His eyes go all pleading. Cowboys-blue, that's how my dad describes the color. A shade close to navy—just like Mom's. In football season, Dad always tells Mom she should root for the Dallas Cowboys because her eyes match their uniform. That's about as good as my dad's compliments get.

"So…yeah?" Cody prompts.

Eventually, I exhale, and he smiles because he knows I'm giving in. No questions. No answers.

This isn't the first time I've covered for Cody, and it won't be the last. I swear trouble follows this kid wherever he goes.

He swings open the refrigerator door and starts rooting through the contents. My focus shifts to the fruit bowl, where Stephen Massets's number is hidden. Something twists inside my chest.

My phone buzzes, and the sound snaps me out of whatever I was feeling. Raf's name comes up with a new message. He's going to be pissed that I didn't show up at Miller's this morning, and he's going to make sure I know it.

> Back to Cray's tonight. Us five, don't invite anyone else.

Cody jostles past me, and I tilt my phone's screen. Just another thing I don't want him to see.

Cody isn't the only one who keeps secrets. He isn't the only one who trouble follows, either.

TITLE: CASE_HPD0149_TEXT MESSAGE TRANSCRIPTS

Recovered thread from +1****797 to an unregistered number. Messages exchanged on Wednesday, November 2, 48 hours before the homicide at Cray's Warehouse.

10:20 You're using the burner?

10:21 Yeah. I don't want my conversations tracked.

10:22 I'm thinking about settling the score.

10:22 What do you mean?

10:24 You'll see.

10:26 Nothing that'll come back on me?

10:27 Not if we're careful.

10:28 Sure?

10:30 Yeah. You know me. Deny everything. Ha.

SAVANA

Friday, August 5

Tara sits in the row of bleachers in front of me, sandwiched between Anaya Burman and Maddie Allen. Their shiny hair is a color palette of hues, ranging from beige blond to jet-black, and all styled and preened to perfection.

Next to me Corinne yawns into the heel of her hand. Her gaze wanders along the rows of packed bleachers, then she glances at her watch. "What's the holdup? Come on, already."

"I think it's about to start," I say, sitting a little higher in my seat to get a better view of the field.

This particular event happens every year toward the end of summer break. A preseason fundraiser football game between Havelock and the neighboring school, Northside Academy. It's our year to host the game, and it feels like our whole school—and theirs—has come out to watch.

This year our student council voted unanimously for the ticket-sale proceeds to go toward supporting the local community garden project, which Corinne has been campaigning for after Northside elected to fund new mascot costumes last year. Corinne's been on a reduce, reuse, recycle kick ever since the vote, and I got roped into handing out campaign buttons.

She gives a half-hearted cheer as the Northside tiger mascot rushes the field.

From the row in front, Anaya gasps and swivels around to face us in a swish of silky black hair. "You're not supposed to root for the away team, Corinne."

Corinne folds her arms. "I'm an impartial spectator. I'm not rooting for anyone." Then she turns to me and adds, "Except maybe the tiger. Since I partially financed that."

"True," I agree, mustering a clap for the Northside tiger.

Anaya grimaces before returning her attention to Tara and Maddie. The trio lean in and whisper between one another.

"Of course Northside got an upgrade on their costume," Corinne says, slumping in her seat, "and all we got was *that*. What even is that?" She gestures to the field, where Brett is parading around in a seven-foot foam shark outfit. "I liked the old shark better."

I scrutinize the goofy smile on the great white's open-mouthed face. "Yeah. Considering ours is supposed to be one of the world's fiercest predators, this one looks a little too jovial."

Corinne plays with the end of her ponytail. "Way too happy. That shark wouldn't last one minute out in the wild."

Her comment sends my thoughts wandering to my journalism project. Behind the jaunty shark's harmless persona, it's still a fierce predator. Sharks don't have to rely on each other to survive. More than that, they're notorious loners. Their social relationships boil down to survival of the fittest.

The players jog onto the field, and Tara starts shushing anyone within earshot. She puts her pinkies in her mouth and whistles as Raf jogs onto the turf.

"If Raf is a social shark," I venture to Corinne, "is he still a shark without the others backing him?"

She glances at me and arches an eyebrow. "Deep," she whispers, aiming an index finger at me. "I like it."

Jesse follows Raf onto the field, bulked out with full shoulder pads and helmet.

Tara whistles again.

"We get it," Corinne groans. "You're dating Raf."

Tara glances over her shoulder at us. "That's not Raf. That's Jesse. In case you haven't noticed," she adds, tilting her chin upward and flipping her platinum hair, "they have numbers on their jerseys. Raf's is ten. My lucky number."

She folds her arms and turns back toward the field. Beside me, Corinne mimes a gag.

It's hard to remember a time when Corinne and I would go to slumber parties at Tara's house or jump rope in Anaya's backyard. But that was back in elementary school, before high school made sharks out of us all.

Down on the field Coach Carson herds the team into a circle and their heads bow as they go over last-minute strategies. I stare at the 10 stitched onto Raf's jersey beneath his inflated shoulder pads.

Corinne lowers her voice. "They all look the same in their uniform. I can't tell them apart from here."

I feel my face flush because I can. At least, my eyes keep straying to number eleven.

Jesse.

Tara cheers again. "Let's go, Freddie!" Jersey number seven

turns and waves to the stands. "Go, Owen!" Tara hollers, and number three salutes her.

Corinne rolls her eyes. "Could she make it any more obvious that she knows them?"

Tara spins around and glares at us. "I heard that."

"Oh." Corinne cringes under her stare. "Sorry."

When Tara turns away again, Corinne looks at me, and I shrug.

Despite Tara's reaction to Corinne's comment, it's pretty clear that she wants us all to know she has a personal relationship with everyone on the team. Or Raf, Jesse, Owen, and Freddie, anyway.

I can't help but bristle the tiniest bit when she calls out Jesse's name, and he waves to her in response.

"Number eleven," Corinne murmurs, nudging me. "How painfully ironic."

"Huh?" I frown back at her. "Why?" My eyes follow Jesse as he jogs across the field, with a giant *11* stitched on his back like a target.

"Because, obviously," Corinne whispers, "eleven is one higher than ten. That doesn't bode well for Raf's huge superiority complex." She snickers.

My gaze wanders back to Raf where he's stretching on the sidelines. When Tara cheers for Jesse again, Raf's attention snaps up to the stands. I see it in the sharp jerk of his head, the crick of his neck, the tension in his movements. It's a warning to Tara, like an animal giving a nip before the big attack.

I see it, and I know she catches it, too, because she sinks a little lower in her seat and falls silent, a candle snuffed out by a cold breeze. No more cheering, no more calling out names. Or at least, no more calling out names that aren't his.

JESSE

Friday, August 5

"We've got to toast this, right?" Dad pops the cork on some imitation champagne, and bubbles fizz over the neck of the bottle.

Mom shrieks with laughter and cowers away from the eruption. She hides behind Mike Lombardi as though the frothing champagne is going to burn her.

"Here's to beating Northside for the second year in a row. I'll do the honors." Dad lines up a couple of mismatched glasses on our kitchen table and starts pouring the wine, sloshing it into the cups.

My jaw clenches involuntarily. This isn't his first *toast* of the night. He was *toasting* during the charity football game and *toasting* in the school parking lot after.

"The boys are going to have a good year," Dad says, looking between Raf and me. "Senior varsity team, and on track for getting scouted." He falters and drags a calloused hand over his mouth, then he turns to me. "I wish your granddad was alive to see this, Jesse."

I clap my hand on his shoulder, and he shakes off the emotion.

His dark eyes crinkle into a smile. "You boys are going places, I'm telling you."

At my age, Dad almost went pro. Almost.

But then I came along right around the time he and Mom finished their senior year, and having a baby at eighteen screwed up all those big dreams. That's the story Mom spins, anyway.

Dad doesn't remember it like that. He says he couldn't have cut it in the major leagues, couldn't make the grade. He never blames me. At least not to my face.

But Mom, sometimes she drops these little digs, little remarks every now and then. She says, *Your dad had so much going for him before you were born.* Or, *You know I was prom queen and voted most likely to succeed. Imagine.* Or my personal favorite, *When I was seventeen, I was discovered by a modeling agency... and then I had you and the dream was all over.* Then she'll laugh, like she's kidding.

But I know she's never kidding.

I smile stiffly as Mike slaps my back in congratulations. He moves on to Raf, gripping his shoulders hard and shaking him. "My kid," Mike says, affectionately grabbing Raf's cheeks. "Star of the football team, eh?"

Raf doesn't look much like a *kid* anymore. He's ripped, just like his dad. They're both six feet tall, with buzz cuts and square jaws, and bulked out from hard-core weight training. I work out, sure, but the Lombardis work *out*.

"Look at you boys," Mike says. "You've done good."

Raf grins at me, and I mirror it.

We used to dream about playing varsity as seniors. We'd lie on the planked jetty outside my house with our fingers skimming the water, two scrawny kids just wasting time wishing we were grown.

"I'll tell you something." Mike carries on. "It's moments like this that have helped me through a tough year."

"Oh, Mike," Mom says, touching his arm. "Of course."

"We're here for you, pal," Dad adds, raising his glass.

Mike runs his knuckles over his mouth. "One big family. I've needed that. After my divorce, and all Lisa's problems..."

I catch Mom's eye and she touches her hand to her heart.

Raf's older sister, Lisa, moved to Boston last year. I don't know much about her, other than she used to date Owen's brother. Freddie and Owen used to have a thing for her, too, along with most of the guys in our grade. She went through some stuff a while back, though, and she's getting therapy after coming out of an abusive relationship. She hasn't been back to Havelock in a while, and Mike is pretty cut up about it. Sometimes I wonder if that's why Raf feels like he's got to stick around, like it's his job to keep Mike happy now that everyone else has gone.

Raf's chest puffs out. "Yeah, well. We're going to have a good year. Jesse and me, we carried the team last season. Coach loves us, doesn't he, J?"

"Yeah." I knock back some of the drink as my mind wanders to a conversation I had with Coach Carson before summer break. He called me into his office, this cramped sports storage closet next to the gym. I sat on a plastic chair, and he looked me dead in the eyes. *I think we need to have a conversion,*

Jesse, he said. *You can be honest with me about what happened. About what you've been doing.*

I grit my teeth and bury the memory. I keep smiling.

"What a year." Mike thumps his fist against his chest, right below where his gold chain rests. "And us, we really are like family now, eh? These boys are as good as brothers. This year has made me realize that there ain't nothing more important than family." I swear he's tearing up; his green-brown eyes have turned red and glassy.

I feel bad for Mike sometimes. Seeing Raf's mom move on so fast after their divorce must have screwed him up pretty bad. She's got a nice little place out of town now with her new guy, while Mike is still microwaving meals-for-one in the same home they once shared.

I like Mike. He's big and loud and bulldozes his way through life, just like Raf does.

For all that front, though, I know Raf's got his issues, his insecurities. Just like I've got mine. He might act like nobody can touch him, but I know what it's like to never feel good enough. To always feel like you've got to *prove* you're good enough.

Not everyone likes Raf. Not everyone gets him like I do.

Mom comes over to me and reaches up to squeeze my shoulder. Her auburn hair is twisted into a complicated-looking knot and she's wearing makeup, like she's made a real effort to show up for our fundraiser game. "I'm so proud of you, Jesse," she says, taking a small sip of champagne.

The words knock the breath out of me.

"Are you?" I ask, because I want to hear it again.

"This time next year we'll be celebrating your college football grant. I can feel it." She clinks her glass against mine. "You'll achieve what your dad never could."

I flinch. Dad must have heard her because his grip tightens around the stem of his wineglass, strangling it. He drains the rest of the drink.

I force a smile and say, "Yeah, maybe. If the team has a good season, and we make state playoffs, I could have a shot. I mean, I've done the legwork, so I've just got to stay consistent and see it through."

"It's in the bag," Mom says, winking. Then she hugs Raf, too, like it's going to happen for both of us. Like we're both her kids.

You can be honest with me about what happened. About what you've been doing.

I set my glass down on the table. "I'll be right back," I mutter before stepping out into the hallway.

I shut the adjoining door behind me. It's dark, quiet, and I stop for a minute, just breathing slowly. I lean against the wall and listen to the sound of muffled laughter leaking out from the kitchen, slithering beneath the closed door.

Cody's footsteps thud above me as he jogs down the stairs. He swerves into the hallway, and when his eyes land on me, he clutches his shirt. "What the *hell*?" He flips the light switch, and the hallway floods with color. "Are you trying to kill me or something? What are you doing creeping around in the dark?"

I stare back at him, blinking in the new light. "I'm not creeping. I'm just standing here."

His eyes move to the kitchen door. "What's going on in there?"

I don't get a chance to answer. The adjoining door swings

open, and Raf slips out into the hallway. He's still holding his narrow champagne glass, and he knocks back what's left. Then he opens his jacket and flashes a baggie tucked into the inside pocket.

"After-party. Cray's. Freddie and Owen are on their way there."

Cody chokes out a sound. "Cray's? Since when have you been going to Cray's?"

Raf just smirks at him, then turns back to me. "Move. We gotta go."

I rub the nape of my neck. "Go without me. I'm not feel-ing it."

"I'll come," Cody says to Raf.

But Raf's only looking at me. "What?" His thick brows draw together. "What do you mean you're not feeling it? After-party, man."

"Yeah. I'm tired." It's an excuse, and he sees it, but I don't care. I've got more on my mind than burning out at Cray's.

Raf chokes out a laugh. "No." He slaps my face—light enough to let me know he's playing but hard enough to shock me. Then he grins. "Sleep when you're dead."

SAVANA

Friday, August 5

It's a warm night, muggy in the clutches of summer. I've opened the French doors leading out from my bedroom, and a light breeze is billowing the drapes. Every so often I hear laughter drifting from the Melos' house, escaping from their open windows. Mr. Lombardi is there, his voice sending tremors through our bay like the rumbles of an earthquake.

I've been at my desk for the past hour, scrolling through social media on the hunt for project fodder. My conversation with Corinne at the game struck a chord with me, and when our team won, and everyone sprang to their feet, cheering and praising the players, those guys became instant heroes. Raf became a hero.

I notice him now through the French doors. He's following Jesse out of the Melos' house. They're gilded by the dying sun as they cross the plank path.

There's something about the way they're walking so rigidly alongside one another that makes me curious. It makes me watch.

"After-party, man," Raf's saying. "How can you say no to that?"

"I said I'll come." Jesse's response carries on the breeze. "But I'm not staying late. Why do you even need me there?"

"Because you're supposed to be my wingman." Raf's voice sounds almost pleading. Almost childlike.

I watch them round the corner onto the driveway. Jesse's leading with his ball cap pulled low, and Raf's trailing behind with his hands stuffed into his jacket pockets.

I frown as they disappear out of sight. It's funny. I always thought Raf was a total alpha—and he is, in a way. But Jesse's not intimidated by him.

The way Raf acts around Jesse is different from how he acts around everyone else. Raf wouldn't give Jesse the withering stare he gave to Tara earlier at the fundraiser game or act like a major sleaze in the way that he does when Jesse isn't around to call him out on it. He doesn't test Jesse like that—his whole demeanor shifts. Maybe that's because they go back so far. Or maybe it's because Raf knows that Jesse isn't scared of him. Raf postures like the alpha, and he fools most people, but I see through it. Jesse's in control. I see it in the way Jesse often walks a step ahead. Or how when it's just the two of them, Raf betrays that he needs Jesse. That he can't do anything, or go anywhere, or be anything, without Jesse backing him.

After I hear their car pull out onto the street, I return my attention to my phone. I have a feeling it's only a matter of time before Tara's postgame photos start popping up on my feed.

A text message from my dad suddenly appears on the screen with a ping.

> Hi, sweetheart. How are you? Natasha and I were
> thinking you might like to spend some time with us
> in Glenview before the weather starts to turn. What
> do you say? Dad.

A strange knot forms in my stomach. I like Natasha—I do. She always goes above and beyond to accommodate me whenever I visit, but that doesn't stop me from feeling like an intruder in someone else's home. And it doesn't stop me from feeling guilty for leaving Mom home alone while I visit her ex-love and his new love in their fancy city apartment.

I gaze at the dimming light beyond the doors. The sunset is gently blushing the Melos' house, painting the deck golden. The sound of laughter trickles out into the evening.

It must be nice to have that uncomplicatedness. A mom and a dad, childhood sweethearts and still happily married all these years later. Two brothers who are clearly super close. I often see Jesse and Cody hanging out on the beach together, skim boarding in the shallows or somersaulting off the jetty.

I want that, sometimes.

I'm fine with just Mom and me. Really, I am. But I wonder what it's like to be them, that's all.

Heaving a sigh, I return to my phone and type out a response.

> Hi, Dad! I'm good. How are you and Natasha? Thanks
> for the offer. Maybe we can figure something out. Say
> hi to Natasha from me!

I can't say no to his suggestion, but I can't bring myself to say yes, either.

As my message is sucked into cyberspace, I toss my phone

aside and reach for my laptop instead. I'm not in the mood to like any more airbrushed Instagram photos of too-perfect lives, but I can at least make notes for my journalism piece.

Who is Raf? More importantly, who is he without Jesse?

A little while after the sun slips away completely, a cold breeze starts to whip at the drapes, tangling the thin material. I hop off my chair and pad across the room to close the doors. As I reach for the handle, something draws my attention outside. A movement in the darkness that makes me catch myself.

Easing back the drapes, I look out over the bay. Everything is dark apart from the beacons of light emitted by the houses. There's no more laughter, only the *shush* of the ocean.

Then a shadow moves near the Melos' house.

I wait for a second, keeping as still as I can.

There's someone out there, a figure standing by their house. Whoever it is, they're staring in through the window, covered by the night.

I hold my breath and wait for them to move on, but they don't.

Something about their stillness sends a shiver over me. They're *too* still. Too hidden.

And then, through the darkness, I see them slowly turn my way and look directly at me.

I quickly pull the drapes and duck out of sight, pressing myself flat against my bedroom wall. The sound of movement outside makes my breathing quicken, and a moment later a shadow passes the drapes.

Once. *Twice.*

I rush back to my desk and grab my phone. Scrolling quickly through my contacts list, I find Jesse's name.

Someone is standing outside your house, I type to him. At the back. You should tell your parents.

I wait a moment. Dots appear while he writes, and then…

What? Can you take a picture?

I edge to the door and gingerly peel back the drapes, but when my eyes search the darkness, there's no one there.

JESSE

Friday, August 5

> What? Can you take a picture?

I stare at my phone, waiting for Savana's response.

> I checked again, and it looks like they're gone. Sorry—
> overreaction!

"Are you dealing, or what?" Raf's voice echoes around Cray's cavernous ground floor, dragging my attention back to him. He's staring at Freddie, waiting for him to shuffle the deck.

"Yeah." Freddie crams a handful of chips into his mouth. "I'm doing it right now." He reaches across the overturned crate and scoops up the cards. He splits the deck, then bends each side and lets the cards fall interlaced. With a quick flick of the wrist, he deals out four hands.

While Freddie passes the cards around, I type out another message to Savana.

> Could have been one of the neighbors. Mr. McAvoy walks his dog at about this time. You okay?

"Jesse," Raf grunts, snapping his fingers. "Come on. Let's go."

I set my phone down and glance between them. All four of us seated on crates and plywood, assessing our cards, silently strategizing how to screw each other over.

Raf is opposite me, catching my eye every time a new hand is dealt. Freddie is to my left, black hair curling around his ears, jersey sleeves pushed up to the elbows. To my right, Owen is cracking with nervous energy, grinding his teeth and tapping his foot on the dusty floor.

"What you got, boys?" Raf calls, throwing down some bills.

Owen checks his cards, then scrubs his hands through his dark blond hair. His gaze jumps to me. He presses his lips together and narrows his stare as he tries to read my poker face.

I grin.

"Fold," Owen said, tossing his cards facedown on the crate.

Freddie's eyes move slowly between Raf and me.

My cards are okay—a pair of kings. Nothing special, but I like the bluff. I like the game.

While Owen looks on, crunching his way through potato chips, Freddie tosses some bills on the crate. "I'll raise you," he says to Raf and me.

Raf catches my eye and gives an almost-imperceptible nod.

I clear my throat. "Fold," I tell the others and fling my cards down on the crate.

A flicker of a smile passes over Raf's face, and I hold back a laugh. He's got nothing. I can tell when he's got a good hand, and this isn't it.

But he and Freddie keep playing, throwing more bills onto the pile. They keep pushing each other, upping the ante. They can't go on like this for much longer. Someone's going to have to break.

Freddie's wavering; he's losing confidence. He licks his lips fast. I give him a look, a nod, a gesture to say *Either show your hand or give up now.* Raf's not going to back down.

He never does.

"Fold," Freddie says after a beat, and he slaps his cards on the crate. "What'd you have?" he asks Raf.

Raf scrapes up the bills. "All your money." He looks at me and laughs.

Owen and I laugh, too, and Freddie tosses a fistful of potato chips at him. The chips scatter across the floor, casualties of a battle lost.

Freddie probably could've beaten Raf with whatever he was holding. I probably could have beaten him with my kings. But I gave Raf this one, just like how he passes the wins to me sometimes. It's not a big deal; all part of the game. Our game, anyway.

I can't keep letting him win, though. I don't know why I do it. Maybe it's because I've always felt sorry for him, because I know how hard he *tries* to win.

"Where's Tara tonight?" Freddie asks. "She was at the game, right?"

"Yeah." Raf flicks through his bills. "She wanted to hang out with the girls after."

Owen leans forward and locks his hands. "Who, Maddie and Anaya?"

"Yeah."

A toothy smile spreads on Owen's face. "Do you think Tara would hook me up with Anaya?"

Raf laughs, a rumble that rebounds in the warehouse. "You've got no chance, bro. Tara's probably already warned her to run."

Owen's lip curls. "From me?"

"Yeah, from you."

"What? Why?"

Raf raises an eyebrow, then he laughs louder.

Owen scuffs the toe of his sneaker on the floor. "Whatever. Whose turn to deal?"

"Mine." Raf scoops up the cards and starts shuffling.

My phone buzzes, and I grab it, checking for Savana's response.

But it isn't Savana. There's a new message from Freddie highlighted on the screen.

Help me take him down.

I glance at Freddie, and he raises his eyebrows. A question. Across the table, Owen's checking his phone, too.

Three against one?

I hold back a grin as I nod to Freddie. I'm already cheating. At least now I can do it fairly—distribute the wealth, and all that. I've always had Raf's back, and he's always had mine, but it won't hurt him to take a couple of losses now and then, like the rest of us all have to.

It still makes me twitchy, though, because if there's one thing I know about Raf, it's that he's not going to like it when we flip the script.

From: Allison Duncan
To: Detective Harrison Bridge
Subject: Ref Case HPD0149

Saturday, November 5

Dear Mr. Bridge,

I have attached the requested information relating to the homicide case HPD0149 at Cray's Warehouse last night, Friday, November 4. Details from the associated Lombardi case dating back to earlier this year have been disclosed from the Boston state district. At present, we have no reason to believe that these two cases are connected.

Parents of the minors present last night have now been contacted and instructed on bail. Please note that at the time of this email, Jesse Melo's parents are still unreachable. Our records are showing no contact number for Melo's mother.

Regards,
Allison Duncan
Administrative assistant at Havelock Police Department

JESSE

Saturday, August 6

I stand in my driveway for a moment, hidden in the darkness, listening to the crash of the ocean behind the houses.

It's a full moon tonight. Or I should say this morning. I probably shouldn't have stayed at Cray's for as long as I did. But when I stopped feeding into Raf's game, the night got more fun. He's pissed at me now, though. But he's more pissed at Freddie and Owen, because he knows one of them started it.

A smile tugs at my lips. He'll get over it.

I start for the front door, but it opens before I reach it.

Mom gasps when she sees me standing on the stoop. She halts in the open doorway, just staring at me with her mouth hanging open.

"Jesse," she whispers. "I—"

"Sorry I'm back so late. You shouldn't have waited up."

Then my eyes land on the luggage propped beside her. My heart thuds hard in my chest.

She doesn't need to tell me; I can see it in her eyes. Eyes that dart from left to right because she can't bring herself to look at me. Her fingers tighten around her luggage strap, and her other hand tugs at the silk scarf that's snaked around her neck.

She opens her mouth to speak, but no words pass her lips.

"Not like this," I murmur.

She shakes her head, and her eyes glisten.

I swear, my lungs feel like they're shrinking. I've been expecting this for a while. I knew it was coming; I just didn't know when.

I've noticed her rummaging through paperwork and sorting through her shit when she thinks no one's watching. Getting everything in order for this moment. Updating her passport, talking in hushed voices on her phone, and calling numbers from infomercials.

Stephen Massets. I can picture his smarmy face staring out from the TV screen. *Call me, Stephen Massets, for a quick and easy way to divide your assets.* Get the hell out of your shitty life—that's what he might as well have been saying. But *shitty life* doesn't rhyme with *Massets*.

She keeps tugging at the scarf. "I'm just... I've fallen out of love."

"With all of us?"

"Your dad and I..." She fumbles. "It's just not working anymore."

"Does he know?"

She bites her lip.

"Don't do it like this." My words are calm. Steady. Everything I'm not. "Leaving in the middle of the night is a shady way out, Mom."

"I didn't know how else to…" Her voices catches, and she trails off.

"How else to what?" I hold her stare, forcing her to look at me. "Bail?" A sound snags in my throat. "Yeah, you're right, better to do it behind our backs than to our faces."

She's silent.

"This'll break Dad."

"*He's* breaking *me*," she says, her fingers tightening around the scarf. "He's drinking again, and I can't…"

The words hit me hard.

I know it, though. I've seen his demons steadily creeping back over the past few months.

I think of my granddad. My strong, stable granddad, and how his death sent my dad into a downward spiral that took him years to come out of. I don't want to go back there.

"So that's it?" I say, gazing up at the dark sky. "You're jumping ship."

My voice must be getting louder because she glances over her shoulder toward the dim staircase inside the house. "Shh." She presses her finger to her lips. "Jesse, please. You'll wake them."

I almost laugh.

"I'll call tomorrow," she whispers. "We'll talk everything through properly."

Too many thoughts spin through my head. But I keep my voice even. "What am I supposed to tell Cody?"

"Tell him that I love him." Tears start streaming down her face, and I turn to steel. "I love you both."

Now I really do laugh. But nothing about this is funny.

"I'm sorry," she whispers. "I'm so sorry." And just like that, she's gone. Out the door. Her shoes are clicking fast along the driveway.

I follow after her, tripping over my feet.

She gets into her SUV, and I bang on the window. "Mom. Wait."

She's crying as she turns the key in the ignition. The sound of the engine twists my heart a little harder.

"Mom." My words are ragged. "Please. This isn't the way." The side window slips from my touch as the SUV rolls forward. She can hear me, though. I know she can. "Mom." My voice is getting louder, more urgent. "Don't do this to Dad and Cody, not like this. I don't want to be the one to tell them."

I run two blocks after her car, and I keep going long after the taillights disappear.

The night dissolves around me, and I stoop to the ground.

Someone grabs me from behind. Arms fold around me, pulling me to my feet.

It takes me a second to register her. Savana.

I don't know how long she's been here or what she saw and heard, but I don't care. All I know is that her arms are around me, and she's here.

SAVANA

Saturday, August 6

I know he's wide-awake; we both are. We're staring up at the shadowed ceiling in my bedroom, lying on top of my sheets, fixated on the shadows that loom over us.

"Thanks for letting me stay," he murmurs into the darkness.

"Of course," I whisper. A long moment passes before I can bring myself to ask the question, "Are you okay?"

He heaves a sigh. "It wasn't supposed to happen like this."

We fall silent, breathing in sync.

I'm hyperaware of his presence, his closeness.

I tilt my head to look at him. His face is next to mine on the pillow, brown hair mussed, deep brown eyes like bottomless pools in the darkness. We've never been like this with each other before, this raw and exposed. I'm so used to seeing him smile, that quick, easy smile that dimples his cheeks and makes my heart skip a little. Now he just looks hollow and lost.

I heard his shouts from my room, and panic spiked through me. I ran out to the street and saw the SUV drive away.

It knots my stomach just thinking about it. Because I care about him.

"I don't want to have to tell my brother," he admits, knotting his hands through his hair. "Or my dad. I don't want to hurt them."

I swallow against a sudden tightness in my throat. "I don't mind doing it."

For the first time all night, he laughs. Just a quick breath, but it's a laugh. My offer was supposed to sound benevolent, helpful. A show of support, or whatever. In hindsight, I probably could have worded it a little better. But I guess it was nice to hear him laugh.

His eyes linger on mine. "You think your mom would mind if I hide out here for the next couple of years?" There's pain behind his smile.

I crinkle my nose. "Do you really want to hide for *years*? That sounds boring."

"I don't mind hiding. Figure I get that from my mom, huh?"

"She might come back. Tomorrow she might wake up and realize she's made a mistake."

"She won't." He traps his lip between his teeth. "It wasn't a mistake."

"I'm sorry," I whisper, leaning into his broad shoulder.

His warm hand folds around mine, and I tighten my fingers around his.

Last time we talked, he asked if I wanted to hang out. Now he's lying in my bed and our hands are locked, but it's...not exactly how I imagined.

Our eyes return to the shadowy ceiling. It's strange, him being here in my room, both of us uttering quiet, secret words into the darkness. I breathe in the evanescence of this moment, the surrealness of his presence. I just hope he finds some comfort here.

When I wake, my room is bathed in morning sunlight. There are sounds, too. A garbage truck on the road at the front of the house, gulls crying over the ocean as they hunt for spoils.

The space beside me on the bed is empty. I'm not sure when he left, but in the cold light of day, last night seems like nothing more than a passing dream. Only it wasn't a dream. Echoes of him haunt the room. The covers are still creased from where he lay. The pillow still smells faintly familiar, making me catch myself.

There's an unread message on my phone from him, too, sent a little after 6:00 a.m. Thanks is all it says.

My stomach turns when I think of the ripple effect of damage that will come from his mom leaving. I have a horrible feeling this is just the beginning.

TITLE: CASE_HPD0149_TEXT MESSAGE TRANSCRIPTS

Recovered thread from +1****797 to an unregistered number. Messages exchanged on Friday, November 4, the morning before the homicide at Cray's Warehouse.

9:15 I had a dream you killed someone.

9:25 That's a messed up dream.

9:27 Yeah. But knowing your family, anything goes. Feel like killing someone for me today?

9:46 That's not funny.

9:46 What makes you think I'm joking?

SAVANA

Sunday, August 7

I've been thinking about Jesse all weekend. Not only Jesse, but Cody and Mr. Melo, too. The SUV is conspicuously absent from their driveway, and I haven't spoken to Jesse since the other night in my room. There've been so many times when I've nearly texted him, only to talk myself out of it a moment later. Right now he needs time to figure everything out with his family. If he needs me, he'll let me know. At least, that's what I'm hoping. As much as I want to see him, that's probably the last thing on his mind. So I'm trying to distract myself, anything to stop myself from imploding with worry.

I'm supposed to be meeting Corinne outside Miller's at eleven o'clock, but she's late. I check my phone for the dozenth time. Her last message just says, Be there in 5 mins. Sooo sorry. That was already ten minutes ago.

I cross the pavement and lean against the boardwalk railing, looking out over the jetties and shimmering ocean.

And that's when I see them. Raf and Tara.

They're standing beneath one of the pier structures on the quiet stretch of golden beach below the boardwalk. Tara's pale hair is fluttering in the breeze.

I almost call out to them, because if there's anyone who knows how Jesse's doing, it'll be Raf.

But their heads are dipped close together in a private moment. He's whispering into her ear. She leans away from him, and her chest heaves. It looks like she's crying.

Snatches of their conversation reach me, merged with the hiss and crash of the ocean as the waves shatter against the shore.

"You actually thought you could get away with this?" Raf's deep voice sounds ghostly in the wind.

Then Tara's, a higher, clearer response. "No. You've got this all wrong…"

He towers over her and grabs her arm.

Gulls cry, shrill, sharp sounds. "No." The fractured word tangles with the birds' calls.

"Hey!" My own voice jumps out, and they both look up with a start. "Is everything okay?"

They freeze and whisper together fiercely before responding.

"Yeah," Tara calls back. She wipes her cheeks with her sleeve. "We're fine."

My attention moves to Raf.

He stares back at me, his mouth turned downward. "We're trying to have a private conversation, Savana."

Tara folds her arms across her chest and looks down at the sand.

"Not that private," I call to them. "I could hear you from up here."

A hand grasps my shoulder from behind, and I jump.

"Hi," Corinne says breathlessly. "I'm so sorry I'm late." She peels the windswept strands of hair from her flustered face.

"It's okay," I say, distracted. "I was just…"

Corinne's focus strays down to the beach, where Raf and Tara are muttering to each other. She shoots me a confused look, and I shake my head.

Tara casts me one final glance before she and Raf start off across the beach, walking away from us. They leave a trail of sunken footprints in the sand.

"What was that all about?" Corinne asks.

I frown as I watch them leave. "I have no idea. They were fighting, I think."

Corinne follows my gaze. "About what?"

"I don't know. It seemed pretty intense." I glance at her. "Do you think we should follow them?"

Corinne laughs, and I stare back at her, my brow furrowed.

She threads her arm through mine. "Savana, I'm starting to regret suggesting you focus your project on Raf."

"What do you mean?"

She gives way to another quick laugh. "You want us to follow them?"

"Okay," I agree. "Maybe that's a little unnecessary."

She grins and pinches her thumb and index finger together. "Just a little."

I muster a smile. "Point taken. But what about Tara? Shouldn't we check that she's okay?"

Corinne waves her hand. "She'll be fine. Those two fight all the time. It's just what they do."

"I guess," I murmur.

"Come on." She nods toward Miller's. "Let's go. I'm in the mood for an iced tea."

I let her lead me toward the diner, but my gaze strays back to the stilts of the pier and the duo of footprints snaking across the damp sand.

JESSE

Sunday, August 7

"Cody." My voice sounds strained, tired. "You need to eat something."

He's sitting at the kitchen table, staring into space. I toss him a packet of Oreo cookies.

It's been two days. My mom hasn't called. I knew she wouldn't.

Cody pushes the cookies aside and stares at me with this strange, vacant look. "Do you think we should check around the hotels?" he asks. "She didn't tell you where she'd be staying?"

It must be the tenth time he's asked me that same damn question.

"No," I mutter. "I have no idea."

"But she definitely wanted to leave?" His blue eyes—the same navy shade as hers—suddenly come alive with a spark of hope and then cloud with concern. Genuine concern. "You don't think she's in trouble, do you?" He threads his fingers through the front of his copper-brown hair. "She might have been caught up in something bad. Should we call the cops?"

I take a seat opposite him at the table and look him dead in the eyes. "Cody. She's gone. She wanted to go, so she left. She's not in trouble." *We are.*

He lowers his gaze. "You don't know that for sure."

I bang the table, urging him to look at me. Face me. Face the situation.

"She left because she didn't want to be here. Stop feeling sorry for her. Stop feeling sorry for yourself. Eat some damn food and move on."

His eyes turn watery.

I rub the nape of my neck. "I'm sorry." My voice still sounds clipped, so I take a breath and try to soften my tone. "I just want you to snap out of it. I want you to eat something. I want you to get up from this table and stop waiting for Mom to come back. It's not going to happen."

He presses the heels of his hands to his damp eyes.

My shoulders tense. I hate it when people cry. I haven't cried in a really long time. My granddad's funeral was the last time—I was ten years old. That guy was everything to us; he looked out for us when my parents were too young to be parents. After he died, our world unraveled. My dad started drinking hard, and my mom started chasing the life that had eluded her, the youth that she'd missed. It was everything I didn't want for myself.

It was around then that I learned how to block out noise. I got really good at tuning out their drunken fights and hateful words. I learned how to turn myself numb, and I stopped crying over the things I couldn't control. So whenever someone else cries, I don't know what to do except look away. Walk away.

My chair scrapes as I stand. Cody's eyes follow me as I cross the kitchen and open the back door. The summer sun is beating down on the deck, but in here, it still feels cold.

"You're going out, Jesse?" The sound of Dad's voice makes me stop.

I turn to see him standing in the kitchen doorway, resting a calloused hand on the frame.

"No." I rub the nape of my neck. "I didn't know you were here. I was just…" I glance at the deck and the gray shoreline beyond the house. "Are you all right?"

"Any coffee going?" He strolls into the kitchen. When he passes Cody, he squeezes his shoulder. "I'll get a pot on."

I scrub my hand through my hair as Dad fills the pot with water. He hums while the faucet runs.

Man. Give me the crying over this fake-happy shit.

"How about we do something today?" Dad says casually. "We could go down to Whitewater Bay. We could go fishing, just us guys."

I catch Cody's gaze and grimace. Nothing against fishing; I don't mind fishing. I like it, actually. But this isn't right, pretending that we're all good, playing happy family with a spontaneous father-and-sons fishing trip.

Dad's eyes snap to me. "What's the face for, Jesse?"

"Nothing. I'll go fishing. Whatever."

Cody knots his hands on the table. "Yeah, I'll go."

"So it's settled." Dad drops the pot down too hard on the counter. "Fishing it is."

Cody looks at me and presses his lips together.

I shrug back at him. *I know*, I respond silently. *Just go with it.*

Cody clears his throat. "We could call Mike? See if we can borrow his boat?"

Dad's false grin stays in place. Teeth bared. "Mike? Yeah, sure, we'll ask if we can borrow his boat. Or we could just take it. I mean, according to the neighbors, Mike Lombardi and I share everything, apparently." He slaps his hand on the counter. "Yeah, I'm sure he wouldn't mind me borrowing his boat, considering he took it upon himself to borrow my wife."

JESSE

Sunday, August 7

I follow Cody onto the driveway. He swiped the keys to my busted old hatchback from the hook on his way out the door. Before I can stop him, he's behind the wheel and revving the engine.

"Whoa." I thump on the hood. "What are you doing? You don't even have your permit!" My head's spinning. His probably is, too.

Mike and Mom?

There's got to be a mistake. They wouldn't do that to Dad.

Cody stares at me through the windshield, his mouth set into a tight line.

"Get out," I tell him. "Get out of my car."

He grips the steering wheel and revs the engine again.

I grab the passenger door and slide into the seat next to him.

He slams his foot on the gas, and we lurch forward. I try to catch the wheel, but we've already shot out onto the street.

Cody's seething. His jaw is clenched, and his eyes are locked on the road.

"Where are we going?" I fasten my seat belt and glance over my shoulder at the back window as we leave our house behind. The front door is still open, swinging after our exit. Dad hasn't followed us. He drops this bombshell, winds up the dogs, and then sets them loose.

"Mom?" Cody chokes out the word, drawing my attention back to him. "And Mike Lombardi?"

I grip the dash as we tear down the street, tires screeching on hot tarmac. "Pull over, Cody. For real. You're going to get us killed."

He swerves around a corner, peeling onto a suburban street.

"Pull over," I say through my teeth.

His jaw is set, rust-colored hair falling over one eye.

"Red light!" I shout.

A car horn blares, and I hold my breath as we speed through the intersection.

My heart's slamming in my chest. I glance back again, half expecting to see Dad's truck tailing us, coming to the rescue. But he's not there. No one's coming for us. "Pull over," I say to Cody, holding my voice steady because he needs me to step up. Because no one else is going to do it. "I get it. You're mad. I'm mad, too." He's panting, shaking, gripping the steering wheel hard. But he's listening; I know he is. See, my granddad would have nailed this conversation if he were here. He would have known exactly what to say and delivered it on point in his calming, gravelly voice. My voice isn't calming, but I'll shoot straight, and Cody knows it. "Come on," I say to him. "It's just me and you. Like always. Stop the car, and we'll deal with this."

He makes a pained sound.

"Please, Cody. Come on."

With a labored effort, he veers to the side of the road, and we jolt to a stop with one wheel mounting the curb.

The engine stalls.

I take a couple of slow breaths in the silence.

"I can't believe she did this to us," he rasps. "To Dad." He slaps the steering wheel.

I lean back in my seat and stare at the leafy sidewalk. "Yeah," I say. "I can't, either." I glance at him, but he's staring straight ahead, jaw locked.

Cars pass us on the road. People going about their day, barely noticing the junked old hatchback that's parked skewed on the pavement, oblivious to the pain that's bursting from the front seat.

We sit in silence for a moment, and his breathing starts to steady. Mine does, too.

He leans his head on his forearms, resting on the wheel. "I'm going to make Mike pay for doing this to Dad," he murmurs.

My chest tightens. "I know. Just don't do anything without me, all right?"

He doesn't answer.

"Cody?" I say, meaningfully.

He grunts, and that's all I get from him.

"Swap seats," I tell him.

He grimaces, but he climbs out of the car. I get behind the wheel and start the engine as he slumps in the passenger seat.

We don't talk on the way home, but the silence between us probably speaks louder than our words could have.

When we reach the house, Cody doesn't go inside. He

stuffs his hands into his pockets and starts toward the beach, head bowed and hair hanging over his eyes.

I watch him leave, standing alone in the driveway with the breeze rippling my T-shirt. My head's still spinning, and I don't think it's going to stop anytime soon.

Mike and my mom?

I clench my teeth hard and pull my phone from my pocket. Usually, I'd be calling Raf right now, firing off about my family's bullshit, but I can't bring myself to hit Dial on his number. Mike's his dad. And no matter what's gone down, blood is thicker than water.

I stare at my phone. Freddie, Owen, Tara—I should call one of them.

My eyes stray toward Savana's house, and it hits me. It catches me off guard, this feeling. Because the only person I want to see right now is her. The way we just lay in the darkness after my mom left, and she didn't make me feel like it was my fault, or like I had to front. I was honest with her, and she got it.

Before I know what I'm doing, I cross the divide separating our houses. She's the only person I want to see right now. Because I know she'll see me, and I know I'll let her.

SAVANA

Sunday, August 7

The profile of an alpha is defined by the drive to be unquestionably in charge, no matter what the situation.

I'm planted cross-legged on my bed with my laptop open, but I can't focus on my project. I must have read the same paragraph five times already, and I still haven't absorbed the text. Every word I write drags me back to Raf and Tara and what I witnessed on the pier earlier.

It's possible I'm reading too much into this. I mean, couples fight. It's no secret that Raf and Tara have a fiery relationship, judging by Tara's occasional cryptic social media posts that allude to drama. But their heated conversation seemed like more than a lovers' tiff. The desperation in Tara's voice and the anxious look on her face. The frustration in Raf's voice, too. The way he grabbed her arm. And the innate gut feeling that I saw something I wasn't supposed to see.

There's a tap on the French doors, and I freeze. A tall silhouette stands on the other side of the thin drapes.

My breath hitches in my throat. *Raf?*

Mom's at work, so I'm home alone. That's never bothered me before, but my pulse has quickened. I stay perfectly still, unable to tear my eyes away from the figure outside my door.

"Savana?" Jesse's voice comes from the other side of the glass. "Are you in there?"

My heart rate normalizes at the sound of his voice. And then it immediately skips again at the realization that it's him. I almost laugh at myself for being so ridiculous, but it doesn't feel funny yet.

I hop off the bed and cross the room, then pull the drapes and open the door to the dulling day.

Jesse's standing on the back deck. "Hi," he says.

"Ever get the feeling you're being totally paranoid?"

He frowns back at me in the open doorway. "I'm not paranoid. Should I be?"

"Never mind. I'm just imagining things." I step aside and gesture for him to come in. "How are you? I've been so worried."

He takes a seat on the edge of my bed and the frame creaks. "I've been better," he answers with a strained smile. "I'll bet you can't guess what happened at my house today."

I sit beside him and anxiously wait for him to continue.

He musses his hair and laughs without humor. "My dad dropped a grenade on us. Turns out, my mom's been having an affair with Raf's dad." His knee starts bouncing. "Isn't that funny?"

I suck in a breath. "Ouch."

"Yeah," he says. "*Ouch* just about sums it up."

"Wow," I whisper. "That's…"

"Yeah," he agrees.

"I'm so sorry, Jesse."

He rubs his brow, pushing away stray strands of hair. "Thanks."

"Does Raf know?" My mind goes back to Raf and Tara, wondering if this could have anything to do with their argument.

You actually thought you could get away with this?

No. You've got this all wrong...

"I don't know." Jesse's voice anchors me. "Probably not. If he did, he would have told me."

I lace my hands in my lap. "How's your dad taking this?" I ask gently.

Jesse's eyes come to mine. "Not well," he replies. "He trusted Mike. They were buddies. They hung out all the time."

I shake my head, lost for words.

His gaze moves to his sneakers. "She never called. My mom, I mean. When she left, she said she'd call, but she didn't."

"I'm sorry, Jesse," I say. "Maybe she just needs a couple of days to get her head together."

He laughs under his breath. "Yeah, right. Take as long as you need. Don't worry about us." His words aren't directed at me; they're for his mom, as though he's secretly hoping the air will catch them and carry them to wherever she is, and perhaps his sarcasm will bite her and make her feel his pain.

He rests his head in his hands for a second. "Mike Lombardi," he says through his fingers. "You know, now that I'm thinking about it, I'm not even surprised. They were always weirdly touchy-feely, him and her. They acted all flirty around each other." He exaggerates a shudder. "Right under my dad's nose, like they didn't care if he caught them or not."

"How did he find out?"

Jesse blows out a sigh. "We didn't get that far into the conversation. My dad mentioned the neighbors, so maybe someone saw them together."

The night when I caught someone looking into their house after the fundraiser football game, Raf's dad was visiting then. Maybe Mr. McAvoy saw them through the window. But the figure in the darkness didn't *seem* like our older neighbor passing with his dog. This person seemed bigger, somehow. More threatening. Although perhaps everyone seems more threatening in the dark.

"I can't believe they did this to my dad." The muscles in Jesse's jaw tense. "*Do* you think Raf knew anything about it?" His gaze comes back to me. He's waiting for a response. Not just any response—he's waiting for me to brush off the remark, tell him he's being absurd and that there's no way Raf could have known and kept this from him.

"I don't know Raf all that well," I say softly. "You know him better than I do. He's your best friend."

Jesse breathes deeply as he stares straight ahead, his eyes trained on the dusky ocean beyond the French doors. "Yeah," he says distantly. "If Raf had known, he would have told me, for sure. He went through it with his own parents last year, with them splitting. He would have given me a heads-up." This time it's not a question, but he answers it all the same. "Yeah," he murmurs, responding to his own thoughts. "He would have told me."

I catch his gaze. "I saw Raf and Tara together on the beach this morning. They were arguing," I add.

He rolls his eyes. "Standard for them."

"I don't know." I pick at a loose thread on my blanket. "It looked intense. Tara was crying, and Raf seemed really angry."

He takes notice now, and his brow knits. "What were they fighting about?"

"No idea." I hold up my hands. "Could it have been over this? Over what happened between your mom and Raf's dad? Maybe Raf found out, too, and he and Tara were talking about it." I feel like I'm grasping at straws, but it could be. Maybe Tara knew something. *Get away with this.* Maybe I misheard Raf's comment. When I'd heard *you*, he might have said *they*.

They actually thought they could get away with this.

Jesse falls silent for a moment as he contemplates my theory. "I'll talk to Raf," he says at last. "Once I come out of hiding."

I offer him a small smile. "Oh, you're back in hiding?"

"I never left," he says with a grin.

"But you're not hiding from me?"

"No," he says. "I don't think I could."

And just like that, something shifts. The energy is different between us, sparking and percolating. It's as though we're suddenly aware of how closely we're sitting. Our arms brush, and I feel it all over.

When he speaks again, his voice is low, just a murmur. "Thank you for being there when I needed you."

"Anytime," I whisper.

His eyes lock with mine, and I can't seem to look away. I don't want to look away. My heart beats faster as my gaze travels over his face. His eyes. His mouth.

There's a knock on the door connecting to the kitchen, and we both jump as the handle turns.

"Savana, do you want some—" Mom appears in the open doorway. She does a double take at the sight of Jesse sitting on my bed. And me, sitting too close beside him, unable to shake my shocked expression no matter how hard I try.

He springs back from me.

A beat of silence follows.

"Jesse," Mom says in a tight voice. Her lips sharpen into a thin line, and she fixes me with a pointed look. Her eyes narrow slightly, expertly conveying *You're in so much trouble.*

"Hi, Mom." I grope for words. "I didn't know you were home. How was work?" I give my best attempt at a breezy smile.

Jesse follows my lead. "Hi, Donna. I was just…"

"Visiting," I supply.

Mom folds her arms across her chest and her hazel eyes land on me again. "Savana, I don't remember you asking if you could have boys over?"

"Boy," I correct. "Just the one." I smile again in the hopes that she'll find me endearing enough to laugh this off. She doesn't.

She arches an eyebrow. "Jesse, Savana isn't allowed to have boys in her room." And then to me she says, "That is not what we agreed when I said you could have private access." She nods significantly toward the French doors, where the cove stretches beyond.

I glance down at the floorboards, wondering why they haven't opened up yet to swallow me whole. I wish they'd hurry.

Jesse jumps to his feet. "Of course. Sorry, Donna. My bad." He mouths *sorry* to me as he heads for the deck.

"Bye, Jesse," I say with a sigh. "Good luck with every-thing."

"You, too," he says.

The drapes flutter in the breeze, and the door clicks shut behind him.

Later that night, just as I'm about to get into bed, there's a knock on the French doors.

Just a quiet tap.

My heart skips a beat.

I quickly comb my fingers through my tangled hair and pad across the room, smiling to myself. A thousand thoughts race through my mind as I prepare to quietly sneak Jesse back in.

I take a breath.

But when I draw open the drapes, there's no one out there, just the murky night beyond the pane.

I cup my hands on the door and peer out into the darkness.

Suddenly, a distorted face appears on the other side, palms slamming the glass so hard that it makes me cry out.

I stumble backward, clasping my hands over my mouth. A spike of fear shoots through me.

The masked face is pressed to the glass, wearing a grotesque plastic sneer. Fingers drum slowly on the pane.

And then they're gone, leaving only the bottomless void of the night and my own reflection trapped in the glass as I cower across the room.

SAVANA:
Was that you?

JESSE:
Was what me?

SAVANA:
Were you at my door just now, at the back?

JESSE:
Nope. Wasn't me.

JESSE:
I just looked out my window. There's no one out there.

SAVANA:
Maybe it was the wind or a bat or something.

JESSE:
Are you okay? Do you want me to go look?

SAVANA:
No, I'm okay. It was nothing.

Audio File_MP3

Title: Case_HPD0149_Savana Caruso Interview

H.B.: Recording now. The date is November 5. The time is approximately nine thirty in the morning. My name is Detective Harrison Bridge. Please state your full name for the purpose of the tape.

S.C.: Savana Caruso.

H.B.: I appreciate this isn't easy for you, Savana, but I need you to talk me through your movements last night, Friday, November 4.

S.C.: Yeah. Um, I was walking through the port, and something caught my eye. It all happened so fast, but I heard a crash. A shattering sound.

H.B.: What were you doing at the port?

S.C.: I was just passing through.

H.B.: You didn't know that five of your friends were inside Cray's Warehouse? Because it seems likely that you'd be going to join them, no?

S.C.: I didn't know anyone was in there. Honestly, I didn't know. They aren't my friends. I wasn't meeting them.

H.B.: They aren't your friends? I've listened back to your 911 call, and I believe you said, verbatim, my friend has fallen from a window.

S.C.: We're classmates. I don't remember what I said on the call. It's all a blur.

H.B.: Okay. What happened next?

S.C.: As you said, I called 911, and I ran over to the warehouse to see if there was anything I could do. But I couldn't. The fall was too high, and…

H.B.: Take a breath.

S.C.: I stayed and waited for emergency services to arrive. And I called my mom.

H.B.: You didn't see anyone else, any of your friends—excuse me, your classmates. You didn't see anyone leave? Or anyone at the window above you?

S.C.: No. It was too high and too dark. I just stayed exactly where I was. When the police came, they escorted people out of the building, but I didn't see any of that. I was at the back.

H.B.: You didn't see anyone else at the marina?

S.C.: I didn't see anyone.

H.B.: Well, if there is a sixth suspect, then I'm sure that will come to light.

S.C.: Sixth? I thought there were only four people escorted from Cray's? Who's the fifth?

H.B.: Savana, I've taken a look through your report and been in contact with your school. There was an incident that happened recently, wasn't there?

S.C.: Me? Is it me? I wasn't even inside the warehouse. I was outside when it happened.

H.B.: And at the moment, we're taking your word for that. But this is a homicide investigation, and your whereabouts need to be verified as much as anyone else's.

JESSE

I lean down to the pool table and take my shot. The balls scatter and my target sinks into the far pocket.

Raf cusses under his breath.

We've wasted way too many hours of our lives at Miller's, shooting pool or racking up high scores on the arcade games in the function room off the diner area.

The back room is scattered with circular tables and lit by dusty lamps. On a Friday night, I swear half the kids from school show up at this place. We even passed Cody and his buddies ordering chili fries on our way in.

Things have calmed down over the past few days. I was right about Raf not knowing about the affair. He was as shocked as the rest of us about it. He said he confronted Mike, and it was just one time and whatever. Like that makes a difference. But it's weird for us now. We're not saying it, but it's weird.

My eyes stray to Savana as she walks into the back room.

She joins her friends at one of the tables, taking a seat with some of the drama crowd.

"Hey." Raf nudges me with his pool cue. "Your shot."

"Oh. Yeah." I get my head back in the game. "Corner pocket." I gesture to the black ball before taking my shot. It sinks into the corner net with a *clink*.

Raf grunts and mutters.

"One all," I say, my lips twitching. "Next game wins?"

"Get ready to lose." He chalks the tip.

While he stacks the balls again, my eyes drift to Savana. Her brown hair is in a ponytail and the ends look lighter from where the salt air and sun have bleached them. Some strands have fallen loose around her face, and she plays with them absently while she talks to her friends.

"I knew you were into her." Raf's voice catches me off guard.

I glance at him and frown. "Huh?"

"I knew it." He points his pool cue conspicuously at Savana. "You're into her."

I grab the end of the cue and push it down. "You wanna shout that a little louder?" I say in a low voice.

He props the cue upright and leans against it, smirking. "So are you going to hit that, or what?"

"Don't say shit like that."

He snorts. "But are you into her? Yes or no?"

I keep my mouth shut. Something makes me hold back. I don't want him to know that I like Savana. He's my best friend, yeah, but I don't want him to know. Because once he knows, then it's just another game to him. It's another competition that he can try to win.

Across the room, she looks up from her phone and glances

my way. Then she stands from her seat and starts making her way toward us, and we fall quiet.

"Hey," she says, leaning against the pool table and meeting my eyes.

Raf steps aside, retreating to our table to get his drink, giving us some space. But he's watching us.

I clear my throat and pretend I can't feel his stare locked on my back. "Hey, Savana. What's up?"

"I just wanted to tell you that my mom's about to finish her shift and she's driving me home if you and Cody need a ride."

I glance at Raf. He's still waiting dutifully at our table. "Thanks. But I'm going hang out a little while longer. I've got a grudge match." I thumb toward the pool table and the unbroken triangle of balls.

"Okay," she says with an easy smile. "See you."

"Wait, Savana," I call as she turns to walk away.

I'm going to say something. Right now. The moment feels right, and I'm going to ask her out, properly. I'm going to suggest a date that she won't want to say no to. Like…something. Something good.

She lingers, waiting for me to speak.

"Uh…" I scratch the back of my neck.

She tilts her head. Still waiting. "What?" she presses.

The words won't come out. The stakes feel so much higher now that we've been spending more time together. If I cross this line, and she doesn't feel the same way, then we're done. We'll say it won't change anything, but it will. No more friendship, no more anything.

She's still leaning against the pool table, waiting for me to speak.

"Could you ask Cody if he needs a ride? He's in the diner. Tell him I walked here so I can't drive him home later."

"Sure," she says.

When she walks away, I squeeze my eyes shut and tap my fist on my forehead.

Raf steps up behind me. "You ready, or what?" he grunts.

"Yeah," I mutter. "You can break."

He picks up his cue.

Savana turns and gives me a small wave when she reaches the exit.

I lift my hand in response. Then I notice Raf's eyes roam over her and his mouth quirks at the edge.

I don't like the way he's looking at her.

She dips her gaze and ducks through the exit fast. I get the feeling she doesn't like it, either.

SAVANA

Friday, August 12

Cody's seated at one of the back booths in Miller's dining area. He's alone, head bowed as he taps on his phone. I cross the busy restaurant and come to a stop at his table.

He looks up, his hair falling over one eye.

"Hey. Your brother's in the back," I tell him in case he didn't realize. Cody's probably the only person sitting alone in this whole place.

"I know," he says.

"Oh. Anyway, Jesse said to tell you that he walked here, so he can't drive you home tonight. My mom can give you a ride, but we're leaving now."

He purses his lips and stares down at the table.

I glance over my shoulder. No one's paying attention to us. Everyone's too busy having fun, laughing and chatting over plates of food.

I lower my voice. "Are you okay, Cody?"

He sucks in his top lip. "Yeah." After a moment he meets my eyes. "Is Jesse leaving soon?"

"Not for a little while, I don't think."

He looks down at the table again.

"Is there something—"

Mom comes up behind me and rests her hand on my back. "Are you ready to go?" She looks between Cody and me. "Where's Jesse?"

"He's staying," I tell her. "But, Cody, are you coming with us?"

Mom's car keys jingle in her hand. "Hang on. How will Jesse be getting home? Does he have his car?"

"No, he walked here."

Her brows pull together. "I'm not sure I'm comfortable with him walking home alone at night."

I sigh. "He'll be fine. He's with people." Sometimes Mom feels like she has to be *everyone's* mom. Or Jesse and Cody's, at least. And she's amped up her maternal instinct another notch since their actual mom left. Kind of cringey, but it's sweet how she gets mad when she hears people gossiping about them on our block. We're aligned on that, Mom and I. The last thing the Melos need right now is to be subjected to neighborhood gossip.

Her eyes fix on Cody. "Come on, then. You shouldn't be out on your own. It's time to go." Obediently, he slides out from the booth. "I'll let your dad know that Jesse is still here," she says, deciding at last. "Perhaps Ric can pick him up later."

As Mom walks on ahead, waving and calling *bye* to the servers behind the counter, Cody and I trail after her through the packed diner.

I glance at him as we weave through the crowd. "Why weren't you in the back room with Jesse and Raf?"

He shrugs, stooping. He's not quite as tall as Jesse, but he's lankier somehow, with loping strides. "Why do you think?" he says under his breath. "Jesse told you what happened, right?"

"About your mom?"

"Yeah. And *him*." He flings his arm toward the entrance to the back room. "That guy's such a liar. I can't stand him."

"You mean Raf?"

"Yeah."

A cold feeling comes over me, making me hesitate. "What, you think Raf knew about your mom and his dad?"

"Of course he knew," Cody hisses. "He probably encouraged it. Do you actually think he gives a crap about us?" He snorts out angrily.

"Jesse says Raf had no idea."

"Yeah," Cody mutters. "Well, that's Jesse for you." When I frown, he adds, "He's too trusting. It'll bite him in the ass one day."

We push through the main doors and step into the dim parking lot just as Tara and Freddie are heading in. They pause and shoot each other a quick look.

"Hi," Tara sings. She slips past us and skips into Miller's with a swish of blond hair and a cloud of smoky perfume.

Freddie lingers in the open doorway, propping it ajar with a lean arm. "Hey," he says. "Where's Jesse?"

"Inside with Raf," I tell him.

Out of the corner of my eye, I notice Cody grimace.

"Where's Owen tonight?" I ask Freddie.

He runs a hand over his curls. "Family time. His brother's home for the weekend, and Owen's parents want them to hang out."

"Oh. That's nice."

"Yeah," Freddie says with a quick smile. "Except Owen and his brother don't get along. The guy's a major tool."

I remember Grant Keaton from school. He always seemed nice enough. Similar to Owen, tall and athletic, with a wide smile and bright blue eyes.

Freddie gives Cody a playful nudge. "Like you and Jesse sometimes, huh?" he adds. "Makes me glad I don't have siblings. You all fight so much."

I glance at Cody. His smile is strained, but Freddie doesn't seem to notice. Freddie's got it wrong, though. It's not that Cody and Jesse don't get along. It's that Cody doesn't get along with Jesse's best friend. I know the feeling.

Across the lot, Mom's taillights come on. I tug on Cody's sleeve. "We'd better go," I say. "Have fun tonight," I add to Freddie.

Freddie lifts his hand in a wave before disappearing into Miller's.

JESSE

Friday, August 12

Shortcutting through the port shaves a couple of minutes off my walk home from Miller's.

It used to weird my mom out whenever I told her I'd cut through the marina at nighttime. There isn't much light around this part of town—a couple of streetlamps lining the waterfront, maybe some secondhand glows cast from nearby buildings. But the port is industrial, built up with warehouses and garages that all shut down by six o'clock. It's fine during the day, but nighttime strips you of your senses, leaves you exposed. The pavement is always littered with ropes and poles that disappear into the darkness. You'd only have to get your foot caught up in a net or stumble into an anchor, and you'd hit the ground hard. Probably hard enough to do some damage. When it gets dark in the port, it gets really dark.

It's that type of darkness now, the type of abyss that makes you widen your eyes, or blink fast, just in case you can trick the color back into the world.

I know I'm being followed. It's a feeling, something intrinsic, validated by the sound of footsteps that are too rhythmic, too steady. But I keep going because there's no point in turning back now. The path narrows and I'm flanked by storage units, locked and abandoned. A cool wind funnels through the chasm, howling at me. Laughing at me.

I think there's two of them, two sets of footsteps. They're moving fast. Faster than my own. Echoes bounce. *Step, step, step.* Mine and theirs, phantoms in the darkness. They're getting closer.

Now's probably a good time to run.

"Cody Melo?" A deep voice jumps out, rebounding in the night.

My steps falter, and I tense. These aren't random guys, looking for an easy fight, or trying to score some cash from the dumb guy walking through the port alone. This isn't chance. They're looking for Cody; they said his name. They're looking for my brother.

Cody, what have you done?

I stop and turn, letting the guys catch up to me. Their shadowed faces come closer, but I don't recognize either of them. One is built, with a bald head and a tattoo across his right cheekbone. The other is smaller, sharper looking. His hood is pulled up, but I can still make out his angular features and stubbled chin.

I take a breath before I speak. "Yeah," I answer. Because tonight, however much it sucks, I'm going to have to be Cody.

I get a couple of good shots in, but there's two of them. Once they get me on the ground, I know I'm pretty much done. I use my arms as a shield and let it play out. I can't even really feel the pain; my adrenaline's already too high.

My mind goes to Savana. I think about the way her bedroom looked in the moonlight when I lay there in pain worse than this. The way she touched my hand, and somehow, everything felt better.

I just focus on that, on her.

And I wait for it to end.

HAVELOCK SUNDAY PRESS
November 6

After reports of an incident at Havelock Port on Friday, November 4, police were called to the scene, where the body of a teenager was later recovered. The initial coroner's report suggests that the victim fell from a considerable height, and it's understood that there were signs of a struggle.

Although the victim's name has not yet been released, a spokes-person from Havelock Police Department has confirmed that the death is being investigated and four high school students were escorted from the former Cray's Warehouse, where the incident allegedly took place.

A local man, who has chosen to remain nameless, has given this statement: "I was working late on my boat that night, and I think I saw them. Four of them went into the warehouse together, and then two more showed up a little later. I got out of there because I didn't feel safe with so many of them boys hanging around. Must have been gang related."

JESSE
Sunday, August 14

"Hey." I step into Cody's room and kick aside the heap of laundry that's blocking the doorway.

He frowns at me from his chair. His gaming headset is draped around his neck, and his laptop is open on the desk in front of him with an ongoing game muted. His eyes roam over my face, taking in the bruises. I told him I got into a fight. I didn't tell him that it happened when I was pretending to be him.

"Yeah?" he says. "What do you want?"

"Nothing."

It's always the same in here, mad chaos with clothes balled up on the floor and greasy bike parts propped against the wall. But one thing's different, and I notice it right away. There's a corkboard on the wall with a ton of printed photos tacked to it, and any pictures that had Mom in the frame have been strategically removed. He's erased her. I don't blame him. I'd do the same, if I could.

"Wanna hang out?" I ask.

"Not really," he grunts. "I'm kinda in the middle of a game."

I cross the room and lean on the window ledge, feeling the lingering ache in my rib cage as I stare out at the ocean. The water looks cobalt blue today, and whitecapped waves are shattering against the small wooden jetties.

"What's been going on with you lately?"

He frowns at me for a second. "Why?"

"Just making conversation."

The frown lines deepen. "Yeah. Why?"

"I got a question for you."

He rolls his eyes. "Make it quick."

"Are you caught up in something sketchy?"

His eyebrows pull together. "No. I'm just gaming." He gestures to his laptop, where a digitized explosion is paused on the screen.

"I mean, in real life."

His jaw ticks. "Like what?"

"I don't know." I take a shot. "Pissed off any drug dealers lately?"

He chokes out a laugh. "No. Have you?"

I slap my hands together. I've got to get this out of him. "A couple of weeks back," I say, changing tack, "when you asked me to cover for you with Mom and Dad—" he cringes at *Mom*, so I carry on quickly "—what did you do?"

His shoulders relax. "Oh, that? Nothing. I found a way into Cray's, that's all. Johnno and me were hanging out at the port." He thumps his fist to his chest. "But then Raf made out like *he* found Cray's, and he claimed it for you guys and all your buddies."

"*You* found a way into Cray's? How come you didn't tell me?"

"Because I didn't want everyone getting in on it and ru-ining it. But then Johnno went and told Raf, trying to score points with him or something, probably." He grimaces.

I drag my hand over my face. "That's it? That's all?"

"Why? What do you think I've done?"

I squint one eye. "What do you think I think you've done?"

We stare at each other.

His lips press together. "I tossed a brick through Lombardi's window."

I sigh. "Cody..."

The corner of his mouth lifts. "You should have been there."

"Yeah," I say through my teeth. "I should have. I asked you not to do anything without talking to me first."

He holds up his hands and shrugs. "Hey. Mike had it com-ing. He deserves a lot more than a broken window and a brick."

SAVANA

Sunday, August 14

Havelock is a lot quieter once the summer season starts to dwindle off. The cove behind my house, which is tempting to some of the off-the-beaten-path vacationers, is now more or less deserted—and it probably will be for the next eight or nine months until the warm sun envelops the coastline again.

But for now, we're safe. The tourists have dissipated, taking their surfboards and brightly colored windbreakers with them. The vacation rentals have been locked up and there are no more loungers in the yards or clothes drying on the balconies.

As for the locals, they don't usually venture out this far. Not when they have easier access to the pristine golden sand bays that fringe the town, where seafood restaurants and bars preface the jetties.

Our little cove doesn't quite boast the same polished allure, but it's great if you don't mind dredging through seaweed and hopping over salt-bleached driftwood. Which, in my opinion, is all part of its rough-around-the-edges charm.

Alone, I stroll along the beach, wading through the shallows. I've rolled my jeans to the knee and cool waves are shattering and fizzing against my calves.

A little farther down the beach, Jesse is jogging along the shoreline, heading in my direction. It's become a familiar sight. Sometimes I see him from my window. I see him leave his house through the back, jump the railing, and then jog down to the sand. He returns half an hour later, damp with sweat and breathing hard.

His pace drops when he notices me in his path, and he slips off his headphones.

By the time he reaches me, he's slowed from a run to a walk to a stop. The frothing waves lap at his sneakers, and the low afternoon sunlight catches the umber tones in his eyes.

"Oh, my God." I press my hands to my mouth. "What happened to you?"

There's a yellow-blue bruise beneath his left eye, and his lower lip looks like it's healing from what was undoubtedly a pretty brutal cut.

He musters a strained smile and shrugs.

I stare at the atlas pattern of bruising on his jawline. "You look terrible."

He quirks an eyebrow. "I think I'm offended."

"Seriously," I say. "What happened to you?"

He bows his head and pushes back some wayward strands of deep brown hair. "Wrong place, wrong time."

"Yeah. No kidding."

"Couple of guys came at me the other night." He kicks a pebble that's rolled in with the tide. "It's no big deal."

I fold my hands over my heart. "That's awful. Are you okay?"

"Yeah." He tilts his head, and his cheeks dimple as he musters another smile, as though he's trying to reassure me. Like I'm the one who needs comfort.

I draw in a tight breath. "Did you see who it was? Did you go to the police?"

"It's fine." He rubs the nape of his neck. "It's just one of those things."

I want to hug him. Then I want to yell at him for this pointless toxic masculinity crap. "What did your dad say?"

He puts on a deep voice and says, "You need to stop getting into fights, son. You're going to get yourself into real trouble one day."

"Wow. Life's really not been on your side lately, huh?"

His mouth lifts at the corner. "Was it ever?"

So I do it. I pull him into a hug. He winces, like he's sore, but his arms lock around me, pulling me closer. I rest my head on his shoulder, letting myself fall into him.

"I'm all right," he murmurs into my temple. "I'm all good."

"I know you are," I whisper back.

But it's a little while before I let go. And the waves keep lapping at our feet.

My conversation with Jesse on the beach plays on my mind well into the afternoon. I can't stop thinking about him, and the cuts and bruises marking his face. It makes my pulse race in fear, in frustration at the unjustness of it all.

The more I replay his words, the worse I feel. There's so much more I should have said or done.

As the sun dips lower over the bay, I leave my house and climb onto the Melos' porch. Taking a shaky breath, I knock on their kitchen door.

A moment later the handle twists and Jesse stands in the

open doorway. The slanted evening light catches in his coppery-brown eyes and blushes the sun-kissed freckles on his nose. "Hey." He frowns a little, as though he's wondering what I'm doing here.

"I had to come over," I say in a whoosh. "I can't stop thinking about how terrible your face looks."

"Oh." He squints one eye and smiles. "Thank you."

"I mean…" I wave my hand in circles. "You know what I mean."

I follow him into the kitchen, and he gestures toward the large oak table.

"Do you want a drink or something?" he asks, hovering at the fridge.

I take a seat at the table. "I've been thinking—you should report this to the police. I can come with you if you want. We could go down to the station together."

"Is that a no to a drink? We've got coffee, or water, or…" He checks a few cupboards around the sink. "That's actually it."

"Jesse." I catch his gaze.

"What?" His one good eye blinks at me.

"You have to report this."

"Savana." He pushes the heels of his hands through his tousled hair. "I wish I hadn't told you anything. I should have told you I fell down the stairs or something. Actually, yeah, I'm changing my story. I fell down the stairs."

I hold his gaze, restlessly twisting one of the rings on my finger. "I just don't think anyone should get away with hurting you like this."

"I'm not hurt. I'm fine."

"You're not fine," I snap.

He glances over my head into the corridor beyond the kitchen, then steps past me and quietly closes the connecting door.

"All right, look," he says, coming to the table and pulling out a chair. "You can't tell anyone, but *this*—" he points at his swollen eye "—wasn't by chance. If I report it, then it'll probably just happen again."

My stomach flips. "What do you mean it wasn't by chance? So you *do* know who it was?"

"No. Not exactly." He lowers his voice. "But they thought I was Cody. They were looking for him. He's obviously pissed off the wrong person. Anyway, it's done now." He extends his hands over the table. "If I go to the cops, it could make things worse."

My heart's beating fast in my chest, the rate accelerating with every word. "Wait, *what*? What did Cody do to warrant *this*?" I motion toward his face.

"I don't know," he says.

"You didn't ask him?"

"It's complicated," he says, gnawing on his lip.

I lock eyes with him. "I'll try to keep up."

He heaves a sigh. "Cody just thinks I got into a fight. And if he finds out the truth, he'll go looking for them because he's a stubborn kid with a quick fuse, and it'll just keep going around and around." He nods slowly, waiting for me to process. "It's done now," he says. "Cody's fine. I'm fine—"

"You are *not* fine."

"I can take it," he says emphatically. "I can walk away. Cody can't. Listen to me, Savana, I know him. Cody can't back down from stuff like this. He's just not wired that way."

"What if this isn't the end of it, though? What if he's involved in something really bad?"

"I'll watch him, believe me. It might have had something to do with Mike Lombardi. Cody threw a brick through their window and—"

"Raf's dad?" I exclaim.

He gestures for me to keep my voice down. "Maybe." He rubs his brow. "But I can't see Mike retaliating like that, so I don't know. Knowing Cody, it could be anything. But you've got to keep this between us. If there's something he isn't telling me, then I don't want to risk it escalating."

I exhale slowly. "Okay," I murmur at last.

"You can't say anything, to anyone."

"Okay," I echo.

I look around the kitchen, taking in the layout and how it mirrors my own house. But despite the familiar structure, our homes feel like polar opposites. The Melos' roof slopes low, meaning the kitchen doesn't catch the light in the same way ours does. It feels sad, somehow. Like it's waiting for sunlight to leak through the windows and wake it from its sleep. As my gaze drifts over Jesse, I recognize the parallel. It's as though the sunlight can never quite reach him.

I press my palms flat on the table. "Well, thank you. For telling me, and for trusting me. I get it."

"Thanks," he says hoarsely.

We fall silent for a moment. When he speaks again, his tone has an air of forced ease about it. "How's your college application coming along? Are you still working on that journalism project?"

"Blatant subject change," I note.

"Yeah," he says, his lips twitching. "We needed it."

"It's going okay," I answer with a small smile. "Maybe you can help me, actually. It'd be good to get your firsthand perspective."

"Okay. What's the project about?"

"That we're all liars."

His eyebrows rise. "And you want my perspective? I'm flattered."

I grin. "I didn't mean it like that. I'm exploring the lies we inadvertently tell that elevate social status. Like how we airbrush reality through social media and attach ourselves to personas. Take you, for example." My gaze passes over him and his classic jock-boy image, with his toned arms and casual confidence. "You're an athlete, and that's your persona. People probably assume they know you because they have a preconceived idea of you, right?"

He laughs softly. "Yeah, but I'm not who they think I am."

"Then who are you really?"

"I'm me when I'm with you," he answers. I notice the way his mouth twitches at the corner and a cute dimple dents his cheek. I notice.

"How about you?" he asks, lowering his voice and leaning a little closer. "Who are you really, Savana?"

I'm your friend, I think. *And I want more.*

But I just keep smiling and say, "Ah. If I tell you, then I'd have to kill you."

It's already dark beyond the Melos' kitchen window. I don't know how the night crept up on us so fast.

"I like that you live next door," Jesse says with a trace of a smile, "and that we can hang out like this."

A smile tugs at my lips, too. "Same."

"We should have been doing this all along."

"Yeah." I glance over the kitchen again, noting the familiar sights. The family photos on the fridge, and the jackets hanging from the hook on the back of the door. I've stopped by their house plenty of times, when we've picked up their mail or needed a neighborly favor, but never like this. Never just me and him, with this new energy between us. I can't quite define what it is, but it's definitely something. Something more than what it was before.

"It's going to be different around here next year when you're at college," he says, drawing my focus back to him.

My eyes linger on his. "What about you, though? Don't you want to go to college?"

He knots his hands on the table. "Yeah, I do. But I'm going to need a football scholarship if I want to make that happen, and it isn't guaranteed. Anyway, I'm starting to think it wouldn't be right to leave my dad and Cody with everything that's going on."

"College is still a year away," I remind him. "A lot can change in a year."

"Yeah. Maybe."

The sound of a car engine on the street outside makes us stop.

I reach for my phone and suck in a breath when I see the time. "Oh, no. That's probably my mom," I say, standing quickly from my chair. "I promised her I wouldn't go out tonight. She'll flip if she finds my room empty."

Jesse clears his throat and stands along with me. "Thanks for coming over. We should do this again, right? I mean, if you want." His nose twitches. "Do you want?"

"Yeah," I say. "Sure."

We cross the kitchen and hover in the doorway for a moment.

"See you," I say, hushing my voice to suit the starry night.

"Yeah," he says quietly. "See you. Tomorrow. Or whenever." He grins and bites his lip. "Anytime. All the time. Whatever."

I laugh as I step out onto the deck. "Night, Jesse," I whisper.

"Night, Savana."

I close the door behind me with a soft click.

As I venture out into the cool moonlit night, a rush of breath escapes me.

Someone is standing on my back deck. They're almost camouflaged by the darkness as they stare into my empty bedroom.

I press myself flat against the wall of the Melos' house, my mind racing as I watch the hooded silhouette merge with the shadows before disappearing completely.

A moment later a car engine rumbles in the quiet night.

I gather myself and race to the street, but all I see are taillights disappearing around the corner.

TITLE: CASE_HPD0149_TEXT MESSAGE TRANSCRIPTS

Recovered thread from +1****797 to an unregistered number. Messages exchanged on Friday, November 4, several hours before the homicide at Cray's Warehouse.

2:04 Payback.

2:06 Relax. It's not worth it.

2:06 Done. For real.

2:11 I can't talk right now.

2:12 I've got a plan. I need your help.

2:13 How?

2:13 Talk later.

JESSE

Saturday, August 20

Owen tears open a bag of potato chips and kicks his feet up on the coffee table. Across the room, Freddie jerks up the footrest on my dad's La-Z-Boy recliner.

I take a seat next to Owen on the couch.

"This is exactly what I'm talking about," Owen says, gesturing toward the TV with a chip. "Their defense has been off since last season."

My gaze stays trained on the football game that's just started on the sports channel. "Yeah. Because they've got Torres playing defense."

Freddie howls in protest as the home team misses a chance to score.

"Tor*res*," Owen yells at the screen.

Cody comes in from the kitchen and drops a pizza box onto the coffee table. "You all owe me six fifty," he says, making himself comfortable on the floor. I toss him a cushion.

"Defense," Owen hollers. He rakes his hands through his hair, tugging at the strands.

Defense. The word bounces around my mind. I told Raf about what happened last week, with those guys looking for Cody. I told him face-to-face because there was a part of me that wanted to see his reaction.

He looked surprised, sounded surprised, and that was enough for me. The more I think about it, the more I realize Mike wouldn't have sent anyone after Cody. No matter what my opinion is of Mike right now, I know he wouldn't do something like that, and it sucks that my head even went there.

That's probably why Raf opted for date night with Tara over this; he feels like he's not welcome here anymore. I hate that.

"Oh, man." Cody's voice pulls me back to the game. "When did I miss a goal?"

"Couple of minutes ago," Owen answers, his eyes still fixed on the screen as he reaches for a slice of pizza. "Rogers."

Cody crams a slice into his mouth and mumbles a response. Something about passes.

It's right around the end of the first half when there's a tap on the kitchen door.

I jump to my feet, almost knocking the pizza box off the table as I trip over myself to get to the kitchen. Because I think I know who's waiting on the other side. I swing the door open, and she's standing there in the porch light with fireflies shooting over her head.

"Hi." She smiles, and I smile.

"Hey, Savana."

"Your face looks better," she says, pursing her lips while she studies me. "The low light helps."

I raise an eyebrow. "Well, that's a backhanded compliment if ever I heard one."

She grins, and my heart does something. An extra beat.

"Is that why you came over, to tell me I look better in the dark?"

"That was one reason, yes."

She's come over nearly every day since I saw her on the beach last week, and every day I like her a little more. Every day I *see* her a little more. The freckles on her cheeks, her dark eyelashes and cherry-colored lips, her kindness and calmness.

"And, also," she says, "to bring you this." She lifts a cake box to eye level. "Bear claws from Miller's. The manager gave my mom a ton to take home because they've been sitting out for so long. They were going into the trash otherwise."

I slap my hands to my face. "Stale food, too? I could get used to this." I take the box from her and pop the lid. "Come in," I say, then take a bear claw from the pile and balance it between my teeth. "Hang out with us," I add through the pastry. "Freddie and Owen are here."

"Okay." She steps gingerly over the threshold and follows me into the living room. "No Raf tonight?"

"He's out with Tara. They've gone to the movies."

"Oh. Good."

I glance at her, and she shrugs, unapologetic. It's no secret that Savana isn't Raf's biggest fan, and I get why.

When we cross into the living room, I place the cake box on the coffee table alongside the pizza. "Gifts from Savana's mom," I tell the others. They all get up to rummage through the box, thanking her as they scavenge.

"You can have my spot," I say to her, gesturing to the place beside Owen on the couch.

"Oh, thanks." She grabs a bear claw before sinking into the cushions. She shuffles to the edge of the couch and pats the empty space between her and Owen. "Here," she says to me. "There's still room."

I take the space between them, then I glance at her, and she smiles. So I smile.

Freddie returns to the recliner, with a bear claw in one hand and a slice of pizza in the other. "Do you watch the Saturday night games, Savana?"

"Sometimes."

"It's our tradition," Freddie says with a grin. "You should join us more often."

An infomercial starts playing on TV, some extraordinary wonder mop that manages to entrance us all for a couple of minutes.

I swear I'm moments away from calling the number and buying the mop, but then Savana snaps me out of it by saying, "Raf and Tara are obviously over that fight they had, then?" I can tell by the way the comment sprang out of nowhere that she's been thinking on it for a while, waiting for an opportunity to drop it into conversation.

"Yeah," I tell her. "They're good."

Her eyes roam over mine, searching for something more.

And then I remember. She has concerns—for Tara. But Raf's not like that. He's loud and hotheaded, sure, but he's harmless. For Savana's peace of mind, though, I raise my voice to catch the attention of the room. "You guys ever notice Raf and Tara argue a lot?"

Owen groans and runs his hands over his face and into his hair. "All the time," he says, dragging out the syllables. "They love it."

Freddie slaps the arm on the recliner. "No, they only argue because Raf gets jealous. He wants to control everything."

Savana catches my gaze and arches an eyebrow.

"You really think that?" I ask Freddie. "Since when?"

"Listen," Freddie says, "Raf's my friend, but he's possessive, right? Especially with Tara."

"Why doesn't that surprise me," Cody mutters from his spot on the floor. "Someone needs to put that guy in his place." He tosses a pizza crust into the box.

My attention stays on him because something in his voice made me cold. I'm suddenly aware of the ocean breeze beating at the windowpanes, rattling the glass and leaking a draft into the room.

Cody stares back at me, his eyes hard.

The sound of Owen's laughter cuts through the tension. He's laughing because he isn't feeling what I'm feeling. He didn't hear what I heard in Cody's voice. The hate. The anger. To Owen, we're just messing.

"But Tara loves it, man," Owen says with a huge smile. "She loves the theatrics. You should see them, Savana. They have these wild fights and then they're making out again a second later."

The pressure eases from my shoulders, and my focus moves back to Savana. "He's right," I tell her, thumbing toward Owen. "I've been there when Raf and Tara have had some heated blowups over the smallest stuff. Tara gets mad if he talks to other girls, then Raf gets mad if she hangs out with other guys. Tara gets mad if he doesn't tell her how pretty she looks, and Raf gets mad because he told her she was pretty and it still wasn't enough."

When I pause, Owen takes over. "They fight, they say

they're both done, and then they get back together and pretend like it never happened."

"Yeah," I jump back in. "Until one of them needs it for ammunition in the next fight."

"Anyway," Owen says, leaning over me to talk to Savana, "we just ignore it. It's better for everyone if we keep out of it."

Savana sighs. "Okay. Sounds kind of toxic to me, but whatever. Not my business."

Freddie's fist starts tapping on the arm of the La-Z-Boy, and he mumbles something to himself. I give him a questioning look, but he just grimaces and turns his attention to the TV.

The commercial break comes to an end and the second half of the game kicks off. We all watch, sometimes commenting, sometimes not.

In the silent moments I realize how close I am to Savana. How our arms bump every time one of us moves. I let my hand brush against hers, and when I steal a glance, she's staring at the TV, but she's smiling.

My mouth tugs, too.

I turn back to the screen, but my mind is somewhere else.

Then there's a bang from the hallway, the sound of the front door slamming. And just like that, I'm on edge.

The others don't seem concerned; it's just my dad getting home from wherever he's been. But I look at Cody, and I know he knows, too. It's the slight differences, barely noticeable to the ear. Like the way the door slammed too hard. Or the irregular heavy footsteps thudding up the staircase, followed by the creaks and thuds from the floor above us as he staggers to his bedroom.

Cody sucks in his top lip and holds my gaze, because he knows. We've been down this road before, once or twice, when things got rough.

I wondered, after Mom left, how long it would be before it all got too much for him. A part of me had believed, though. Believed that he'd be stronger this time, especially after how hard he worked to get sober, to keep his demons under control. But I feel like I've been holding my breath.

The demons are back.

My voice comes out strangely loud. "Do you guys wanna go hang out at Cray's?" I can see the confusion on their faces, Freddie and Owen, eyebrows drawn, looking at me like I just suggested we leave a castle to go play in lava. Man, I must be desperate if going back to the port is a better option than this.

Freddie is the first to shoot me down. "Uh, no." He snorts at me. "I wanna watch the game. That's why I walked fifteen blocks in the rain to get here."

I glance at Cody, and his jaw clenches.

"Owen," I try. "Didn't you say your folks are away this weekend?"

He glances at me, distracted as the home team makes a play for the fifty-yard line. "Yeah. They're staying with my brother for his court-case bullshit."

Savana gasps. "What did Grant do?"

"Lying, as usual," Owen mutters. "I don't have time for that shit. If you're a shady person, just own it, you know? Own your shit and face the consequences." His head jerks at the sound of cheers erupting from the TV. The supporters in the crowd are on their feet. "Come *on*!"

I glance at Freddie, and he looks down at his sneakers.

Owen doesn't usually talk about his family, just like Freddie doesn't talk about his, and I don't talk about mine. Raf and Tara, too; it's one thing we all recognize in each other. Tara once confided in me that she and her parents don't get along, and they disapprove of her relationship with Raf. Sometimes I wonder if that's part of the reason she and Raf have lasted so long.

More bangs come from the ceiling above us. Heavy stumbling footsteps. My eyes are on Cody. We're communicating silently, speaking a wordless language that only we understand.

And then I'm on my feet. "Let's go to your house," I say to Owen. He blinks up at me from the couch.

"Right now? The game isn't over yet."

Cody's on his feet, too. He's already shrugging into his jacket.

"Yeah, I know," I say to Owen. "But my dad's home and he's going to claim the TV. I'll drive. We can be at your house before the fourth quarter."

Owen and Freddie swap a look, then stand. Savana does, too. Freddie's eyes still linger on the screen as I try to herd them through to the kitchen.

"Are you coming with us?" I ask Savana.

"No." She pats my arm as she slips past me, heading for the back door. "I'd better get home before my mom sends out a search party." She rolls her eyes.

My heart sinks because the last thing I want is for her to leave. But I hear the thump of footsteps descending the staircase, and I know he'll inevitably come into the living room, and he'll slur and stumble, and they'll see, and they'll know.

So Cody and I get everyone out of the house, and we don't

look back. But we both know we can't run forever. Dad's a ticking time bomb, and it's only a matter of time before he explodes.

SAVANA

Sunday, August 21

Corinne sits cross-legged on my bedroom floor as she applies her makeup in the full-length mirror.

"Ooh, this is new," she says. There's a *clunk* as she rummages through my meager makeup bag.

I glance up from my phone. I've been reclined on my bed for the past half an hour, idly scrolling through Instagram. My feed is clogged with posts from my classmates, and I've immersed myself in the photos with their heavy filters and altered features. Everyone's climbing the ladder to be seen, to have the best image and the most followers and likes.

"What do you think of this shade on me?" Corinne leans closer to the mirror as she dabs on a layer of scarlet lip gloss. She turns to me and pouts.

"I like it. It suits you." The rich red contrasts with her dark eyes and silky jet-black hair.

Her gaze moves back to her reflection and she tilts her

head from left to right, tucking her hair behind her ears to inspect her contouring.

My attention returns to my phone. I've landed on a post from Tara Kowalski's account. It's a picture of Tara and Raf, captioned *Date night with this one #everything* and punctuated with flame emojis and hearts. Raf is looking intently into the camera, his jaw squared and a slight sneer on his lips. Tara is on his lap, inclining her head so that her pale blond ponytail skims his shoulder. It looks like she's applied a color filter, because her baby blue eyes are suddenly piercing, dramatically framed by heavy lashes. According to the time stamp, she posted the photo last night, right around the time Jesse and those guys were watching the game at the Melos' house.

There are a couple of comments beneath the picture, mostly from girls in our grade, fawning over what a cute couple Tara and Raf make. How perfect they are. Tara has liked and replied to every single comment, affirming with *Right! He's so hot* and *I'm so lucky.*

I wrinkle my nose.

There's only one comment she hasn't reacted to. A comment from Freddie, posted a little after ten o'clock, not long after everyone left Jesse's house.

It just says *We're at Owen's place. You should come.*

Tara may not have commented on it, but Raf has. *She's with me.* A perfectly innocent response, sure. Just letting his friend know where they are, and that they're together at the movies downtown.

Innocent enough, despite the curtness of it.

Freddie has responded to Raf's remark, writing, *I know.*

I read over the exchange a couple of times, dissecting it way more than necessary. Reading the tension in the words.

I imagine them as two stags, bowing their heads, warning each other that they're about to combat.

We're at Owen's place. You should come.

She's with me.

I know.

I tap over to Tara's page and scroll over the rows of thumbnail shots. My eyebrows draw together. Nearly every single picture on Tara's account features Raf. Either Raf and Tara together or Raf on his own. There's one of him leaning out of his car window and throwing up a V sign, and there's an artsy shot of his broad-shouldered silhouette strolling along the beach at sunset.

They've only been dating for a few months, and Tara has had her Instagram account since at least freshman year. In theory, there should be three years' worth of photos. Three years of Tara at parties, or dances, or on vacation. Three years of her drinking coffee with Anaya and Maddie, or posing for selfies. But everything pre-Raf has been deleted. Erased.

After spending some time with Owen and Freddie last night, I'm starting to think that the group of five everyone is so obsessed with is sort of just smoke and mirrors. They seemed like pretty normal, friendly guys to me, and I already knew I liked Jesse. All the weirdness and the shutting people out… I think maybe it comes down to these two. Raf and Tara. And I want to know what that's all about.

Freddie was quick to call out Raf's controlling behavior last night, and Owen made it clear that he's all about authenticity and morals himself, a what-you-see-is-what-you-get kind of guy. So if Raf's all persona and bluff, what is it that Tara sees in him? More importantly, who is Tara beyond the carefully crafted image she's created for herself?

I'm so lost in my thoughts that I barely notice when Corinne hops up from her spot in front of the mirror and skips across the room.

She drops down beside me on the bed. "Uh, Savana?"

I glance at her. "Yeah?"

"Why are you Instagram stalking Tara Kowalski?"

I shuffle over and angle my screen toward her. "Look at this…"

Her eyes stray over the screen. "What am I supposed to be looking at?"

"It's all Raf." I point to the rows of pictures, hovering my finger over the tens of photos.

"Yes. But we knew this already. For some unimaginable reason, Tara is obsessed with Raf Lombardi."

"Okay, but why delete all her pre-Raf photos?"

Corinne squints back at me. "Wait. Are you devising a conspiracy theory? Are we going to have to wear tees saying *Free Tara* and protest on the boardwalk?"

My gaze stays on the page for another moment. "Okay." I turn to Corinne. "I hear what you're saying. I might be over-thinking this. But Raf *is* controlling, and jealous," I say, raising an index finger as I remember Freddie's direct words from last night. "Maybe she felt pressured into doing it. Maybe he *made* her do it."

"Oh, come on," Corinne scoffs. "Tara is the queen of smug. I'm sure she deems her pre-Raf life irrelevant, and she wants to make it abundantly clear that she's dating him." She mimics Tara's sugary-sweet voice, overaccenting her words, "And they're ex-clu-sive."

I sigh. "Yeah. I guess."

"And because she thinks he's the hottest guy ev-ver," she adds, holding up both hands and extending her fingers wide.

I smile, but I can't shake the feeling that Raf isn't the innocent bystander here. The way he smirks and leers at the camera—it gives me the creeps.

"I hate that guy," Corinne carries on, pretending to flick the screen where Raf stares out at us, unnerving me with his frozen sneer. "I don't know why everyone kisses his ass. He's such a Neanderthal."

I remember a few months back, when Corinne and I were walking along the school corridor toward homeroom, Raf pushed past us and *accidentally* stuck his foot out just enough to make me stumble and trip. One of the many *accidents* he has on a daily basis. Then, as Corinne helped me to my feet, Raf looked at us, wide-eyed and apologetic, as I fumbled to regain my scattered textbooks. He targeted us just because he could. Because he thinks we're weaker than him, probably.

My teeth clench at the thought.

"All of them," Corinne says, grimacing in a way that makes me think her mind has traveled to the same place mine did. "Tara, Raf, Freddie, Owen, Jesse. I don't trust a single one of them."

I fall silent, holding back the fact that I don't share those same feelings. At least, not about Jesse. Not about Freddie and Owen, either. Maybe not even about Tara.

"We shouldn't give them our energy." Corinne gently pries my cell from my hands and closes the app. "We'll talk about this again when their *Dateline* episode comes out and we're all trying to figure out where Raf hid the body after he killed her."

Her remark was said with ease, just a joke, because she doesn't really believe those words could ever come true.

But I don't laugh.

From: Allison Duncan
To: Detective Harrison Bridge
Subject: Ref Case HPD0149

Saturday, November 5

Dear Mr. Bridge,

Please find attached the file correlating to Jesse Melo's criminal record, as per your request.

According to the obtained document, he was formally charged for the incident that took place some months earlier. There was no further action against him, and the injured party did not press charges.

Further to this, I would like to inform you that his father, Mr. Ric Melo, has now been contacted and the details of last night's homicide at Havelock Port have been relayed to the family.

Regards,
Allison Duncan
Administrative assistant at Havelock Police Department

JESSE

Sunday, August 21

Freddie drags an overturned crate across the warehouse and drops it next to mine. He takes a seat beside me and clasps his hands together.

Cray's feels too barren now that the warmth of summer has slipped away and marine winds are biting at the walls.

But any refuge away from home feels good to me right now, no matter how hard the cold hits me.

Freddie sparks up a cigarette and the end crackles and glows in the dim building. On a crate opposite us, Owen takes a bottle of whiskey from his jacket pocket.

"Courtesy of my dad's liquor cabinet," he says with a toothy grin. He takes a swig, then hands the bottle to me.

I pass it back. "No, thanks."

Freddie stares at Owen and clicks his tongue to the roof of his mouth. "How did you get away with taking that? My folks would lose it if I pulled half the crap you do."

Owen smooths over his gelled hair. "That's because you

always get caught. You've just got to get them while they're preoccupied. My parents won't even notice it's gone." He takes another swig, then shudders and screws up his face.

The faraway sound of a door thudding reaches us, followed by footsteps bouncing off the walls in a trick of acoustics.

Raf and Tara emerge from the shadows. Tara skips over and takes a seat on one of the overturned crates. "Hey, boys." She steals the cigarette out of Freddie's hand and takes a long drag, then blows a stream of smoke high up into the multistory levels.

Freddie cracks a smile. "Long time no see, Tara. How've you been?"

She shrugs. "I've missed you guys."

Raf's eyes stay on her.

"Hey," Owen says. "Did either of you bring anything we could mix this with?" He shakes the bourbon bottle.

Raf grimaces. "Go to the store yourself, lazy ass." Then he grins and ruffles Owen's hair before swiping the bottle.

Owen laughs and slaps Raf's awaiting hand.

Raf claims the crate next to mine. "Come over here." He beckons to Tara. "Sit with me."

She sighs and stands, then skips over to Raf. He pulls her onto his lap, and she shrieks as he dips her.

They do this a lot—all this PDA junk that makes the rest of us uncomfortable.

"So, guys," Tara says, untangling herself from Raf long enough to look between us. "Who's down for a little night swimming?"

Owen's brow creases. "In the port?"

"Yeah." Tara's catlike eyes dance. "You're not scared, are you, Owen?" She coils a strand of hair around her index finger and leans forward so that her top slides down and we see the red lace on her bra. I look away.

"Nuh," Owen says, puffing out his chest. "But there are shitloads of fishing nets and rocks out there, and I don't feel like dying tonight."

"Nope," I say. "I'm not doing it, either."

"I'll go," Freddie says. His sneaker starts tapping on the floor, and it echoes louder than it sounds.

Tara claps her hands. Her pink-painted fingernails glisten in the dull light. "I can always rely on you, Fred. Glad to hear that at least one of you losers has some balls."

Freddie sits taller, smiling only at her.

My attention flickers to Raf, and I notice it. That pinched scowl, the tension in his back.

His arms lock tighter around her. "How about just me and you go swimming?" he murmurs into Tara's ear.

She sighs and combs her fingers through her hair.

"Come on," Raf says. "Just us." He stands and she slides up with him.

"Just us?" She laughs, but it's stilted. "What about these guys? We only just got here, babe."

"So?" he says, wrapping his arms around her and resting his chin on top of her head. "I think they'll survive without us." He turns to me and winks. I don't know what he's trying to convey, that I'm supposed to encourage her, too? That we're in on some secret, me and him?

If only he knew the secrets I know about Tara, he wouldn't be looking at me like that.

Tara makes a whimpering noise. "But I want to stay here and hang out for a little bit," she says, grabbing both of Raf's hands and twisting on her tiptoes as she gazes up at him. "It's been ages since we hung out like this, all five of us."

He snorts. "We hang out all the time."

I watch them out of the corner of my eye. Maybe I'm more aware of it now after talking to Savana, and hearing Freddie's take on it, too. Raf *is* controlling. But Tara's arms lock around his waist and she nuzzles into his chest. She's wielding some big-guns power of her own.

"These guys are boring as hell," Raf says with an easy laugh, and she laughs, too. "Come on." He lowers his voice, just for her. "We should go hang out upstairs."

When they start making out, I look away. Owen seizes the opportunity to untangle the bottle from Raf's grip.

I hear him audibly wince as he takes a swig.

Next to me, Raf and Tara's kiss amps up.

Just leave, I think. They're practically standing right over me. *If you want to go, just go.* I lean away from them.

Tara giggles when they break apart. "Okay, fine," she says, breathlessly. "Let's go upstairs and jump into the water from one of the windows."

Raf's eyes dart to me, and I half smile.

"She called your bluff," I say.

He grimaces. No one but Tara could think swimming in the port is a good idea.

She grips Raf's hand and hauls him away through the vast room. Their voices and bursts of laughter echo even after we can't see them anymore.

And then it's just the three of us again.

Freddie kicks the crate next to him and it skids across the dusty floor.

Owen and I both turn to him.

"What?" I ask. "You didn't actually want to go with them, did you?"

"No," Freddie says. "Of course not."

I swap a glance with Owen, and he takes another swig.

The occasional tremors of Raf's and Tara's laughter haunt the building.

Owen's leg starts bouncing. "Is Raf pissed at us or something?"

Freddie burrows his hands into his sleeves, retreating from the cold draft. "Nah. He just hates it when Tara wants to hang out with us over him."

More of Tara's high-pitched giggles ripple through the warehouse.

Owen's leg keeps twitching. "What, Raf thinks we're going to shoot our shot with her or something?"

Freddie presses his lips together. "Probably. You guys saw how he reacted when I said I'd go swimming." He slaps my arm to catch my attention. "You saw."

"Forget it. He didn't mean anything by it."

More giggles rebound through the warehouse.

Owen lowers his voice. "Whatever. Let's just let them do their thing," he says to Freddie. "They wanna do couple-y stuff."

"I know." Freddie sits up taller. "I get that. But Tara's our friend, too, and I swear, he's stopped inviting her out with us."

I frown at him. "She's always busy with Maddie and Anaya."

He aims his finger at me. "That's Raf's story."

"I'm not down for swimming, anyway," Owen says. "She must be out of her mind. I heard about some guy who got his leg caught in a net and straight up drowned."

Freddie's eyebrows rise. "For real?"

"Yeah, man. Like, last year or something."

I let their conversation disappear into some distant corner of my consciousness.

Something about tonight doesn't feel right to me. Cray's was a novelty for a while, but it's cold and damp, and there's nothing to do here except waste time away. I'm tired of wasting time.

I stand and the crate scrapes the floor. "I'm out."

They both look at me.

Owen's brow furrows. "What?" His eyes catch the light from the low-watt bulbs hanging over us. "You're going home already?"

"Why?" Freddie's eyes are on me, too.

I run my hands over my face. "I don't know. I've just gotta get out of here."

They swap a look.

"Wanna go somewhere else?" Owen asks. "We could hang out at my house and game?"

I shrug, and Owen takes that as his cue to stand.

Freddie glances across the room. "What about Raf and Tara?"

"Don't worry," Owen teases, tousling Freddie's curls, "they'll be okay without their third wheel." Freddie hops to his feet and they scuffle and play fight as I start for the door.

"Hey," Freddie calls after me. Their footsteps beat behind me. "Are you good to drive?"

"Yeah."

We venture outside into the bracing night wind. The clangs of the marina accompany our footsteps as we cross the quay. My car is parked on the street, bathed in lamplight.

I slide into the driver's side. Freddie rides shotgun, and Owen climbs into the back seat.

The next thing I know, my foot is on the gas and we're tearing through the suburban streets of Havelock.

On this dark stretch of road, my mind wanders. I try not to think about my mom. I try to pretend she never existed, but the memory follows me like a shadow. I swear I can still feel the pain that burned in my chest when her taillights disappeared. That night, for a second, I actually believed I could convince her to stay, and then I'd find a way to fix everything.

I lie to myself all the time; it's just what I do. I fool myself into thinking that I'm the person who can make things right, who can help my dad stay sober, who can protect my brother from the pain I know he's in. But I'm not that person. I've never been that person.

School's about to start up again, and I've got to figure out how to get Cody through the year now that Mom's gone and Dad is sliding again.

"Whoa." Freddie tugs at his seat belt. "Slow down, Jesse."

My foot stays on the pedal. "It's fine. I'm good." I crank up the music, drowning out my thoughts.

Owen starts singing in the back, wailing along to the song.

The night road stretches out before me, lights bleeding and blurring. Streetlamps, starlight, porch lights. My hands grip the steering wheel tighter.

Owen sings, wails.

Freddie thumps my seat.

Music.

Lights.

Cold air in my lungs.

"Slow down," Freddie calls over the sound system. "You're way over the speed limit. We'll get cops tailing us."

"Shit," I mutter. "Right. Sorry."

My foot slips off the gas. And then I hit a corner too fast. I brake, but the back tires keep sliding, screeching on tarmac. The steering wheel spins, torn from my grasp.

I get ahold of it just as we hit the curb and mount the sidewalk. I jerk forward with the motion, and I see the tree a moment too late.

The windshield shatters, my airbag pops and punches me back hard.

The impact is fast and hurts like hell.

SAVANA

Sunday, August 21

The sound of the doorbell merges into my dream. It takes me a couple of seconds to realize that I'm awake and the chime is real and not some ethereal part of my subconsciousness. The bell rings again, loudly. Too loudly for the dead of night.

I fumble for my phone in the darkness, then squint to read the time from the bright screen display. *11:56 p.m.*

Above my room, I hear Mom's bedroom door creak open, followed by the quick pad of her footsteps moving across the hallway and down the stairs.

I jump out of bed and hurry to join her.

"What's going on?" I call to Mom as she turns the dead bolt on the front door.

"I have no idea." Her voice is groggy, and her eyes are puffy from sleep. She swings the door open. "Ric?"

Jesse's dad is on our doorstep, lit by the soft glow of the streetlamp outside.

"Hi, Donna," he greets my mom. He's breathing strangely.

Too shallow. Too quick. "I'm so sorry to wake you, but there's been an accident. My boy's been in an accident."

My heart skips a beat. "Jesse?"

Mom wraps her arm around me. "Is he okay?" She's alert now, wide-awake. We both are. "How can we help?"

Mr. Melo's face looks sunken, streaked and distorted by long shadows. "I have to get down there, across town. Cody's trying to get through to a cab company now, but it's going to take too long, by the time they get here." His eyes are darting every which way. "I can't drive. I've been drinking. Please, Donna." His breathing quickens.

Mom is already grabbing her coat and keys. "I'll drive."

"I'm coming, too," I say as I unhook my parka from the rack and slip my arms into the sleeves. I tug the wool lining close to my chest as we brave the night wind.

Cody's on the sidewalk with his cell pressed to his ear.

"It's okay." Mr. Melo signals to him. "Donna is going to drive us."

Cody lowers his cell. His grown-out hair is rumpled and he's gnawing on his lip. When Mom's car unlocks with a beep, Cody shoots her this strange, helpless look.

She places her hand on his arm. "Everything's going to be okay," she says firmly.

His jaw clenches.

I swallow my nerves as Cody and I climb into the back seat. "Is Jesse okay?"

"EMTs are there," Mr. Melo says. His seat belt clicks into place, and Mom starts the engine.

I take a steadying breath. Next to me, Cody is shaking. He must be cold, wearing only a T-shirt and jeans. His hands are clasped, thumbs pressed together.

"Everything's going to be okay," I whisper to him. But it sounds more like a question.

He nods, all the same.

In the seat in front of me, Mr. Melo rakes his hands through his disheveled graying hair. "Take a right here," he says, gesturing beyond the car window. Mom follows his directions as we glide through the deserted lamp-lit streets.

Minutes later we turn onto Hill Street, where flashing blue lights are sweeping over the pavement.

My breath escapes in a rush. Jesse's car is totaled. It's half on the sidewalk and the hood has accordioned against a tree, and the passenger side has bowed inward.

Beneath the pulse of the blue light, two paramedics are carrying someone on a stretcher, heading for the ambulance parked opposite.

Freddie, I realize with a bolt of fear. He's not moving. He's lying on the stretcher, perfectly still, his arms folded over his chest as though they've been placed that way.

A little farther away, Owen is being checked over at the side of the road.

My heart feels like it's in my throat.

Across the pavement, my eyes land on Jesse. He's sitting on the sidewalk with his head in his hands, and there's blood smeared across his brow.

I stand back as his dad and Cody race toward him, their shoes crunching over shattered glass.

Jesse catches my gaze and presses his lips together hard. Even as his dad and brother hug him, and ask him fast questions, his eyes don't leave mine.

And mine don't leave his.

I'm sorry, he mouths.

JESSE:

Owen says they let you out of the hospital?

FREDDIE:

Yeah. Dislocated shoulder. I'm home now.

JESSE:

You okay?

FREDDIE:

Yeah. No biggie. You?

JESSE:

I shouldn't have been driving like that. I'm sorry.

FREDDIE:

We're good. No worries.

JESSE:

Cops didn't come down on you over this, did they? I told them it was all me. I told them you asked me to slow down.

FREDDIE:

It's fine, they know you were driving.

JESSE:
Can I drop by your place later?

FREDDIE:
Can't. Got to rest up.

JESSE:
I'm sorry.

JESSE:
Freddie's out of the hospital.

                     SAVANA:
                     How is he?

JESSE:
Healing from a dislocated shoulder.

                     SAVANA:
                     Poor Freddie.

JESSE:
I don't know why I did it. Drove. I was distracted, I
wasn't concentrating.

                     SAVANA:
                     Learn from this, right?

JESSE:
I will. I have.

                     SAVANA:
                     I know you have.

TITLE: CASE_HPD0149_TEXT MESSAGE TRANSCRIPTS

Recovered thread from +1****797 to an unregistered number. Messages exchanged on Friday, November 4, a few hours before the homicide at Cray's Warehouse.

5:46 Wanna know my plan?

5:47 Yeah?

5:47 Going to settle the score. Are you in?

5:59 What's the plan?

6:01 Meet me at Cray's and I'll walk you through it.

6:02 When?

6:03 I'll let you know when I'm ready. We're doing this tonight.

JESSE

Thursday, September 1

I knock on Coach Carson's office door.

"Come in." His voice sounds muffled.

I twist the handle and push the door ajar. "You wanted to see me, sir?"

He sets his pen down on the cluttered desk. "Yes. Jesse. Come on in." He gestures to the plastic chair opposite him, and I put down my backpack and take a seat.

I gaze around at the tall cupboards that take up most of the cramped space. The shelves are filled with gym equipment and half-hidden behind burlap sacks bursting with bats and poles.

"Welcome back," he says. "Did you have a good summer break?"

I muster a smile. "Yeah. Did you?"

"I did, thank you. I noticed Freddie Bass isn't in school today." He says it conversationally, but there's something in his tone. A question, maybe. "I heard about the accident you boys had," he adds. "Sounds like you were all very lucky to come out of that alive."

"Yeah." I clear my throat. "It was my fault. I'm sorry." It's a compulsion—the need to apologize to him. The guy has this fatherly energy that makes it suck to disappoint him. I search his eyes, wondering why he wanted to see me today. My behavior outside of school will probably warrant subbing me from this year's team.

My heart slams. That's probably why he called me to the sports office. He's going to tell me I'm out.

I can't help but think of my mom. How excited she was when she thought I had a shot at getting a football scholarship. She said she was proud of me. If I want any opportunity of getting scouted, and actually doing something with my life, then being on the team is the only chance I have. The kind of money it takes to get to college… I don't have that.

I grip my collar.

Coach Carson waits a moment before speaking. "Have you had a chance to think about what we discussed before summer break?"

My breath stops. *You can be honest with me about what happened. About what you've been doing.*

I remember that night in my kitchen, toasting the fundraiser game. I'd buried his words because I wasn't ready to go there.

He leans back in his seat and folds his arms across his wide chest. "Lombardi hasn't been cutting it, and you've been taking the fall for a lot of his mistakes. That's what I think's going on."

I look down at my hands.

"Or tell me I'm wrong," he says, picking me apart with his

stare. "Maybe you have been slipping up, and not passing to him. That's what he says, isn't it?"

My voice fails me.

"I want you to shoot for it this year." He clasps his thick hands together and sits forward. "We've got some big games coming up, and if you're looking to get scouted, you've got to show it."

His eyes are fixed on me, trying to pull the truth out of me.

I grasp for words. Raf was having a rough year, between his parents' separation and finding out about his sister being in an abusive relationship. He needed a break.

I know he's been telling the guys I don't pass to him, or my throws are off, and I go along with it, because he doesn't deserve to get subbed over a few mistakes.

"You've got potential," Coach Carson says. "If you pull this out of the bag, you're in with a real shot. People are going to be watching you, though."

My throat feels dry. "What about Raf?"

He stares steadily at me. "Lombardi's not cutting it, and I think you know that. I'm looking at making some changes this season. To be clear," he adds, directing his index finger at me, "I'm not guaranteeing you a scholarship, especially with a driving offense on your record. But I'm going to try to help you make up for it and make your odds as good as I possibly can. If I'm going to stick my neck out for you, you can't let me down. Gun for it. Sound good?"

I chew on my lip. "Yeah."

The lunch bell rings shrilly, tremoring through me.

Coach Carson slaps his palms together. "That's all I wanted to talk to you about. Go get some lunch." He picks up his pen and gestures toward the door.

I stand and sling my backpack over my shoulder. As I head for the door, he returns to his paperwork.

"Good luck this season," he calls without looking up. "Give me your best."

Savana's strolling along the corridor as I come out of the sports office.

"Hey," she says with a laugh. "You look—" she waves her hand in front of my face "—spacey. Are you…in there?" She peers into my eyes, exaggerating wonder.

I glance over my shoulder. There are too many people around, too many bodies weaving past us as they head for the cafeteria.

I gesture for Savana to follow me.

I lead her to a classroom doorway where we're out of the path of hallway traffic. "Coach Carson just called me into his office."

She tucks a strand of wavy brown hair behind her ear and frowns. "Oh, no. Why? Was it about the accident?"

"Yeah, but other stuff, too." My focus strays to the people passing us and the buzz of voices. "Raf messed up a couple of times last year, and I took the heat over it."

Her eyebrows rise. "Oh."

"Maybe more than a couple of times." I run my hand over my mouth. "But I don't want him to get subbed."

She narrows her silvery-gray gaze. "Okay. But that's kind of not up to you, right?"

"Do you think I should tell Raf?"

She shrugs. "I don't know. Maybe that's a conversation Coach Carson needs to have with him."

"He said he's changing things around this year. I know he wants us to get to state playoffs."

"Well, yeah. That's always the aim, right?"

"Yeah."

Farther down the corridor, I notice Raf and Tara heading this way. Their heads are bowed in conversation, but they're going to walk right past us.

I give Savana a look. "Pick this up later?"

She nods. "Let me know how it goes." Then she touches my arm. "I'll see you later."

"Yeah," I murmur.

She leaves me alone in the doorway and merges into the sea of bodies moving along the corridor.

SAVANA

Tuesday, September 6

Coach Carson is announcing the new football lineup today.

It's raining pretty heavily, so a bunch of seniors have gathered in the gym, taking up a couple of rows on the bleachers as they wait for the coach to read out this year's team. The spectators are mostly the players, and some friends, and girlfriends or boyfriends. And me, a curious bystander.

A little way along the bleachers, Jesse, Raf, Freddie, and Owen are seated together.

Coach Carson's shoes squeak on the orange floor as he walks to the center of the gym. His bald head shines where the light hits it, and he runs his thumb along his jaw as he considers the printed list in his hand. There's a whistle hanging around his neck, and it moves up and down with the rhythm of his broad chest.

He glances up when Principal Harland crosses the gym to join him.

Suddenly, the double doors swing open and Tara rushes in.

Her cheeks are flushed, and her hair looks windswept. She slides onto my bench.

"What have I missed?" she hisses, smoothing down some flyaway strands.

I stare at her for a second, wondering why she's sitting next to me. My row is closest to the gym's entrance, sure, but Tara Kowalski would normally walk an extra couple of rows up and climb over as many people as necessary to sit with Raf and the guys.

"Nothing," I answer after a pause. "They haven't announced yet." Mr. Carson and Principal Harland are standing together, heads bowed as they study the printed list and mutter between one another. "Looks like they're still finalizing," I whisper to Tara.

She exhales and her slim shoulders drop. "Okay, good. Raf would have been so mad if I'd missed this." Her eyes narrow. "Wait, why are you here?"

"Journalism project for my college application." I reach for an excuse that isn't related to Jesse, because a) not her business, and b) not looking for her opinion. "I'm investigating how the status of being a high school athlete elevates social ranking." It's true enough. This is research. Ninety-five percent research. Five percent something else.

"Oh." Tara flips her glossy highlighted waves. "Social ranking? You can interview me, if you want, since I'm way up at the top of the pyramid."

"That's actually not a bad idea."

"Savana, I'm kidding," she says with a laugh.

She's right, though. If there were ever an example of a person whose life standing has elevated because of the way she crafts her social media, with airbrushed photos and a timeline of her "perfect" relationship with the high school wide receiver—or perhaps after today, *former* wide receiver—it's Tara.

We turn our attention back to Coach Carson as he claps his enormous hands to command the attention of the room.

"I'm sure you're all ready to find out who'll be playing on this year's boys' varsity team," he booms, and the voices around the gym simmer. He begins reading the names on his list, followed by a cheer from the bleachers after each position is called. Freddie's name gets called, followed by Owen's.

Then he announces, "Finally, number eleven, Jesse Melo, you'll be starting quarterback."

There are a few claps around the hall. I glance across the bleachers at Jesse. He's leaning forward, chin rested on his fists. He isn't smiling, exactly. He's just staring steadily ahead, absorbing the coach's words.

Finally, as in, that's it. Raf's name didn't get called.

Tara's gaze shoots to me. "Raf's been subbed?" she hisses.

"Sounds like it."

"Ouch," she murmurs. "He's going to be so pissed. I mean, seriously."

My gaze shifts back to the boys. The muscles in Raf's jaw are bulging, Freddie is drumming his finger on his teeth, and Owen's face looks frozen in surprise. Jesse's staring down at his sneakers now.

"He'll be so jealous of the others right now," Tara purrs.

I glance at her, and she almost looks like she's suppressing a smile.

"Jesse's dead," she whispers.

TITLE: CASE_HPD0149_TEXT MESSAGE TRANSCRIPTS

Recovered thread from +1****797 to an unregistered number. Messages exchanged on Friday, November 4, an hour before the homicide at Cray's Warehouse was called in to Dispatch.

10:01 You ready?

10:02 Yeah.

10:03 You know where I'll be.

10:05 What's the plan?

10:06 I'll tell you when you get here. Don't back out. You owe me this, remember? Delete these messages from your phone.

JESSE

Thursday, September 8

Half the team is still in the locker room after first practice with the new lineup. Dominic Campbell took Raf's spot, and although I'd never admit this to Raf, Dom was good.

Raf took being subbed better than I'd expected. But I can tell it's eating away at him. I see the way he looks at me, too, like this is my fault.

I scrub my hair with a towel before dropping it onto the bench. The locker room is always humid and toxic with body spray. Metal doors clang and voices sound tinny.

Freddie steps out from the shower block with a towel wrapped around his waist. He leaves wet footprints on the tiles as he crosses the room.

He gives me a nod, then swings open his locker and fishes out a T-shirt.

I pull on my sneakers and tighten the laces.

Out of the corner of my eye, I notice him stretching his shoulder, pulling his arm across his chest and then shaking it out. I think this practice hit him hard. I doubt his doctor would have approved contact sports this early into his recovery.

I clear my throat. "Are you all right?"

"Yeah," he says.

"Is your shoulder okay?"

He pulls the T-shirt over his head and shakes a hand through his wet curls. "Yeah. It's healed now."

I must be frowning without even realizing I'm doing it because he gives me a look.

His jaw tightens. "I said it's fine, so it's fine. Who are you, my mom?"

I return to my sneakers, tightening the laces for a second time. "All right."

He looks over my head as Owen and Raf cross the locker room.

Raf shoulders past me while I'm still pulling at my laces, one foot propped on the bench. It catches me off guard and I have to steady myself.

My eyes shoot to him.

"Sorry, man," he says, slapping my back. "I slipped."

I stand to full height, but he's already turned his attention to Freddie.

"Word?" Raf nods toward the corner of the shower block, and Freddie follows him across the room.

Owen and I glance at each other as they leave.

"What's that about?" I ask.

"Raf's got some stuff to help Freddie's shoulder," he says.

"Like what?"

He shrugs. "Dunno."

Our eyes linger on them as they talk in hushed voices across the room.

"How did you think Freddie was today?" I ask Owen under my breath.

"A mess." Owen's voice is lowered, too, and his eyes move between them and me. "Man, he was all over the place."

I rub the nape of my neck. "He shouldn't be doing this," I grumble. "If he's not ready to play, then he shouldn't push it."

Owen presses his lips together. "Don't go saying that to Freddie. He won't want to hear shit like that."

My gaze strays back to Raf and Freddie. Owen's right. Freddie won't want to hear it, especially not from me. This wouldn't even be a problem if it wasn't for me.

"You know your dad's outside?" Owen's tone eases as he switches the topic. "I saw his truck in the lot when I was at the vending machine."

"Okay." I pull my backpack from my locker. "I better go." I nudge the metal door shut and Owen claps my shoulder.

"See you tomorrow," he says.

I nod, then call *bye* to Raf and Freddie as I leave.

The locker room door thumps shut behind me. I'm back in the cool, bright corridor, but it's empty now, stripped of the usual flow of people and cacophony of voices.

Dad's been giving me rides since my car was totaled in the accident, partly because he's doing me a favor, but mostly because he wants to keep tabs on me. His truck is parked near the field. The last of the daylight is falling away and bleeding orange over the turf. Darkness is creeping up on us earlier now.

I slide into the truck's passenger seat and pull the door shut.

"Thanks for the ride."

"No problem," Dad says. "Did you have a good day?"

I search his eyes. They're clear, focused. Dark brown like mine, and sharp, not the eyes of someone who's been drinking.

"Yeah," I answer. "You?"

"Not bad."

"I wasn't expecting you to come today," I tell him. "I know it's late."

"Are you kidding?" His eyes crinkle with a smile, and he reaches out and grips my shoulder. "I wouldn't have missed your first practice."

"You watched?"

"You did good," he says with a nod. "Nice hustle in the second half." He gives a low whistle. "Better than I could have done at your age."

He's lying. He was really good. Like my mom used to say, he had so much going for him before I came along. Maybe she'd still be with him if I hadn't knocked his life so out of whack.

The thought of her, and the things she used to say, the clues she used to plant about how dissatisfied she was with her life...it makes my lungs tighten.

"I talked to your coach," Dad carries on, oblivious to the raw places my mind has wandered. "He thinks you've got a great shot at getting scouted. What do you think?"

I run my hand over my face. "I hope so."

"Cal State is looking. Your coach thinks he should be able to get you an interview at the end of the season."

"What do you think about that?"

"It's a fantastic opportunity, Jesse."

"It's a long way from home, though. What about you and Cody?"

He laughs, just a quick sound. "Don't worry about us. We've got to get you on the right path. That's all I'm thinking about right now."

I stare beyond the windshield to the field.

Dad clears his throat. "You've really pulled yourself together these past couple of weeks. I've noticed." He aims a finger at me, his tone serious. "That doesn't mean you're off the hook. But community service, knuckling down at school, football. You're putting in the work, and I see it."

My focus strays to the orange sky. The moon has faintly appeared as the day starts to dissolve.

"Proud of you," Dad says. "Your granddad would have been proud of you, too." He squeezes my shoulder again before bringing his hands to the steering wheel.

As the engine rumbles, I notice Raf, Owen, and Freddie coming out of school. They split apart and head toward their cars. But my eyes only follow Raf. I don't look, but I get the feeling Dad's eyes are doing the same.

SAVANA

Monday, September 19

Tara and I have fifth-period English together. Her desk is next to mine. That wasn't a deliberate arrangement. We don't usually say more than *hey* to each other during the entire hour.

But today, right before the bell, she slides her phone onto my desk. The screen is lit by a picture of her, a selfie. It's been retouched and filtered with a cool bluish tone.

"What do you think?" she whispers. When I glance over at her, she curls her top lip. "Is it too thirsty?"

"What do you mean?" I whisper back.

"The photo," she says, looking at me expectantly. "Should I post it or does it look like I'm trying too hard?"

I frown. I'm not entirely sure why she's asking me, or why she suddenly cares about my opinion, but I take another look at the selfie before the screen fades to black.

"It's cute," I tell her. "You know your angles." I hand the phone back to her.

"You think?" she says as she reopens the screen and in-

spects it with a tilted head. "My nose is so…" She exaggerates a shudder and presses the tip of her nose.

Her nose is perfect, of course. Completely straight and
flawless from every angle.

"So you think I should post it?" She stares at me, tapping
her pen on her lips.

My eyes stray to Mr. Greggory, who's at the front of class
grading worksheets. "Yeah," I whisper. "It's a good photo."

Tara's thumbs move fast over her screen. "Thanks. I'd usually ask Maddie or Anaya for their opinion, but you've probably noticed we're not talking right now."

I glance over my shoulder to where Tara's girlfriends are
sitting side by side at the back of the classroom, focused on
their work. "How come?"

She sighs. "Who knows with them. I think they're jealous or something."

I decide not to respond. I'd prefer not to get pulled into
Tara's drama.

"They've got a problem with Raf," she elaborates. "But it's
whatever." When I frown, she adds, "Maddie says he makes
her uncomfortable. It's such a joke, I can't."

I blink at her. "Oh."

"I probably should ask him before I post this picture," she
mutters to herself. "But oh, well."

"I wouldn't worry," I whisper back. "I'm sure Raf loves
everything you post. He's completely obsessed."

I think back to Tara's Instagram page and the time I casually stalked her Raf-themed feed. Of course he'd love everything she posts, because more often than not, it's shots of him.

She shakes her head, blond ponytail swishing. "No way.
He thinks my pictures make me look trashy and desperate."

I do a double take. "What? He actually says that?" This is
the side of Raf that I've been suspicious of in my fantastical
theories about how he pulls the strings in their relationship.
But to hear it from Tara makes it feel a little too real.

"He's just protective," Tara adds. "He doesn't want other
guys thinking I'm easy." Her eyes are still fixed on her cell
as she crops the image into a perfect square.

"That's called possessive," I tell her, "not protective."

She shrugs, and her attention stays on her phone. There's
a faint tapping sound as she types out a caption to accompany her selfie.

I turn back to my paper.

A second later Tara prods me with her pen. "You wanna
get coffee after school? I feel like going to the pier and I need
girl time."

I stare back at her, dazed into silence.

I glance over my shoulder, because surely that invitation
wasn't intended for me? But no one else is looking our way.
Tara smiles, waiting for my response.

I decide to squash my default reactions, like: *Since when do
you and I go for coffee?* And: *Since when are we friends?* How have
I become the replacement for Maddie and Anaya all of a sudden? Unless Jesse has said something to her...

She's still waiting for my answer, so I settle for "Um, what?"

The bell rings, and Tara springs from her chair and threads
her arm through mine, hauling me to my feet.

"Hold up," I say, staring at her as the class starts moving
around us. "Did I fall asleep and wake up in an alternate
reality?"

She smirks. "If you did, then you just got lucky, bitch."

Tara jumps into fast chatter about some shows she's watching on Netflix, telling me how I *need it in my life*. And it's *everything*. Ev-er-y-thing.

To my shame, I'm kind of buying into it. The show, the strange new camaraderie, the *girl time* and *coffee at the pier*. I'm going along with it, my arm linked through hers as she tows me down the hall. In a weird way I'm almost enjoying the effervescence of her company. Right up until the moment I see Corinne waiting at my locker.

And then I cringe.

"Hey, Corinne," I say, cutting Tara off midstream. "Do you want to come to the pier with us?"

Corinne stares back at me, her expression frozen somewhere between a mocking smile and a horrified scowl. "With us?" she echoes. "And *us* is…" She trails off and her eyes skate over Tara.

Tara's face has fallen, too. Clearly, she hadn't envisioned Corinne as part of our new coalition.

Before I can respond, Corinne arches an eyebrow. "Actually, I have to get home. But have fun, girls." There's a lilt to her voice, and she gives me the look. The pursed-lipped, raised-eyebrow look that says, *What the hell are you doing and why the hell are you doing it?*

I slip my arm free from Tara's. "Are you sure you won't come, Corinne?"

She crinkles her nose. "Another time. Oh, and by the way, Tara," she adds, "you might want to check in with Raf. Principal Harland called him out of chem. People are saying he's been busted with drugs."

JESSE

Monday, September 19

I catch up with Freddie in the parking lot just as school's getting out.

He's pacing toward his Camaro.

"Hey," I call after him. "What happened?"

He reaches his car and slams his palm on the hood.

"Whoa." I jog the rest of the way to reach him. "Why'd you get pulled from class?"

"I'm done!" He throws his backpack onto the tarmac and kicks it. The bag skids across the ground and knocks into a nearby car's tire. "Expelled."

"What?" I take a step back, knocked by his words. "What are you talking about?"

He licks his lips fast. "Raf sold me out. Someone found steroids in the boys' locker room and Raf said they were mine to save his own ass."

I stare back at him. "What? Who had steroids?"

"Raf!" he exclaims, throwing up his hands. "He was getting them. He offered some to me for my shoulder, but I said no." His mouth pulls into a grimace. "They were *his*, and he set me up." He's breathing hard. "Who's going to believe me over him?"

I squeeze my eyes shut for a second. "This can't be happening," I object. "You can't be expelled. There's got to be something you can do." I glance over my shoulder. There are people coming out of the building, but no one's close enough to hear our words. "Can't you just deny everything?"

"Raf's already pinned it on me! He told me I should keep his stash in my locker just in case I needed it. He said it like he was doing me a favor." His teeth clench. "Raf set me up, and who's going to believe me over him?" he says again, and my chest tightens.

He rubs his hands roughly over his face. "I'm done. I'm out." He swings open the driver's door, and the next thing I know he's behind the wheel and revving the engine.

I jump aside as the Camaro lurches forward. "Freddie, come on." I rap on the hood. "Get your folks to talk to the school, explain about your shoulder. We'll all back you. It's probably not as cut-and-dry as you think. Raf wouldn't have done you like that."

His window rolls down. "Oh, yeah," he shouts. "Because Raf's such a good guy." His expression changes and his Adam's apple bobs as he swallows. "You wanna know who Raf really is? He told me to keep this from you because he said it'd screw with your head if you knew. Remember over the summer when those guys jumped you in the port?"

My heart starts beating fast because those words are enough. I already know where this is going. I already know how the sentence ends.

I know it. I *knew* it.

"Raf set it up." Freddie's words cut through me like a steel blade. "Because Cody threw a brick through his window. Those guys were coming for your brother and they got you by mistake—"

I don't hear the rest because I'm already running through the parking lot, dodging all the students who are heading for their cars.

I'm pushing past people, shoving my way through, because I can see Raf in the hallway. He's strolling toward the exit without a care in the world. Without a speck on his conscience.

I take a swing at him. And another.

Arms are around me, pulling me off. But I only see him.

His lies.

His betrayal.

He came for my brother, and now I'm coming for him.

From: Allison Duncan
To: Detective Harrison Bridge
Subject: Ref Case HPD0149

Saturday, November 5

Dear Mr. Bridge,

Please see the attached text message transcripts from the cell phone belonging to Jesse Melo that was recovered from the incident site.

As you'll see from the attached file, a text conversation takes place between Jesse Melo and Savana Caruso shortly before the incident. In the messages, Melo requests that Caruso join him at Cray's Warehouse on the night of Friday, November 4. He asks for her help with something unspecified.

Savana Caruso's phone records have been subpoenaed, along with the phone records of the other people present that night. We are awaiting transcripts. Attachments to follow.

Regards,
Allison Duncan
Administrative assistant at Havelock Police Department

SAVANA

Monday, September 19

I walk fast alongside Jesse as we head toward the cove. He's breathing hard. His shirt is still bunched from whatever just went down at school between him and Raf.

I brace myself in the crisp autumn air. "What happened back there?"

One minute I'm in an alternate reality arranging to go for coffee on the pier with Tara; the next minute half our class is pulling Jesse and Raf apart as they go at it in the corridor.

"He's a snake, Savana." Jesse's voice is raised. "He's twisted."

We stride quickly along the suburban street, past picket fences and neat lawns.

"Raf was the person who sent those guys after Cody," he says through gritted teeth. "It was him."

My breath comes out in a rush as I piece his words together. "Oh, my God," I murmur. "You're kidding?"

"Nope."

"We have to do something," I say, fumbling over my words. "We have to tell your dad, or the police, or something." I glance at his profile as we walk. His jaw clenches.

"No," he says, shaking his head. "This can't get back to Cody. He'll lose it."

The wind whips at my hair, and my eyes stray over the sidewalk. "But he can't just..."

"He set up Freddie, too. Freddie's been expelled because Raf set him up with steroids."

My stomach flips. "We can't let him get away with this."

"I always knew there was another side to Raf. But I never... *never*..." He trails off, as though he can't bring himself to finish the sentence.

I hold my breath. "I'm so sorry, Jesse," I whisper. "I know this must hurt."

He gives way to a fractured laugh. "Yeah. It does." He catches my gaze, and we pause, standing still for a moment. The wind tousles his hair. "That's it, isn't it?" he says. "We're not coming back from this. Me and him, we're done."

I take a small breath.

"Be careful around him," he says. "For real. He knows how I feel about you, and I don't trust him."

I swallow and nod, lost for words. Instinctively, I reach out to catch his hand, and his fingers lock with mine. The touch is safe, familiar. An innate communication that we're on the same page.

His eyes linger on mine, as though he's seeing something deeper. He moves his thumb along my hand. "Sorry. I shouldn't have said that. I didn't mean to scare you."

"You didn't," I assure him. "I'm not scared of Raf."

He musters a smile. "Good. You don't have to be. I've got you."

"I know." I squeeze his hand, and we carry on walking.

TARA:

Hey, girlie. Wanna watch football training with me after school?

SAVANA:

Can't. Gotta work on my journalism project.

TARA:

Aha, then I have some resources for you.

SAVANA:

Like what?

TARA:

Just come. You'll see.

SAVANA:

Tara wants me to watch football practice with her after school today.

JESSE:

?

SAVANA:

I feel like I'm betraying you if I hang out with her.

JESSE:

Why? Tara's not Raf.

SAVANA:

Okay. So you're fine with it?

JESSE:

Yeah. Are you going to do it?

SAVANA:

I guess.

JESSE:

Will you wave at me from the stands?

SAVANA:
Maybe. If you wave back.

                                         JESSE:
                                        You know it.

SAVANA

Tuesday, October 4

Without a doubt, the past few weeks at school have been... *different*.

Jesse and Raf's usual five-strong lunch table has dispersed. Freddie is gone, expelled for allegedly bringing drugs on campus, and the Jesse-Raf bromance is well and truly over. Raf and Tara sit on one side of the cafeteria while Jesse and Owen sit on the other. Jesse and Raf don't acknowledge each other in class, and they keep enough of a distance to make it clear to everyone that their friendship is officially done.

After school I head over to the football field and climb the bleachers to join Tara. *Tara*, my new friend-type person. Yet more proof that the equilibrium is shot.

It started out as curiosity, getting a closer insight into who Tara Kowalski, the persona, really is. Turns out, I actually kind of like her. She's fast-talking and seems to have a never-ending supply of candy in her purse. I feel like I'm on a sugar high whenever I hang out with her.

The team is jogging laps around the field, while Coach Carson stands in the middle and hollers at them to pick up the pace.

Tara pats the space beside her. "So I'm thinking," she says, sweeping her long hair to one side and twisting it, "for your project we should assess who's most likely to make homecoming queen this year." She fans her face with her hands. "No pressure to say me. Wink, wink."

I crinkle my nose. "Is that it? You said you had resources."

"Yeah. I am the resources. Also, I need you to be here." She tugs her coat tighter around herself. "I'm bored and I need company."

"Sneaky."

She feigns a mortified gasp. "Sneaky? I think you mean *resourceful*."

I glance at the field. The team and the subs are still running laps like sharks circling the water. "Why are you even out here?" I ask Tara.

"I like to watch the practices," she says.

I resign myself to accepting the seat beside her. The truth is, I kind of feel sorry for her. Tara fronts like she's the queen, but I don't buy the act. At least, not anymore. Now that the group has splintered, I've noticed Tara spends a lot of time on her own. Well, either on her own or with Raf. Frankly, I don't know which is worse.

"Thanks for coming." She shudders and huddles close to me. Her nose is flushed from the cold air. "I need someone to talk to. Even if we have to talk about your boring project." She flashes me a quick grin. "Kidding."

I swat her arm. "If I stay out here with you, you need to at least pretend to be interested."

She flutters her eyelashes. "Is that not what I'm already doing?"

"So things aren't any better with Maddie and Anaya, I take it?"

"Nope." She blows out a sigh. "But I don't have time for negative energy. I'm only about positive vibes this year." She beams at me, all teeth and sparkly eyes. "Now," she says, "wanna scroll through TikTok mindlessly with me? I have snacks." She pulls a bag of M&M's from her shoulder bag and pops it open. "See? More resources."

I take a handful and lean in as she opens an app on her phone, and we start working our way through the videos.

I shade the screen with my hand as a trending sound bite plays on a loop. "You know," I say, squinting to make out the video, "this would be a lot easier to see if we were inside."

"I know, but Raf needs me here," she says, crunching on one of the M&M's. "He's really down right now." Then she pauses and sighs. The video keeps playing, but Tara's gaze has moved to me. "I'm sure you've noticed he's fighting with Jesse and Owen, and he's annoyed about this whole Freddie thing." She looks at me in earnest, and I frown. "Okay, like apparently—" she hits Pause on the video and lowers her voice, not that anyone can hear us from here "—Freddie brought steroids into school and when he got caught, he tried to blame it all on Raf, even though Raf didn't know anything about it. Now everyone hates Raf for it. It's so shady, Savana, you have no idea."

"Funny," I mutter. "I heard it the other way around."

She tilts her head. "What? From who?"

Dropping Jesse's name will only add fuel to the already-blazing fire, so I just shrug. Since Tara hasn't mentioned Cody in this, I suspect Raf hasn't disclosed that part of the story to her, either.

"Freddie was taking them for his shoulder," Tara says. "That's what I heard. But Raf can't understand why Freddie tried to pass the blame onto him. Raf's just so confused and hurt."

My gaze drifts over the field. The team has split off into smaller groups now and they're passing balls back and forth between each other. Jesse and Owen are in a group together, and Raf is way across the field with some other guys from our grade.

I turn back to Tara. "Have you talked to Freddie since all this happened?"

"No." She starts unpicking a knot in her hair. "Do you think I should call him?"

"Yes."

"Don't tell Raf, though. He'll hate that."

I sigh into the cold air. "Just call Freddie."

"Maybe. But Freddie's got the others in his corner. Raf doesn't have anyone." Her sky blue eyes stray to the field, lingering on number eleven. Jesse.

The team has regrouped, and the coach keeps yelling at Jesse for not passing to Raf, shouting *Lombardi's open*. It ripples through the field.

"All of Raf's best friends have turned against him," Tara states. "It sucks for him."

My eyes stay trained on Jesse. He won't pass to Raf. He won't go near Raf.

Coach Carson blows the whistle and signals for the boys to take a break. They jog to the sidelines to retrieve their water bottles.

While the others roam around on the field, Raf climbs the bleachers toward us, grinning at Tara. When he reaches us, he pulls Tara into a kiss.

She shrieks with laughter. "Ew, babe, you're all sweaty!"

I shuffle over, averting my eyes from the heavy-handed PDA. Because ick.

Jesse's still on the field, looking our way.

I lift my hand in a small wave, but his expression is stony, preoccupied. He takes a sip from his water bottle, and his eyes don't leave Raf's back.

Corinne has drama club after school on Tuesdays. Since I'm here way past my usual fleeing time, I meet her at her locker. Tara has already left in a whirlwind of *byeee*s, and M&M's, and air-kisses.

"Hey," Corinne sings when she sees me waiting at her locker. "What are you doing here so late?"

"Oh, you know me, ever the loiterer." The true admission that I've been watching football practice with Tara doesn't seem to want to leave my lips. I'm not even sure it has a place in my vocabulary.

"Well," Corinne says, accepting my vague response, "I'm glad about your loitering ways because it means I have someone to hang out with. Miller's on the way home?"

I gasp and touch my hand to my heart. "It's like you're reading my mind."

Corinne tosses her books into her locker and shuts the door with a clang.

A little farther down the hall, the boys' locker room opens and Raf strides out. His head is bowed, eyes fixed on his phone as he walks.

He passes us with quick strides, and his shoulder knocks hard into Corinne.

She lets out a cry.

I suck in a breath and reach out to steady her.

Raf stops and looks up from his phone. "Oh, shit, Karen," he says. "Sorry. I wasn't looking where I was going." He stands close, towering over us. Then he places his hand on her shoulder, just because he can. "Sorry," he says again, and he smirks. Corinne shakes his hand away.

"You're a bully," Corinne shouts after him as he continues on his way. "You know what, Raf? Sooner or later you're going to get what's coming to you."

He raises his middle finger high and keeps on walking.

TARA:
Party tonight at Owen's place!

SAVANA:
I don't know, I'm kind of tired.

TARA:
No! You have to come! It's open invite, everyone's going to be there, you do not want to miss this.

SAVANA:
I'll think about it.

TARA:
Please!

SAVANA:
Do you want to go to a party tonight?

CORINNE:
Whose party?

SAVANA:
Owen Keaton's.

CORINNE:
That'll be a colossal NO from me. I've officially reached my quota for attending parties where Raf will be. Is this still "research"?

SAVANA:
Kind of. But I also just want to hang out with Jesse.

CORINNE:
Aha, I called it! Are you going to make your move?

SAVANA:
Maybe. If I'm feeling brave enough!

CORINNE:
You'll be fine, he obviously likes you, too. Good luck and be careful. Text me updates. Love ya!

JESSE

Saturday, October 22

I sit with Savana on the Keatons' couch, my eyes straying over the framed photos hanging on their living room wall. Owen at a football game in full gear; Grant at graduation in his cap and gown; Mr. and Mrs. Keaton wearing colorful leis at a hotel resort. Owen's parents are in Boston visiting Grant, so Owen threw a party and put out an open invite to everyone in our grade.

The house is crammed, and music is tremoring the walls.

I lean in close to Savana, trying to hear her voice above the clamor. Her words brush my ear in the best way.

She speaks. I speak.

She laughs. I laugh.

I want to stay in this bubble with her forever, close enough to count the freckles on her cheeks. Close enough to see the different shades of gray in her eyes. I'm all kinds of happy here.

And then *he* shows up and bursts our bubble.

"Hey," Raf says, casting a shadow over us.

I look up at him from the couch. "Yeah? What?"

His jaw juts out. "You over it yet?"

Something rushes inside my chest. "Am I *over it*?" My grip tightens around my water bottle, and Savana rests her hand on my arm.

"Yeah," he grunts. "Whatever lies Freddie told you. See, he hasn't shown tonight because he knows he's lying."

I grind my teeth. "He hasn't shown tonight because he doesn't want to see *you*."

His Adam's apple moves when he swallows. "Savana, give us a minute."

She glances at me, and I crick my neck. I don't like the way he spoke to her, the bluntness of his tone.

"Okay," she says slowly.

"No." My eyes stay fixed on Raf. "You and I don't need a minute."

He sneers. For a second it looks like he's going to leave, but then he stops. He looks at us again. His eyes rove over us. "Are you two together now or something?"

"You need to go," I say.

And this time he does.

SAVANA

Saturday, October 22

I squeeze my way through the Keatons' crowded hallway and head for the staircase. Owen's making his way down, slapping hands with various loiterers. We pass midway on the stairs, and he high-fives me. His light blue eyes are bloodshot and bleary from alcohol.

"Bathroom?" I call above the pulse of music.

He points vaguely to the second-floor landing.

"Hey," he says before I continue my ascent. "You and Jesse." He gives me a thumbs-up. "It's happening, yeah?"

I can't help but smile with every inch of my face.

Owen presses his index finger to his lips. "He likes you. I can tell. And I'm here for it. Holler if you need a wingman."

I can't hold back the grin. "I like him, too. Watch this space."

I laugh at the sound of Owen drunkenly cheering as I carry on up the stairs.

It's quieter up here, with most of the party contained to the main floor. Upstairs seems to be reserved for couples making out in dark corners, or in-depth conversations in doorways. I slip into the bathroom and close the door behind me with a quiet click.

Before I've had a chance to pull the lock, the handle twists and the door opens.

"Hey." I move to push it shut, but Raf forces his way into the bathroom. He nudges the door shut and twists the lock.

My heart gives a slow thud. "What are you doing?" My voice sounds weak. I take an involuntary step backward and my spine presses against the sink.

"I want to talk to you." His words are slurred, thick. "Without Jesse and Tara around."

There's a beat of silence, and his eyes shift to my lips.

I frown as he reaches for me, his big hand folding around my wrist.

"*Hey.*" I pull my arm back, but his grip holds fast. He leans closer and lowers his lips to mine and kisses me.

I jerk my head away from him. Time seems to warp, moving too fast and then too slow. All I can think to do is shove him as hard as I can and get to the door. The instant I'm out of the bathroom, I run for the stairs.

SAVANA

Saturday, October 22

I should never have gone to Owen's party.

Jesse's footsteps are moving fast behind me.

"Savana, wait." His words reach me over the howl of the night wind.

I take an unsteady breath and slow my pace. Jesse catches up with me on the sidewalk, but we keep going. I can't bring myself to stop.

"What happened back there?" He glances over his shoulder, toward Owen's house.

I wrap my arms around myself tightly as I continue along the street.

"Savana, you're scaring me." I can hear it in his voice; he *is* scared. He's walking fast beside me, his footsteps in perfect sync with mine. His arm keeps twitching, almost reaching out. It's like he wants to pull me into a hug or something. But he doesn't.

"What happened?"

I shake my head. I can't speak, not yet. I can't find my voice. I couldn't find it back there, and I can't find it out here, either.

We keep striding along the sidewalk under the streetlamps. Jesse's eyes dart between me and the road as he waits for me to talk.

"Did someone say something to you?" His hands ball. "Did someone *do* something to you?"

My skin prickles and a shiver slides over me.

Of course Jesse's confused. Of course he has questions. Just a little while earlier I was fine, happy. We were lounging on the Keatons' sofa, talking, laughing, smiling. He was going to save my spot while I went to the bathroom. But when I came back, I just grabbed my purse and told him I was leaving.

I squeeze my eyes shut, pushing the thoughts as far down as I can bury them.

"I'm okay." I manage to get the words out.

He exhales in relief.

I'm lying. I'm not okay. I want to scream. I want to cry, but there are no tears coming to the surface. They're all frozen, just like I have been ever since…

"Raf grabbed me." My voice jumps out, shattering the night.

There's a beat, a pause, where everything shifts.

"What do you mean?" Jesse says.

"He followed me into the bathroom, and he grabbed me and kissed me."

The rhythm of our footsteps halts as Jesse stops walking.

I stop, too, and I drag my gaze to his.

He's breathing fast.

Too many thoughts spiral through my mind. He doesn't believe me; he didn't see. I scramble for my voice as Jesse yanks his phone from his jacket pocket.

"What are you doing?"

He presses his cell to his ear. "Calling the cops."

"No!" I grab the phone from him and end the call. "No, don't. This isn't a police thing. It was just…"

We stand rigidly in an orb of yellow lamplight, staring at each other.

My heart is racing, thumping in my ears. "Please, Jesse. Don't." There's a catch in my voice; I can hear it. I can hear it and I hate it.

"Okay," he murmurs, holding my gaze. "It's okay. I won't do anything you don't want me to."

My grip tightens on his phone, my fingers locked firmly around it. "I don't want you to say anything to anyone. I'm not even sure…" I let out a broken breath and shake my head. "I'm not even sure. I just feel…"

Disempowered. The word rushes through me, because that's how I feel. The gut-wrenching realization that Raf managed it. He managed to make me feel small. Smaller than him.

Jesse grimaces and casts another glance in the direction of Owen's house.

"Don't go back there," I whisper.

"I won't."

I start walking again, heading toward the coast and the sanctuary of home. Jesse lopes alongside me with his hands shoved into his jacket pockets.

"Don't tell anyone." My words sound hoarse. I can't bring myself to look at him.

"I won't. You can talk to me," he says. "Just me."

So I do. I tell him every muddled memory I have, starting from the moment I stepped into the bathroom.

JESSE

Sunday, October 23

I drum on Cody's bedroom door. "It's me," I call from the hallway.

"Yeah?" his voice comes back, muffled behind the walls and dense wood. "What do you want?"

I push the door and step into his room.

He's seated at his desk with his gaming headset slung around his neck and his laptop open in front of him. "What the hell, man? I didn't say come in."

"Oh. My bad." I glance around the room, figuring out a path through the chaos of balled-up clothes and bike parts.

Resigned to my presence, he untangles himself from his headset and tosses it onto the desk. "What do you want? Make it quick."

I sit on the edge of his bed and thread my fingers together. "I need your help."

He snorts out a laugh and swivels around to face me. "Oh,

man. It must be bad. You're really scraping the barrel if you're coming to me."

I squeeze my eyes shut and my knee starts bouncing. "If I tell you something, it's got to stay between us."

"Yeah."

My eyes shoot to his. "Swear down."

"Yeah," he says with a shrug.

"All right." I press my palms together. "This girl, my friend—"

"Savana." He rolls his hand for me to continue.

"No," I say, feeling heat rise to my neck. "Not Savana."

"Fine. Not Savana." He rolls his hand again.

"Something happened to her, my friend. Not Savana. A guy made a move on her, and she didn't want him to."

His expression changes; he sobers. "Oh, shit."

"Yeah. She managed to get away from him, pushed him off her and stuff, but he kissed her, and she's pretty shaken up. But she won't tell anyone, and I don't think she should keep this to herself."

He leans back in his seat. "Sucks, but it's not your call."

I drag my hands over my face. "Should I tell her mom or something?"

He holds up his palm and shakes his head. "I wouldn't do that."

"I know *you* wouldn't, but what should *I* do? I told her I wouldn't tell anyone, but I can't just let this guy get away with it, right?" My knee starts bouncing faster. "I can't just leave her feeling this way."

"Wait." He sits upright and raises an eyebrow. "You told her you wouldn't tell anyone? You've just told me. Good to know you can't keep your mouth shut. Noting that for future reference."

I roll my eyes. "You don't count. Cody, I need help with this. I'm going out of my mind."

He leans back in his seat again and folds his arms. "Do you know who the guy was?"

I swallow and nod.

"Can you go face up to him or something?"

"She doesn't want me to."

"You can't tell her mom, Jesse. That's shady as hell."

I fall back on the bed and stare up at the ceiling. "Then do I tell Dad?"

"What, *our* dad?" He chokes out a laugh. "No! Because he'd get drunk and tell her mom, anyway. They live right next door."

I sit up. "Cody, it's not Savana. And don't ever tell Savana I told you this."

He scoffs. "Please. Unlike you, I know how to keep my mouth shut."

I stare down at my hands, and my fists clench. "So that's it? I just do nothing?"

"Yeah," he says. "Be there if she wants to talk and whatever."

"And this guy gets away with it?"

"For now."

The bedroom door creaks, and my stomach drops. Dad is standing in the open doorway with his jaw clenched. "All right, Jesse," he says gruffly. "I'm going to need you to start from the beginning."

SAVANA

Monday, October 24

"How could you do this, Savana?" Tara's voice is extra high. Extra shrill.

I bow my head and keep walking across the school parking lot. My car is just ahead, sandwiched between two silver convertibles. If I can just make it to my car...

Tara's shoes click fast behind me. "How could you kiss my boyfriend?"

I keep my eyes forward. "It wasn't like that, Tara." The words sound weak as they leave my lips. "I've tried to explain—"

"What, he turned you down, so you told the school?" She scoffs.

She's wrong. *I* didn't report Raf's behavior to the school; my mom did, right after Jesse's dad relayed the whole story to her. And there wasn't much the school could do, other than ensure that we're kept apart, which subsequently got the word spread fast around our grade. I keep walking; just a few more feet and I'm home free. I clutch my keys and press the automatic unlock button. The Bug gives a cheerful beep in response.

But now there are other footsteps behind me, too. Other voices. Jesse's voice. "Leave her alone, Tara." He sounds tired, beaten.

"Gladly," Tara yells.

"Please, Savana." Jesse's right behind me as I swing open the Bug's driver's-side door. "I'm so sorry. Please talk to me."

I slide into the seat and Jesse hovers at the open door, his hand gripping the edge. His eyes have turned ruby brown in the afternoon light. They look pained. Good.

When Mr. Melo showed up at our house, I almost didn't believe it at first. I didn't believe Jesse would ever betray my confidence, but he did. He lied, and now everything's different.

I stare up at him from my seat. "Why did you do it?"

"It was an accident, I swear," he stresses. "I was talking to Cody. I had no idea my dad was standing outside the room."

I blink back at him in disbelief. "You shouldn't have been talking to Cody!"

"I know," he says quickly. "I know. I just needed advice, and I trust Cody. I never meant for your name to come out."

I glance beyond him into the parking lot where some junior girls are getting into a nearby car. I grimace and lower my voice. "Raf won. He knows he got to me. Now he's pretending like I came on to him and he rejected me, and I'm the one who has to feel embarrassed."

"You shouldn't feel embarrassed. *He* should," Jesse says through his teeth. "You've got nothing to be embarrassed about. Everyone's on your side."

I gesture with my keys in the direction Tara went. "She isn't on my side. We're supposed to be friends and she didn't even hear me out."

"But I'm on your side," he says emphatically.

"I told you in confidence, and now everyone knows."

"I'm so sorry," he murmurs.

I jam the key into the ignition. "Bye, Jesse."

"Please, Savana," he says, holding the door frame. "I'm so sorry. I'm so, so sorry." His distraught expression makes me look away. "Please forgive me."

I grab the internal door handle and yank my door shut, then I press my foot on the gas and drive away fast so that he doesn't see me break.

JESSE

Monday, October 24

My chest tightens as I watch her car swerve out of the parking lot.

"You've got to be kidding me." The voice behind me makes
my skin crawl. "You're seriously siding with her over me?"

I grit my teeth and turn around to see Raf leaning against
a nearby car. He runs a hand over his mouth.

"Unbelievable," he rumbles.

My heart starts beating fast. Too fast. "Walk away from
me," I say. "For real. Walk away."

His jaw squares. "You're going to screw me over like this?
Backing that bitch over some lie that ain't nobody going to
believe, anyway? After everything we've been through together, J?"

I shoulder past him, but he follows me across the lot.

My dad's already had it out with Mike, some misplaced
blame over what his kid did. Raf should be the one taking
the heat for this. Not Mike. Not Savana. Him.

"I can't believe you're taking her side." His voice gets louder. "Just so you can hit it? You're supposed to be my best friend."

I stop walking and choke out a laugh. "Oh, man," I say, turning around to face him. "If *I'm* your best friend, then you really are screwed."

His face falls. "What? We're like brothers, you and me. We scrap, we get over it."

Pain rises in my chest, tangling with the anger. Because he's right; we were like brothers, once. We looked out for each other; we backed each other, no matter what.

I see the glassiness in his eyes, and I look dead into them.

"What you did to Savana is the lowest, and you're not my brother. My *brother* is the kid you put a hit out on."

He licks his lips fast. "Hey, Cody was coming after me." He slaps his hand on his chest. "He threw a brick through my window. You think I was going to just let that slide?"

I shake my head and start walking again. "You're messed up," I shout without looking back. "You deserve everything you're going to get."

I can hear his footsteps crunching the gravel behind me. "You really wanna go up against me?" he calls. "Because I'll come for you, Jesse. I swear to God, if you turn your back on me, I'll *ruin* your life."

My lips twitch into a smile and I turn to face him. "Come for me," I tell him, extending my arms wide and holding up both middle fingers. "And then see what happens."

RAF:
I heard you got your college scout interview lined up
for tomorrow. Congrats, man. That's big.

RAF:
Listen, I know we said some stuff, but I didn't mean
any of it. I'm sorry, man.

JESSE:
No, you're not.

RAF:
I am. Can we just meet up? I'll explain everything.

RAF:
Please. Just me and you.

RAF:
There's something else you should know. Your mom
called my dad last night. I wasn't going to tell you like
this over texts. I wanted to talk to you in person. She
asked me to pass on a message to you. You probably don't want to hear any of this, but I'll be at Cray's
tonight if you do.

JESSE

Friday, November 4

My heart's beating fast, and my breath is fogging the cold night air. I stand outside Cray's, hidden in the shadows.

I saw them go in, all of them.

Raf, Tara, Freddie, and Owen.

It's meant to be just Raf, alone. That's what he said in his message. Just him and me.

I'm supposed to be home, preparing for my scout interview tomorrow, but his words got into my head. *He* got into my head, and now I'm here.

The sounds of the wind groaning and buoys sloshing in the water make the hairs on the back of my neck stand on end.

I don't like the port. I have every reason not to like the port.

But I'm here now, and I've got to see this through.

The wind whips at my jacket.

Here we go.

JESSE

Friday, November 4

I freeze at the sound of glass shattering. The warehouse creaks and groans, alive with phantom noises roaming the darkness. Clanks, voices, echoes. Footsteps thump above me, patterning from different directions.

My own voice rattles around my mind. *Run.* But I don't leave.

The rasp of my breath, the thud of my sneakers, and the clang of the metal steps.

I hear their voices, frantic, high-pitched. I keep going, first floor…second floor…third floor…fourth floor…

I stumble into the room. Their faces are streaked with moonlight. The window is smashed. Shards of glass glint on the floor beneath the ledge, and jagged edges spike from the frame, teeth in gaping jaws.

Tara is panting, shaking. Owen is raking his hands through his hair, pacing the length of the room with long strides. Freddie is standing at the window, his fist pressed to his mouth.

There's this beat of silence, this eerie stillness that haunts us. Only our breaths speak.

And then I ask them, hoarsely, "Where's Raf?"

PART TWO
After

Audio File_MP3

Title: Case_HPD0149_Jesse Melo Interview

H.B.: Recording now. The date is November 5. The time is approximately eleven thirty in the morning. My name is Detective Harrison Bridge. Please state your full name for the purpose of the tape.

J.M.: Jesse Melo.

H.B.: Thank you for your cooperation. Why don't you talk me through what happened last night, Friday, November 4? Starting with what you were doing at Cray's Warehouse.

J.M.: I was there to meet a friend. He asked me to meet him there. He said he had a message from my mom that she wanted him to pass on.

H.B.: Your friend's name?

J.M.: Raf. Rafael Lombardi.

H.B.: And this message, he couldn't have done that at your house? Over a phone call, perhaps?

J.M.: Apparently not.

H.B.: So what was the message?

J.M.: I didn't get a chance to find out. I didn't see him.

H.B.: You couldn't have called him?

J.M.: I lost my phone that morning. I don't know where I left it.

H.B.: Go on, then. Tell me what happened. Who was at the warehouse with you last night?

J.M.: Freddie, Owen, and Tara.

H.B.: And Savana Caruso?

J.M.: Savana? Savana wasn't there.

H.B.: Savana Caruso is the person who made the 911 call last night. Another friend of yours, is she?

J.M.: She's my neighbor. She called 911?

H.B.: What happened in that building, Jesse? You and your friends got into a fight or something? An argument? Maybe something to do with this message you were supposed to receive?

J.M.: I told you I didn't get the message. I didn't see Raf.

H.B.: Okay, you're going to play ignorant?

J.M.: I'm not playing anything. I don't know why I'm here.

H.B.: You're telling me you didn't see the broken window? You didn't go up to it, take a look down?

J.M.: I saw the window. But no, I didn't go near it. I don't know why I've spent the night in a cell.

H.B.: Well, then I'm sorry to have to tell you that you're being investigated for the murder of your friend Rafael Lombardi. So you'd better start talking.

JESSE

Saturday, November 5

We stand in the port with the wind rippling our clothes. Owen, Freddie, Tara, and me. We must be out of our minds to want to come back here, less than twenty-four hours after we were escorted out. Cray's is cordoned off with police tape and barriers. The wind flutters the yellow tape; I can hear it clicking above the moan of the gusting air.

It's a murder scene.

We all stare in silence.

"What the hell happened?" My voice sounds hoarse. I didn't sleep last night. I spent it in a jail cell, separated from these guys. Judging by their drawn faces and glazed eyes, I doubt any of them slept much, either.

Tears are streaming down Tara's cheeks. She's quiet, just crying. Freddie puts his arm around her. He's breathing slowly, calmly. But he's not calm. None of us are.

Owen's hands are balled, and the muscles in his jaw are bulging. He's standing too close to me. His shoulder is pressed against mine, like he's leaning on me. Like he's about to keel over.

"I didn't see anything," Tara whispers. "Did you guys see Raf fall?"

Freddie shakes his head. "The window was broken, but I didn't see anything."

My heart beats faster when I remember hearing the glass smash, and the clang of the iron staircase as I raced up from the ground floor. The thud of their footsteps, all coming from different directions.

"Whatever happened," I say, my voice stolen by the howling wind, "whoever pushed him, just own up. End this."

Tara's watery eyes dart to me. "Shut up, Jesse," she hisses. "Just shut up."

I shatter into a huff. "What? You're not wondering the same thing?"

"Just shut up!"

"Guys," Owen placates us in a weak voice. "Come on." He grips my shoulder.

But Tara's glassy blue eyes are still on me. "You wanna know what I'm wondering?" she seethes. "I'm wondering why *you* killed my boyfriend."

"Hey," Freddie soothes. "Take it easy, Tara." He pulls her closer, and she leans into him.

I choke out a sound. "*You* were in the room before I even got there!" I remind her. "You all were."

"We all heard you run out of the room right after it happened, and you only came back once we were all there to make yourself seem less guilty." Tara turns her attention away from me, and Freddie shoots me a helpless look over her head. Owen's shoulder presses against mine.

Sounds echo in my head. The smash of glass, the thud of footsteps.

Run, says the voice in my mind.

"It could have been an accident," Owen murmurs. "Maybe he just slipped and fell."

I swallow. "Then why are we being investigated for murder?"

I look at them. All three of them. They're silent.

We're all silent.

And that's how we're going to stay.

SAVANA

Saturday, November 5

There's a knock on the French doors. I freeze, holding still on my bed as a silhouette moves beyond the drapes.

I hear someone walking across the deck and the shadow disappears. A moment later the front doorbell rings.

I scramble off my bed and rush into the kitchen, where Mom is clattering around.

"Don't answer that!" I hiss.

She jumps when she sees me. The teakettle whistles, and she takes it off the stove. "Savana..." She looks tired and disheveled in the same way I do—hair fastened into a messy bun and a strange, sallow complexion. A night at the police station will do that to a person, I guess.

"It's Jesse," I tell her in a strained voice. "I think it's Jesse."

Her eyes cloud. "I have to answer the door, Savana. We can't just leave him standing out there."

I grab the edge of the counter. "Okay," I concede, "but tell him I'm not here."

She nods, saying nothing.

While Mom heads for the corridor, I retreat to my bedroom and quietly close the door behind me.

As I listen to their tense, muffled conversation on the front stoop, the sound of his voice tugs at my heart.

But I'm not ready to talk to him.

I reach for my phone, then crouch at my closed bedroom door to reread his messages from Friday night.

Come to Cray's Warehouse tonight.
My response: What? Why?
Just come. I need your help.

And that's it. That was all he said.

Later that night Raf Lombardi was killed.

I wait until I'm sure Mom's asleep before I sneak out. I pull my coat tightly around myself and close the back door with a soft click.

My breath mists the air. Inside the Bug it's almost as cold as outside. The windshield is fogged by the night chill, and frost holds the windows tightly. My headlights throw long beams over the tarmac as I pull out of the driveway and wind through the lamp-lit streets toward the port.

I wasn't in Cray's last night, so I didn't see what the others saw—the room, the window, the broken glass. The police know something I don't—they clearly suspect it's murder, and I want to know what led them to reach that conclusion.

When I get to the marina, I cut the engine and sit for a moment, safe inside the Bug. My eyes rove over the darkness. It's quiet and calm across the port, but the stillness isn't comforting.

Clutching my phone, I hold the flashlight high and leave the sanctuary of the car, then half run across the square toward Cray's. I lift the police tape from the door and duck beneath it, cloaked by the night. The desolation of the warehouse aches. It swallows me whole.

The metal steps clang faintly as I climb to the fourth floor, my fingers locked around my phone and the flashlight bobbing with my every movement. Shadows watch me; they follow me.

I count the doors as I pass them, searching for the room, the exact room, and the exact window. And I find it. It's untouched, glass still scattered across the floor like razor-sharp snowflakes.

I crouch at the ledge, running my light over everything. The floorboards are scuffed at the window, and some of the glass is crushed as though it's been stepped on. There's a chalk outline beneath the ledge—just a small circle indicating that something was found there. I move my light slowly up and down and left to right, then finally settle on the scuff mark and what looks like a footprint.

"No sand," I murmur to the darkness. I track the light around the area, just to make sure. Nothing. No grains among the glass.

The floorboards creak beneath me, and I almost feel a presence. Raf's presence, as though the final echo of him still lingers here.

I shiver and try to suffocate the memory of him falling, his arms clawing through the air. His body on the ground.

My heart starts jackhammering in my chest.

Suddenly, the reality of the situation knocks the breath out of me. What am I doing here?

I run the whole way back to my car.

JESSE

Sunday, November 6

This won't break me. Nothing breaks me.

I lie on my bed, staring up at the ceiling and tracing the cracks with my eyes. There's a spider in the far corner. It's been there for a while, sometimes moving, mostly not.

I focus on it, watch it.

Footsteps sound from the hallway outside my bedroom.

I fold my hands together on my chest, waiting for the knock to come.

Tap, tap.

The handle twists, and the door creaks open.

Cody lingers in the doorway. He drags a hand through his messy hair. "Can I come in?"

I raise an eyebrow, but I don't lift my head from the pillow. I give him a nod, and he takes that as his cue to step into the room. He pushes the door shut behind him and sinks onto the floorboards next to my bed. His gaze travels to the window overlooking the dark tide and jetties.

We're silent for a minute, but Cody's twitchy, bursting with words. He knots his fingers through his hair and mutters under his breath.

"Can't hear you when you talk like that." My focus strays back to the spider; it's moved again.

"What should I say if the cops want to speak to me about what happened to Raf?" His gaze is fixed on his sneakers. The laces are dirty, and the toe keeps tapping.

I press my tongue hard against the back of my teeth. "Just say whatever you want."

"I don't want to say anything."

"Then don't say anything."

He starts rubbing at the frays on his jeans. "Do you think they'll want to talk to me?"

"Maybe. But you don't have anything to hide." I link my fingers behind my head, watching the spider's journey along the ceiling. It's halfway across the room now.

I don't have anything to hide.

Eventually, Cody looks at me. His bloodshot eyes drift over my face, then anchor back to his sneakers.

"Are you all right?" he asks, head bowed. His question haunts the room.

I breathe hard, then I reach over and clap his shoulder. "I'm good." He needs me to say it. He needs me to keep my shit together. He doesn't need to see my hands shaking, or me dry heaving over the toilet because I've got nothing left inside.

A few minutes pass before he speaks again. "Do you think

the cops will be looking at you?" His voice sounds distant, even though he's still right next to me.

I stare up at the ceiling, but I can't see the spider anymore.

"No." I swallow the pain in my throat. "I didn't do anything."

UNKNOWN NUMBER:
Hey, Savana.

                                    SAVANA:
                                    Hey. Who is this?

UNKNOWN NUMBER:
We should talk.

                                    SAVANA:
                                    Is this Jesse?

UNKNOWN NUMBER:
Nope. Guess again.

                                    SAVANA:
                                    Who is this?

UNKNOWN NUMBER:
Keep guessing.

                                    SAVANA:
                                    I'm blocking you now. Bye.

UNKNOWN NUMBER:
Wait. There are some things you should know.

SAVANA:
Such as?

UNKNOWN NUMBER:
Jesse is going down for murder.

SAVANA

Monday, November 7

I'm not a Monday person. And I'm definitely not a Monday person when that particular Monday happens to fall after the weekend when one of my classmates fell from a window, and I witnessed the whole thing. Oh, and that particular classmate also happens to be the guy who forcefully kissed me in a bathroom at a party a few weeks earlier.

Corinne is at my car before I've even cut the engine.

She swings open the driver's-side door and stares down at me. "Oh, my God. You're actually here." She tucks her sleek hair behind her ears and purses her scarlet lips. "Why are you here?"

I look up at her from my seat. "Um, because I go to school here."

"Are you okay?"

"Define *okay.*"

"People are going to be grilling you, Savana." She glances

around the parking lot, assessing the targets with a sniper stare. "If you're not ready for that…"

"I'm going to have to deal with the questions eventually," I say with a sigh. "It might as well be now."

She drops her hand from the door and steps aside for me to leave the privacy of the Bug. More cars are pulling into the lot, and their drivers are glancing my way.

I'm undoubtedly on everyone's radar. People I know, people I barely know, people I'd swear I've never even seen before. It doesn't matter if I know them or not. They know me. At least, they've heard my name thrown around. The girl who was there. The girl who called 911 when Raf Lombardi fell from a window in Cray's Warehouse.

Aside from my mom and the police, Corinne's the only person who knows my account of what happened on Friday night. She's heard it twenty times over already, while I tried to process it without tailspinning. She knows about the nightmares and the constant replay that I can't seem to switch off. Arms clawing through the air…

I lower my voice. "I have to tell you something," I say, swallowing. "Last night I got a ton of text messages from an unknown number."

She frowns.

I take a breath and glance over my shoulder to check that we're not within earshot of any eavesdroppers. "They called Jesse out as a murderer," I whisper. Corinne's eyes cast downward, so I carry on. "Who would text me anonymously like that?"

"I don't know," she murmurs.

Her vibe is off. She's not asking to read the messages or jumping to Jesse's defense. But then, why would she? She's witnessed Jesse and Raf butt heads as much as everyone else in our grade has. Of course the logical conclusion is that Jesse pushed Raf through that window.

And there's still one detail that Corinne doesn't know.

The fact that Jesse texted me on Friday, asking me to come to Cray's, and that's why I went.

I want to tell Corinne about his message, and I will tell her, eventually. But there are too many questions I don't know the answers to. There are questions I'm scared to even ask myself, because I'm afraid I *already* know the answers.

Namely, why did Jesse want me there?

Corinne threads her arm through mine as we begin toward the school. "Don't worry," she says, guiding my thoughts back to the anonymous texts. "It's probably just someone's sick idea of a joke."

I try to control my spiraling thoughts. More curious stares roam over me, but I raise my chin and forge on.

Corinne squeezes my arm. "Are you sure you want to do this? It's not too late to run."

I blow out a breath, fogging the cold air. "What's the point in delaying the inevitable? I've got nothing to hide." My shoulders tense as I say the words.

She musters a smile. Side by side, we step through the fallen leaves that muddle the path—a crisp red river snaking through the school grounds.

Inside, I keep my head down and beeline for my locker. I avoid any eye contact from passersby and busy myself selecting books from the lower shelf.

It's only when I hear Corinne take an audible breath that I force myself to look up. Jesse is heading toward us. His brown hair is pushed to the side, a little messier than usual. When his eyes land on mine, my stomach tightens.

The first warning bell rings and bodies start flowing around us, heading to their respective classrooms.

Jesse comes to a stop at my locker. He glances at Corinne before fixing his deep brown stare on me. "Can we talk?" He shifts the weight of his backpack on his broad shoulder.

Evidently, Corinne takes that as her cue to leave. She squeezes my hand and says, "See you in homeroom."

My heart plummets when I realize she's actually leaving. It's happening. I have to face Jesse, and I do not feel ready for this conversation. I didn't feel ready when he knocked on my door on Saturday, and I still don't feel ready now.

I watch Corinne disappear into the sea of corridor foot traffic.

"I didn't know you were there on Friday," Jesse says, his voice lowered just a little.

I stare back at him, silently.

"I went over to your house on Saturday," he adds. "After I found out you were at the port that night. But your mom told me you were out." He tilts his head, like it's a question. He wants to know if I was really out, or if my mom concocted the story because it was *him* at the door.

His attention wanders to the gray floor tiles as some juniors pass us. Their conversation simmers, probably because they're suddenly more interested in trying to catch snippets of ours.

Jesse and I look at each other, waiting for them to pass before we speak again.

"Did your mom tell you I lost my phone?" he asks. "That's why I couldn't call you or text you."

"Yeah," I say. "She told me."

His gaze flickers to the ceiling and the bright strip lights above us. The general whir of voices in the corridor has quieted. Most people have gone to their classrooms, apart from a few stragglers and latecomers.

"I thought you'd come over," he says, tapping his knuckles on a locker in steady raps. "I waited for you all weekend. I get that you're still mad at me about my dad telling your mom about Owen's party. But I thought you'd want to talk after what happened at the port on Friday. After Raf..."

I shake my head, gazing up at him. "What, am I supposed to *thank* you or something?"

He's silent for a second, and he blinks. "What?"

My pulse quickens with a sudden rush of adrenaline. I knew I'd have to deal with this confrontation eventually, but in my head I'd imagined myself being totally Zen. I'd be cool, calm, and collected. That was the plan. But I'm not getting those feels right now. "Why did you ask me to come to Cray's on Friday?" The words rush out. "Was *this* what you needed my help with?"

He cringes and glances along the deserted corridor. "What are you talking about?"

"Why did you want me to go there?" My chest tightens in fear. Fear of what he's done, and what he's dragged me into. What he's dragged us *both* into.

He shakes his head, staring blankly back at me. "I didn't want you to go there. Why would you think that?"

"You texted me!"

"No, I didn't."

The main doors swing open and a few more stragglers bound in. They notice us, huddled together at the wall of lockers, muttering back and forth. Their pace slows and their ears practically cock.

Jesse and I pause again, looking anywhere but at each other.

I dip my voice once the dawdlers have passed. "You texted me on Friday asking me to go to Cray's."

His jaw clenches. "No, I didn't, Savana."

I fumble to pull my phone from the front pocket of my messenger bag. With a quick swipe, I unlock the screen and scroll through my messages. I hand him the phone and watch his eyes skim over the text displayed on the screen.

"I didn't send these." His breathing sounds shallow.

I study him, trying to assess his expression. He's biting on his lower lip, his teeth pressed down hard.

"Are you serious?" I whisper.

"I swear to you." He holds his fist to his chest. "I didn't send those messages." More latecomers trot into the hallway, but apparently, Jesse doesn't care who's walking by anymore. His voice is coming out too loud, too fast. "I lost my phone. I haven't had it since Friday morning, before these messages were sent." He pushes my cell back into my hands.

The world seems to stop for a moment, freeze.

A second bell drills through the corridor. I flinch. Jesse does, too.

Students start to filter out from the rabbit's warren of rooms, flooding the hallways again.

Jesse runs a hand over his brow.

"There's more." I show him the messages from last night, the texts sent from an unknown number.

He holds my gaze as the din gets louder around us.

"You believe this?" he asks.

I know instantly what he's referring to. The last message sent in the conversation. *Jesse is going down for murder.*

"Do you think I did it?" he presses.

I can't seem to find the words to respond, so I say nothing. But I see the look of sheer disbelief on his face as he walks away.

JESSE

Monday, November 7

I catch up with Owen in the locker room in the afternoon. A couple of guys are coming out from the shower block, and their stares slide over us. They give each other a "look" when they think we won't notice—lips pressed together, eyebrows slightly risen.

Of course we notice.

I clench my teeth, and Owen bows his head. We take a seat on the damp bench in the changing area.

"We shouldn't be here," I mutter.

Owen gnaws on his lip. "I feel like I'm in some screwed-up nightmare and I can't wake up." His hands shake and he balls his fists. "Raf's dead."

My heart does something, a heavy thump in my chest. I can almost hear Raf's laughter, still rebounding through the locker room. His loud, quick laugh. It haunts me.

Owen nudges me. "Are you okay?"

I swallow. "Yeah. Yeah, I'm just…" I glance up as a couple

more guys pass us. They muster smiles, strange commiserating smiles that I don't know how I'm supposed to respond to.

"Have you spoken to Tara or Freddie?" Owen's lowered voice jolts me back.

"Not since Saturday," I tell him. "I don't know what I'm supposed to say to them." I look down at my hands because I know we both feel it. We don't know how to act right now, either. The truth is, none of us knows how to be, or if we can even trust each other. We were the only people there. One of us knows something. One of us *did* something.

I rub my brow. "Is it possible the police are wrong? Was this somehow an accident, and Raf just fell?"

Owen exhales slowly. "It has to have been, right? Me, you, Freddie, Raf… I know things have been off lately, but we go back a long way. None of us would have…"

"Tara," I blurt out. "What about Tara? It could have been her." I wait for his response. He doesn't agree or disagree; he just leans forward and locks his hands in front of him.

"What the hell happened on Friday, Owen?"

He chews his lip and shakes his head.

That feeling is back, the tension hovering between us. The distrust, the doubt, the fear that we don't know each other anymore, and never will again.

Our silence haunts the room, just like the echoes of Raf's laughter.

Audio File_MP3

Title: Case_HPD0149_Freddie Bass Interview

H.B.: Good morning. I'm Detective Harrison Bridge. The date is Saturday, November 5, and the time is approximately 8:00 a.m. Your name, please?

F.B.: Freddie Bass.

H.B.: What were you and your friends doing at Cray's Warehouse last night, Freddie?

F.B.: No comment.

H.B.: There was an incident between yourself and Rafael Lombardi, wasn't there? At school, resulting in your expulsion. Did you boys get into a fight about that? Did you get into an altercation last night?

F.B.: No comment.

H.B.: Rafael Lombardi is dead. This isn't a game, son.

F.B.: I need a lawyer. It's my right to have a lawyer present.

H.B.: What happened last night, Freddie? Because if you know something, and I have a hunch that you do, then now is the time to start talking. Who pushed Raf? Was it you? One of your friends, Jesse Melo, Owen Keaton, Tara Kowalski, Savana Caruso?

F.B.: No comment.

H.B.: Which one of you was it, Freddie?

F.B.: I'm not answering any more questions without a lawyer present.

JESSE

Monday, November 7

I trudge up the porch steps and jam my keys into the front door just as a familiar chrome Jeep speeds along my street. It rolls through a puddle of rainwater pooling along the curb and jerks to an abrupt stop.

Raf's Jeep.

It takes me a second to remember that it won't be him behind the wheel. I'm so used to seeing that Jeep, so used to seeing Raf in it, cruising around Havelock with one arm slung out the window, that for a second I actually do see him behind the wheel. I see him getting out of the car, walking toward me with a wide grin and one hand risen, ready to clap mine.

But it's not him.

It's his dad. Mike.

Not all that long ago, this guy was like a second dad to me, a buddy, but the look in his eyes as he gets out of the car makes me cold. He slams the door hard.

I glance at the Jeep's passenger side, half wondering, half

expecting my mom to be there. She should be here. What-ever went down before, she should be here now. For all of us.

But it's just him.

My keys are in the front door, and I freeze up. I swear the blood drains from my face.

Mike is crossing my lawn, steaming toward me.

He grabs my shirt and slams me hard against the door. It happens fast. One second his hands are on my shirt, next they're around my throat. I wheeze for breath, clawing at his thick fingers. Then the door gives way from behind me, and we both stumble.

I hear Cody's voice as Mike's hands slip away from my throat. My dad is here, too, somewhere in the blur of all this. We're all outside, all four of us, stumbling onto the lawn.

I wipe my lip and notice the blood smeared across the back of my hand.

Mike is a big guy. My dad isn't small, none of us are, but we're not jacked like the Lombardis.

I wipe my lip again and jump between my dad and Mike. "Dad." I press my hand to his chest, pushing him back as Mike runs his mouth to anyone who's listening on our street. "Dad, leave it." He's breathing fast and his eyes are fixed on Mike. The faint trace of whiskey on his breath makes my heart sink.

Mike is backing off toward the Jeep, and Cody's yelling after him. "Put your hands on my brother again and we'll call the cops on your ass."

But Mike is only looking at me. "They've got you," he hollers. His finger is aiming at me, firing the only bullets he can. "Evidence against you."

I swallow and say nothing, but my mind is racing. *They've got you.*

Cody is next to me; his hand is on my shoulder. Dad's halfway down the drive, tossing out empty threats. Across the street a couple of curtains are twitching.

Mike holds up his phone as he backs toward the Jeep. It looks like he's taking a picture. Or a video.

His words sound fuzzy to my ears because I can't believe what I'm hearing.

This is the boy who killed my son.

Audio File_MP3

Title: Case_HPD0149_Jesse Melo Interview2

H.B.: Good afternoon, Jesse. Thanks for coming back in. Once again, my name is Detective Harrison Bridge, and I'll be asking you a few questions in relation to the death of Rafael Lombardi.

J.M.: Okay. Yeah.

H.B.: For the purpose of the tape, the date is Monday, November 7. The time is approximately six thirty in the evening, and I have in my possession a cell phone with a scratch across the back and a cracked screen. All right, let's get started. Do you recognize this phone, Jesse?

J.M.: Yeah. It's mine.

H.B.: And what about this?

J.M.: It's a photo of my phone.

H.B.: For the purpose of the tape, the interviewee is being shown a printed copy of a photograph taken during the forensic search of Cray's Warehouse on Friday, November 4. Jesse, why was your cell phone recovered from beneath the ledge of a fourth-floor window at Cray's Warehouse on Friday night?

J.M.: I lost my phone earlier that day. I told the cops that already.

H.B.: You exchanged some text messages with Lombardi on the morning of the incident. In these messages, he asked you to meet him at Cray's Warehouse that evening. Is that correct?

J.M.: Yes.

H.B.: Is it fair to say your response to him was blunt? Frosty?

J.M.: Yes.

H.B.: Okay. We're going to need to keep hold of your phone as evidence for the time being. Let me be frank with you, son. The forensic team found marks on the floorboards, and the way the window broke shows Rafael must have collided with it at a force that would have been hard to hit on his own. This is murder, and I think you know it. Now, I'm going to ask you again. Why was your phone recovered from beneath the ledge, Jesse?

J.M.: I don't know.

H.B.: Okay. I appreciate your cell might have, let's say, slipped out of your pocket while you were inspecting the broken window. But my problem here, son, is that that story doesn't align with what you told us previously. You said you lost your phone earlier in the day. You also said you didn't approach the window at all on Friday night. So naturally, I'm wondering how your phone wound up there?

J.M.: (PAUSE) Someone put it there. Someone planted my phone at Cray's.

H.B.: Who do you think would have done that, Jesse?

J.M.: I don't know.

H.B.: Wild guess?

J.M.: Someone who wanted to make it look like I killed Raf.

SAVANA

Monday, November 7

I lie in bed with the covers bunched around me.

It seems strange now to think of how hard I bargained to get this room, a ground-floor bedroom with its own access. Back when we first moved here, this room seemed beyond perfect. I thought I'd love it, and I did love it. But the past few months have changed that. Now, when I see shadows pass the sweeping drapes, or whenever the wind taps at the glass doors, I bristle and my mind wanders to the what-ifs.

What if someone is standing outside? What if someone is trying to get in?

Rain patters against the French doors now, making them vibrate. Another shadow moves. Another tap on the glass.

I flip the lamp on and light floods the room. In the illumination, I feel braver. Or at least, I can fool myself.

The guilt of what happened at school this morning between Jesse and me is gnawing away at me. I can't stop picturing the pained look on his face when I nearly accused him of killing

Raf. I shouldn't have jumped to that, regardless of the text messages. I know him better than that. More than anything, though, I miss him. I've missed him every day since our fight after Owen's party.

Across the room my jacket is hanging over the back of my desk chair. I grab it and wrap it around myself before quietly twisting the lock on the French doors.

It's dark out, apart from a ripple of moonlight bouncing off the tide. Rain is pattering on the planked deck, pooling on the boards. There's no one out here. No silhouettes stalking the night. No masked face lurking in the darkness.

I slip into my shoes and make a dash for the Melos' house. I'm pretty sure Jesse's bedroom faces out to the cove, top left window. His light is on—at least, I think it's his light. I'm almost sure, and I'm willing to wager it. I root around for a small pebble and launch it at the window. It bounces off the glass.

My pulse accelerates while I wait for movement beyond the window.

The curtains move, and Jesse appears. He frowns down at me.

I offer him a small wave and then wait in the rain as he vanishes from the window. A moment later the back door swings open.

"You don't have your phone," I start, shivering a little in the darkness. "I didn't know how else to…"

He nods and steps aside to let me in.

I barely make it across the threshold before the words tumble out. "I'm so sorry about how I handled things at school." My voice is hushed, lowered for his ears only. "But I'm just so confused. If you didn't send those text messages to me on Friday night, then who did?"

Standing in the dim kitchen, he takes a deep breath and links his hands behind his head. "Probably whoever took my phone and planted it at the window ledge in Cray's." He slides two chairs out from the oak table and takes a seat on one of them.

But I stay standing, shivering. I comb my fingers through my damp hair. The house is quiet, and I can hear the patter of rain hitting the roof. I glance over the cabinets, barely noticing them.

I think of the chalk circle I saw at the crime scene, wondering if that was where his phone was found. It was right beneath the ledge.

The news about Jesse's cell being recovered from Cray's has already spread—aided, in no small part, by a slanderous video posted online by Raf's dad, which is currently being shared across social media more times than I can keep track of.

This is the boy who killed my son. Accompanied by a frame of Jesse standing on his front lawn, lips parted and blood smeared across his mouth. His dad and brother are flanking him, their faces drained of color.

"Do you think it was deliberate?" I ask. "All of it. Someone taking your phone, texting me, then leaving your phone at the window?"

Jesse stares down at the table, clenching and unclenching his fists. "I didn't send you that message. Someone else sent it, deliberately, from my phone. From me."

We're silent as rain continues to pelt the slanted roof. I take in the familiarity of the kitchen. It's got pieces of Jesse everywhere, echoes and memories. His. Mine.

It would be so easy for me to assume that Jesse sent that message, asking me to come to Cray's. It was sent from his phone. And after everything that's gone down between Jesse and Raf lately, it almost makes sense. Jesse wanted me there to witness it, or to help him. That's what the message had said; he needed my help. He was planning on pushing Raf from a high window, and he did it. His phone slipped from his pocket in the scuffle, landing beneath the ledge, and in the fight he didn't notice it fall. Then he lied to cover his tracks. It adds up.

But I don't buy it. Even if there's a tiny part of me that questions it, there's one thing I know in my core, and that's that I can trust Jesse to be honest with me. After everything we've been through, I trust that.

"I believe you," I whisper. "We have to figure out who took your phone. If this was all premeditated, then whoever took it wanted us both involved." I take a breath and gingerly sit down beside him.

He exhales, and his eyes close for a second. "You really believe me?" His relief is palpable, and it tugs at my heart a little.

"Yes." I reach across the table, moving my hand closer to his. "Besides," I say, my mind wandering back to my flashlight in the abandoned warehouse. "There was no sand."

He frowns.

"I mean, at the window, where the scuff marks were. What shoes were you wearing on Friday night?"

"Just the same sneakers I always wear."

"Can I see the bottoms?"

He twists his ankle, and I noticed that the ridges of his sneakers are embedded with sand, just as I'd expected them to be.

"You jog on the beach practically every day," I point out. "You know what it's like living here. Sand gets into everything, particularly the grooves of sneakers. If there was an altercation at the window, enough to scuff the floor, then surely some of those grains would have come loose?"

He drops his foot back down. "You think that's enough to prove my innocence?"

"No," I say. "But it's a start. When was the last time you remember having your cell?"

"I don't know. Friday morning, maybe."

"The police will check the fingerprints."

"But the guys use my phone all the time. Their fingerprints could be on it, anyway. Raf's, too."

I fiddle with the ends of my damp hair. "So the people who were there that night. Me, you, Owen, Freddie, and Tara."

His eyes stay on mine. "You didn't see anything?" he asks. "You didn't see anyone else come out?"

"No. I only saw Raf fall. Did you see anything from inside Cray's?"

"I heard the glass smash," he says. "I heard footsteps coming from different places. I ran upstairs, and the others were there, too. Then the cops showed up and arrested us."

"Okay." I fold my hands on the table, listening to the tick of the wall clock. "Let's just say, for argument's sake, that this *was* premeditated..." He rubs the nape of his neck, and I keep going, holding his gaze in the muted light. "Who out of the five of us had motive?"

He laughs under his breath.

Right.

Us.

SAVANA

Tuesday, November 8

"'Raf Lombardi fell from a fourth-floor window in Cray's Warehouse on Friday, November fourth'—"

Corinne's voice makes me jump and I slam my laptop shut. She's leaning over my shoulder in the media arts room. It's late and the sun is setting beyond the long rectangular windows. This room is usually quiet; the only people who come in here are the art kids working in their aprons on the paint-stained tables, or the photography students using the darkroom in the corner for developing prints. Along the back wall, there's a bank of charging units beneath the windows that overlook the football field.

Corinne pops upright and smooths her hair. "What is this?"

I swivel around in my chair to face her and muster an uneasy smile. "Nothing."

"Savana," she says, folding her arms, "I really think you need to pull the plug on this project. Raf is..." She hesitates and lowers her voice. "Raf's dead. And this," she says, gesturing toward my laptop, "is not a good idea right now."

"I know," I murmur. "I'm just trying to piece everything together. I feel like if I write it down, it'll suddenly make sense."

She arches an eyebrow. "And does it?"

My gaze wanders across the room to the closed door. The glass panel frames a few passersby in the corridor. "Not yet," I answer, my focus still trained on the door. "But it was one of them."

"Yeah. No kidding, Savana. I think it's looking pretty cut-and-dry that it was Jesse."

"No." I trap my lip between my teeth. "I meant one of the *others*. Tara, Owen, or Freddie."

She hops up onto the table opposite and crosses her legs. "I'm listening."

My eyes flicker to the door again. We're alone, and the red light above the darkroom is off, signaling that's empty, too.

"There's something I haven't told you. I had a text message on Friday night, asking me to come to Cray's. From Jesse."

Corinne's forehead creases. "Okay," she says slowly.

"But the message wasn't from Jesse. It was from his phone, but he says he didn't send it."

She purses her lips. "Hold up. Let me get this straight. Jesse—or his phone—asked you to go to Cray's on Friday, the same night that Raf…" She lets the sentence trail off.

"Yes. At the same *time* that Raf…" I don't need to finish my sentence, either.

"Okay." She sucks in her lip. "Jesse says he didn't send the message, and you believe him." It's not a question, but there's enough incredulity in her voice to make it seem like it should be in question.

"I believe him. He wouldn't lie to me about this." I would have known what Corinne was thinking even without her scrunched-up expression. Even *I* can hear how weak my logic sounds—because it isn't logic; it's instinct. "If he says he didn't send it, he didn't send it."

Corinne clicks her tongue to the roof of her mouth. "Oh-kay."

"So I want to know who did send it," I carry on, ignoring the cynicism still crinkling her brow. "And *why* they sent it."

She raises both hands. "Okay. Let's just say, for a second, that I'm buying into this. Maybe Tara stole Jesse's phone, then pushed Raf in a jealous rage because of…you know. What Raf did at Owen's party."

"Plausible," I agree. "Or Freddie because Raf set him up to get expelled. Maybe Freddie wanted me there to frame Jesse and me because we're logical suspects, given everything that's gone on lately."

She nods along with the theory. "Or Owen," she adds. "Because Raf always seemed to have control over Owen, like Owen always wanted to please him, to stay on his side. Maybe the lackey didn't want to play nice anymore."

"I'd buy that."

"Or Jesse," she says quietly. She picks at a streak of dried paint on the table, then shoots me a meaningful look. "Because if we're including those three, then we have to consider him, too, right? Isn't that what any good journalist would tell you?"

"Or me," I murmur, holding her gaze. "Because I was

there, too. By that rationale, I'm involved in this as much as any of them. Do you suspect me?"

She laughs quietly. "Just don't be blinkered. That's all I'm saying."

"I won't," I answer.

"Don't assume you know the whole story."

I catch her gaze, waiting for more.

"Who knows what dirt those guys have on each other," she says. "Before their squad fell apart, they were in each other's business, big-time."

My gaze drifts to the door. The corridor has gone quiet now.

She follows my gaze. "Maybe there's more to that night than we know about," she whispers. "You only saw what happened outside. For all you know, they were all in on it. Or, to that point, none of them."

Audio File_MP3

Title: Case_HPD0149_Tara Kowalski Interview

H.B.: Good morning. My name is Detective Harrison Bridge. The date is Saturday, November 5, and the time is approximately nine o'clock in the morning. I'd like to have a chat with you about your actions last night. How does that sound?

T.K.: Why am I here? What's going on?

H.B.: We'll get to that. Can you tell me your full name, please?

T.K.: Tara Elisa Kowalski. Have my parents been called? Is Raf okay?

H.B.: Your parents are on their way. Are you comfortable getting started without them?

T.K.: I guess. I don't know.

H.B.: What's your relationship with Rafael Lombardi?

T.K.: He's my boyfriend. He fell through a window last night. He was pushed. Jesse Melo pushed him.

H.B.: Did you see that happen?

T.K.: No. But I know. Is Raf going to be okay?

H.B.: (PAUSE) Tara, I'm sorry. Rafael is dead.

T.K.: (INAUDIBLE.)

[Interview terminated at 9:12 a.m.]

SAVANA

Wednesday, November 9

The moment I cross into Miller's I'm hit with the sugary smell of sweet food and freshly ground coffee. The rows of booths are already pretty full, as they usually are after school on a weekday. Right away I feel eyes wander my way. Like it or not, Friday night has become a part of my identity. I'm the girl who saw.

I was hoping Mom would be here, but there's a new guy behind the counter. I guess her shift has finished already.

"Hey," I say to the barista. I don't recognize him. He's exuding college-kid vibes, wearing a retro band T-shirt and a bandanna over his long hair. "Can I get a coffee to go, please?"

"Sure," he says, tapping at the cash register and frowning.

While I wait for him to ring up the order, I glance over at the seating area. I shrink a little when I catch sight of Tara sitting alone in one of the booths near the back. Her usual glossy blond hair is falling limply around her shoulders, and she's sipping delicately from a mug.

Her gaze lands on me and she offers me a thin smile.

I haven't seen Tara in a while, and I haven't spoken to her in a really long while. It's been less than a week since Raf's death, and she hasn't been back in school since. My pulse races at the sight of her, because while I know I'm supposed to offer support given that she just lost her boyfriend, I can't help but wonder if she did it. If she's the person who texted me from Jesse's phone, tricking me into showing up.

When Bandanna Guy steps away to prepare my order, I take a deep breath and cross the diner.

"Hi," I say, bracing myself as I tentatively approach Tara's booth. "Are you okay?"

Her heavy lashes sweep downward. "No." She clenches her teeth and swallows. "What can you do, though? It's not like we can bring him back."

"I'm sorry," I murmur.

"Maddie's in the bathroom," she adds. "It's hilarious, really. She and Anaya were totally cool with ditching me when Raf was still here, saying he weirded them out and whatever. But now that he's gone, they're all in on grieving for him, talking about memorials and bullshit plaques. There hasn't even been a funeral yet." She hugs her arms around herself. "Maddie will not stop questioning me about Friday. I feel like I'm being interrogated, and honestly…" She squeezes her eyes shut for a beat. "The police, people from school, my mom… I just don't want to think about it for, like, five seconds. I guess that's too much to ask."

I press my lips together.

She inhales, gathering herself. "Are people interrogating you about it, too?"

"Yeah." I muster a strained smile. "That's why I avoid people."

"Is that why you've been avoiding me?"

The comment surprises me. "I haven't been avoiding you, Tara."

"Well, I've been avoiding you," she says. "For a while." She looks up to meet my eyes.

"That's okay," I tell her. "I get it."

"For what it's worth, I've missed you. I liked hanging out with you."

I dip my gaze. "Yeah," I whisper. "You, too."

I stare at the black-and-white floor tiles as Maddie comes out of the bathroom in the back.

Thankfully, Bandanna Guy calls my order before I have to figure out what I'm supposed to say next.

"I'd better go," I say to Tara. "But thanks. Take care."

She nods, then, under her breath, she adds, "Wish me luck. Five seconds, right?"

I summon a smile and cross my fingers.

As I collect my order from the counter, I hear Maddie pressing Tara on what we were talking about.

Do you think she did it?

Maddie's words knock the wind out of me. I stumble through the exit, out onto the cold street.

I was wrong. I'm not just the girl who saw. I'm the girl who might have done it.

JESSE

Wednesday, November 9

"What have the cops got on you?" Cody's voice spills out into the night.

I lean my head against the wooden mooring on the jetty outside our house. My hand folds around the damp rope as I stare up at the starry sky.

"Nothing," I say.

"Then why did they call you back in for questioning?"

"My phone. They found it near the ledge in Cray's."

He cusses under his breath.

"Don't worry," I press. "The cops found my phone, but all that shows it that I was there. They knew that already."

There's a pause, and I wait for him to speak. I can practically feel him scrambling for words.

"Are you worried?" he asks.

"Nope." The lie sounds easy. I like that.

We're silent again, just listening to the water slosh and slap beneath the jetty as we stare up at the endless expanse of black sky. We sit out here sometimes when we have nowhere else to go. It's easy to disappear out here.

"Are you worried about Dad?" He's trying to keep his voice steady, but there's a waver. A kink of fear.

"No," I answer. Numb. "Yeah, he's drinking again, but he'll get it under control. I know he will."

"What are we going to do if he doesn't?"

"We'll do what we always do. Bury our heads in the sand and pretend like everything's fine." I glance at him and smile, but I don't know if he can see it. It's dark enough for the shadows to trick our eyes and make our expressions morph and bend into something else.

But he half laughs. "Pretend? I don't know what you're talking about. Everything *is* fine."

Another smile tugs at my mouth. I return my attention to the stars, imagining patterns, imagining worlds that aren't here. Realities that aren't this.

It's not my fault that he's drinking again, I tell myself. *It's not my fault.*

"It's not your fault." Cody echoes the words in my mind, and it floors me for a second. My eyes snap to him. I almost wonder if I spoke those thoughts aloud. But then he says, "What happened to Raf. It sucks that the cops are coming after you, but it's not your fault."

I don't respond.

He taps his knuckles on the planks. "Do you miss him?" he asks after a moment. "Raf, I mean."

My eyes travel to the waning moon as I contemplate the question. "Yeah," I murmur, knowing that there's no one else in the world I can be this honest with. "Sometimes I miss him so much it hurts. It's killing me to think about what happened to him, and the way that it happened to him. But then I remember who he was." I catch Cody's gaze in the darkness. "And then I can't forget that."

UNKNOWN NUMBER:
I know what happened.

SAVANA:
If you don't stop harassing me, I'm taking these messages to the police.

UNKNOWN NUMBER:
Maybe I want you to.

SAVANA:
Tell me who you are.

UNKNOWN NUMBER:
I want you to know the truth, like I know the truth. I know what happened between you and Raf.

SAVANA:
Everyone knows that.

UNKNOWN NUMBER:
But I know the truth. The real story. I know everything.

SAVANA

Thursday, November 10

I tap on the Melos' back door and wait for Jesse to let me in.

He ushers me into the kitchen and closes the door on the wintery chill that's batting at the walls.

I hand him my phone without a word.

His eyes wander over the messages displayed on the screen. He hits dial on the number, and I faintly hear the line go dead.

"Tried that already," I tell him.

We fall silent and he passes the phone back to me.

"Maybe you should show the cops," he says at last.

"What, and show them this?" I scroll back through the anonymous thread, landing on the text that names *him* as the murderer. "Whoever's sending these is clearly more than happy to throw you under the bus."

He sinks into a seat at the kitchen table and pushes his hands through his hair. "Who do you think is behind this?"

I take the chair opposite him. "Someone who knows about

what happened between Raf and me at the party? Which is pretty much everyone."

"But they said they know the truth? What does that mean?" His hands twitch on the table.

The memory of that night slithers through my mind in the worst way and it makes me shiver.

Jesse's gentle gaze lands on me. "Sorry," he says quietly.

I shake my head, brushing off his sympathy.

"About everything," he adds.

"It's fine." I exhale. "We've moved on. Life's moved on."

"Can I…?" He reaches across the table and tentatively folds his hand around mine.

A quiet breath escapes me as I thread my fingers through his. This is the first time we've been close—physically close like this—since the night of the party. After that, everything kind of just imploded. It feels nice to be back here, in this place. Even with something so simple, something so elementary school, as holding hands. Butterflies.

"Whoever's texting you," he says, running his thumb along mine, "we'll figure it out."

"Yeah. And whoever pushed Raf, we'll figure that out, too. We've just got to trust each other and be honest with each other, no matter what." I hesitate for a second. "We need to stay calm, Jesse. The fact of the matter is one of them did it. One of them pushed Raf, and we're all on the chopping block until we figure out who it was."

He nods. Then after a moment he says, "What if it was Tara?"

I wait for him to elaborate.

"It's just something I've been thinking about," he says. "Maybe she got mad at Raf that night at Cray's. He humiliated her, right? Going after you while they were supposed to be together. She was *at* Owen's party, just down the hall. That's got to sting."

My gaze wanders around the dimly lit kitchen. The wind is rattling the panes and a draft is leaking beneath the back door.

"I saw Tara at Miller's yesterday," I tell him. When his eyebrows rise, I add, "It was okay between us. I think she was trying to offer an olive branch or something."

"Yeah? How did she seem?"

"Sad, mostly. It's going to take time for her to process losing Raf."

He bows his head. "Yeah."

I pause for a second. "You really think it could have been her?"

"I don't know. But those messages..." He glances at my phone on the table. "Whoever's texting you said they know the truth. Maybe Tara is trying to fix things with you now that she knows."

"But why would she have that conversation with me at Miller's and then text me a day later from a burner phone?" I press. "It just doesn't seem like something she'd do."

He falls silent, mulling over my words. "How well do we really know her, though?"

My gaze breaks away from his. "How well do any of us know each other?"

His hand twitches around mine.

"All three of them were there," I say, bringing my eyes back to him. "Tara, Owen, and Freddie. Someone left *your* phone at the window ledge. Someone texted *me* to come to Cray's, pretending to be you. Whoever killed Raf probably doesn't like us very much, either."

SAVANA

Friday, November 11

Tara's back in school on Friday. I notice her crossing the parking lot at the end of the day, so I pick up my pace to catch up with her. Jesse's theory nagged at me all night, and I'm glad I don't have to wait for another chance encounter to see her in person.

"Hey!" I call as she unlocks her Prius. She turns, and her fingers grip the open driver's door. A breeze streams into her car and flutters the heart-shaped air freshener that's hanging from the rearview mirror.

I come to a stop a few paces away from her. "How are you feeling?"

Her dark lashes sweep downward, and she shrugs.

I take a deep breath. "Tara, can I talk to you for a second?"

She glances around. Classes are over and the parking lot is bustling with people retreating to their cars. Fortunately, no one seems to be paying much attention to us. The November wind has thrown us a lifeline, and everyone seems more concerned with escaping the icy chill than eavesdropping on us.

"Sure," she says at last, dragging her gaze back to me. "Right here?"

"This won't take long."

"Okay." She combs her acrylic nails through her shiny hair. Today she looks more like the Tara I'm used to seeing, with carefully applied makeup and styled hair. It's like she's put on her armor, ready to face the world again.

I feel like I need a little of that armor, too. I straighten my shoulders and take a breath. "I have to ask you something."

Her brow creases as she stares back at me. "What?"

"Is it you?"

Her head tilts. "Is what me?"

"Did you text me last night from a burner phone?"

"What?" Her eyebrows pull together. "What are you talking about?"

"I promise I won't go to the police," I add, quickly. "I just have to know. Was it you?"

She tucks a strand of hair behind her ear and stares blankly back at me. "I haven't been texting you, Savana."

Her answer deflates me way more than I was prepared for. I guess I'd been hoping for a different response. If the messages were coming from Tara, then suddenly they don't feel so threatening anymore. Jesse's logic fits. Mystery solved.

Sure, maybe she's lying. Maybe it is her. But there were no hidden cues in her body language. No telltale glance to the side while she constructed her lie. No falter, or overacted response. Just a blank expression and a tired sigh.

"What's going on?" She folds her arms and rubs her hands

up and down her sleeves as a bitter wind funnels between the parked cars.

"I've been getting texts," I say. "From a number I don't know. About Raf."

She shakes her head, confused. "Saying what?"

"That they know things," I answer vaguely. I'm still not entirely sure if I can trust Tara. Or anyone. After all, someone is lying. Someone killed Raf, and Tara is as much of a suspect as anyone.

"What kind of things?" she presses. "You mean, like, they know who pushed him?"

"Maybe," I say, holding up my hands. "Or maybe they're just trying to scare me because they think I saw something. I have no idea."

"Shit. Have you shown the police?" She starts fiddling with her necklace, twisting the little gold pendant between her thumb and index finger.

"No."

She lets the necklace fall and presses her hand to her chest. "Babe, if you're being harassed, you should take it to the police. It's probably Jesse."

I prickle at the remark. "It's not Jesse."

She rolls her eyes. "Don't tell me you're still defending the guy? He killed my boyfriend, Savana."

"He didn't." The cold air steals my voice. I glance over my shoulder, checking that we're still alone. A junior guy is climbing into a car a few spaces away, but he slams the door shut and the engine rumbles. "Jesse didn't do it."

Tara puffs out a laugh. "Come on, Savana. His phone was under the window ledge. The police are just waiting for enough evidence to pull him in. What more proof do you need?"

I brace against a blast of cold air. "That's not proof, Tara. No one saw anything that night. I didn't. Did you?"

She lifts her chin.

"Exactly," I carry on when she doesn't respond. "So you can't go around saying it was Jesse if you didn't see him do it."

"Oh," she says, folding her arms, "so if you *don't* think it was him, you're saying it was either me, Owen, or Freddie." She ticks off the names on her fingers. "Thanks a lot."

I open my mouth to speak, but she jumps in fast.

"I know you believe anything he tells you," she says, "because you can't see who he really is. I know because I've been there myself, with Raf. Those two, they're more alike than you realize. They only show you what they want you to see."

A rush of heat rises to my face, despite the wintry air. "Tara, Jesse's your friend."

"He was *never* my friend," she snaps. "As soon as he and Raf stopped hanging out, he dropped me, too."

"Probably because Raf was feeding you a bunch of lies about him!"

"Who's to say Jesse isn't the liar?" she says with a grimace. "I think Jesse's the worst liar of all. *Worst* because he's the best at it." With that, she gets into her car and slams the door behind her.

I curl up on the porch swing and rock back and forth on beat with the waves. Wind ripples the gray water, skimming the surface.

I tug a blanket around myself, combating the chill in the air. But a blanket won't thaw the memory of Tara's icy words.

Or the memory of Raf.

The fall. The sight of his lifeless body on the ground.

And everything that came before.

I don't want to think about the night Raf made a move on me, but it creeps back every now and then. No matter how hard I try, I can't seem to squash the aftershock of that feeling. The bolt of fear that rose in my throat when his hand clamped down on my arm. The feeling of his weight pushed against me, and the sour taste of his lips.

I squeeze my eyes shut, focusing on the hiss of the surf. *I got away from him*, I remind myself. And I certainly never wanted *this*, what happened to Raf. I didn't want retribution; I didn't want anything.

The kitchen door creaks open.

"You look like you could use this." Mom steps onto the deck, carrying two steaming cups of cocoa. She hands one to me before taking a seat beside me on the porch swing.

"Thanks." I wrap my hands around the mug and let the sweet steam drift upward. "Don't you have to be at work?"

"Not for a little while." She hesitates, trailing her finger over the rim of her cup. "Is that all right with you? I don't want to leave you home alone tonight if you're not feeling up to it?"

Goose bumps spread over my skin. Mom's been avoiding late shifts for the past week, but I knew that'd have to come to an end eventually.

"I'm fine," I tell her. "It's fine."

The bench swings slowly back and forth.

"Maybe you could go visit your dad this weekend? Get out of Havelock for a while." It sounds like she's forcing the words out, trying to make the suggestion sound way more positive than it is.

"Yeah, maybe," I say.

I do owe Dad a visit. And maybe getting out of Havelock is exactly what I need right now. Although, it kind of feels like I'm running from something. From someone.

And I don't want to run.

I glance at my phone on the cushion next to me. My pulse accelerates at the reminder of the anonymous texts hidden inside.

Mom takes a sip of her cocoa. "How are you feeling about everything?"

I force a thin smile. "Okay, I guess. You?"

"Oh, you know." She nudges me with her elbow and smiles. "It's been a strange couple of months, hasn't it? My heart goes out to that poor boy's family. No matter what my personal feelings were toward him." She takes another small sip, and her gaze lands on me. "Think about what I said, though. Perhaps some distance from this place would be good for you." Her eyes skate over the Melos' house.

I stiffen on reflex.

"I mean," she adds, "I'll have to clear it with the, uh, police, just in case they need to ask you any more questions, but I'm sure it'll be fine. You'll only be visiting your dad, for God's sake."

Right. We'll have to get permission because I'm still a suspect, after all—no matter how much Mom tries to sugarcoat it. Now is not the best time to plan a trip. Although I get the feeling that Mom's suggesting I visit Dad has less to do with a vacation, and more to do with orchestrating a separation.

I catch her gaze. "I thought you liked Jesse."

She sucks in a breath, as though she's actually surprised I uncovered her ulterior motive, her ploy to separate me from my "bad influence" neighbor. "I do like Jesse," she says.

I study her face and her mouth twitches.

"Oh," I say, picking apart her comment. "You like Jesse, just not when he's around me?"

She heaves a sigh. "Savana, I do like Jesse. Sure, he's made some mistakes lately, but he's a good kid. Most of the time." I frown and she continues, "But with everything going on with this investigation, Jesse's in serious trouble, and I think it's time for you to step back."

Our attention drifts to the Melos' house. It's quiet over there; the curtains are drawn.

Of course Mom wants me to step back from Jesse. She's just trying to protect me. But it's too late. I'm already in way over my head.

"I don't want to visit Dad right now," I murmur. "When this is all over..." I trail off.

Her smile turns rigid. "Okay, Savana."

"He didn't do it," I tell Mom. "Jesse didn't do it."

She doesn't respond. She takes a slow sip of cocoa and stares out at the snapping jaws of the ocean.

Audio File_MP3

Title: Case_HPD0149_Owen Keaton Interview

H.B.: For the purpose of the tape, the date is Saturday, November 5. The time is approximately ten o'clock in the morning. Your full name, please?

O.K.: It's Owen Keaton, sir.

H.B.: What happened last night at the port, Owen?

O.K.: I have no idea. The guy—the policeman from last night—he didn't tell us anything. What's going on?

H.B.: How do you know Rafael Lombardi?

O.K.: School, I guess. Through our families, too. Why?

H.B.: And you and Rafael were good friends?

O.K.: Yeah. We're tight.

H.B.: Explain to me what happened at Cray's Warehouse last night, Owen. Talk me through it.

O.K.: I honestly don't know. I went into a room on the fourth floor, and the window was broken. We were trying to see down, but it was dark. Then the police came.

H.B.: What made you go to that room, Owen?

O.K.: I heard the glass smash—the window, I figure—then I saw two of my friends coming from down the hall. They heard it, too, so we started checking the rooms.

H.B.: Your friends' names, please?

O.K.: Freddie and Tara. Then Jesse showed up right after.

H.B.: Are you aware that Rafael Lombardi is dead?

O.K.: What? (INAUDIBLE) Is this for real?

H.B.: I'm afraid so.

O.K.: No. No way. No way.

H.B.: Do you need to take a break?

O.K.: Can I call my parents? I've got to call my parents. This can't be real.

H.B.: We'll take a short break, Owen.

[Interview terminated at 10:17 a.m.]

JESSE:
New phone. Jesse.

FREDDIE:
Hey, man. We need to meet.

JESSE:
Yeah. Where you at?

FREDDIE:
Port? Half an hour?

JESSE:
Yeah.

JESSE

Saturday, November 12

I meet Freddie at the port on Saturday afternoon. We sit on the edge of the seawall and watch the tankers pull into the harbor.

"You sleeping much these days?" he asks. The wind messes with his jet-black curls.

"Nope." I pick up a pebble and launch it into the harbor. The murky water swallows it whole. "You?"

Freddie bows his head. "Cops are coming at me over what happened at school between Raf and me, with the steroids and him setting me up. It's stressing me out hard."

My lungs tighten. "How have they been with you?"

"They think I did it." He drums his knuckles on the seawall. "I'm a Black kid with a drug record. It doesn't matter that I'm getting my GED at the community college. That I'll graduate. That the stuff that went down at school is in the past. It's like they don't even hear me. They're still looking at me, you know?"

I stare out at the horizon.

"Are they looking at you, too?" he asks.

A cold wind steals the air from my lungs. "Yeah. Did you hear about my phone being found under the ledge?" *Do you know who put it there?* I want to ask. But the words don't come out.

Was it Tara? Owen? *Raf?*

Freddie's voice pulls me back. "Yeah, but that doesn't mean anything."

"My fight with Raf does, though."

"We've all fought with Raf."

His words hang over us, weighing down on us.

"Did you see anything that night?" I ask him.

He shakes his head. "Raf told me to meet him upstairs. I was looking for him and I heard the window smash. When I went to check it out, I saw Tara and Owen coming from down the hall. I never saw Raf."

"I didn't, either," I murmur.

"Have you talked to Owen and Tara much at school? Did they see anything?"

I exhale into the misted air. "Not that I've heard. I see Owen, but Tara's been avoiding me. I figure because she thinks I did it."

He rolls a pebble between his palms. "Man. Sorry."

"Tara's been off with me for a while, though. Way before that night at Cray's. After you left school, it got bad between Raf and me. Tara stuck by him."

The muscles in his jaw twitch. "Yeah. Listen, about that day... I'm sorry I told you in the way that I did, about Raf sending those guys after Cody." He rubs his brow. "That wasn't the way to do it. I'm sorry I didn't tell you sooner, too.

I should have, but Raf…" He sighs into the wind. "The guy could be persuasive, man."

My hands ball, but my expression stays neutral. Calm. "It is what it is."

"He'd get into your head, you know?" Freddie's eyes become lost on the tankers and their wailing horns. "He could make you think something was a good idea, even if you knew it wasn't."

"I hear you," I mutter.

"That thing with Cody," Freddie carries on. "Raf made out like it'd be worse if you knew. It'd mess with your head, and he only meant to scare Cody. Just a warning."

I grit my teeth and stare out at the rippling water. I don't want to hear this.

But Freddie keeps talking. "And on that Friday night, the night Raf died, I only went to Cray's because Raf called me and said it was you who screwed me with the drugs. I don't know why I believed him. I *don't* believe him."

"Wait, what?" My eyes snap to him. "Raf said what?"

"He said you told Coach Carson about the steroids."

I choke out a sound. "You're kidding?"

He shakes his head. "He said you wanted me off the team, in case I got scouted instead of you. He said you got him off the team for the same reason."

"You believed him?"

"For a minute, yeah." His focus moves to the gray water sloshing beneath us. "Raf was a good liar."

Something else trips on my mind. I blink, trying to make sense of it all. "What does this have to do with you going to Cray's that night?"

"I don't know," he says. He cricks his neck. "Raf. He wanted us to talk."

The cold wind folds around me and musses my hair. "About what?"

"He just wanted us to put things right, or whatever." He hesitates and presses his knuckles to his mouth. "So you haven't spoken to Tara since that night at the warehouse? It's been a week."

"Nope. But I know she thinks I did it."

His eyes come to me. "Did you do it?"

The question hits me hard in the rib cage. "No. Did *you*?"

He blows out a breath, fogging the air. "No. Do you think it was Owen?"

"Could have been any of us."

"Maybe Raf and Owen had some bad blood lingering, you know? Maybe it wasn't all good with them."

"Maybe."

It doesn't surprise me that he didn't throw Tara's name out there. He'd rather suspect his buddies, Owen and me, before he doubts Tara. Because he thinks she's someone who needs saving. Personally, I don't think she wants to be saved. But Freddie's always had her back. He's always looked out for her.

And man, did Raf hate that.

It crosses my mind, just like it's probably crossing his mind, and Owen's, and Tara's, none of us can trust each other anymore. I feel the divide between us, this invisible force pushing us apart. Because any one of us could have snapped that night, and whoever did do it is setting me up to take the fall.

HAVELOCK SUNDAY PRESS

November 13

New evidence has been found in the investigation of the death of eighteen-year-old Rafael Lombardi.

The teenager's body was recovered from Havelock Port on Friday, November 4, and four high school students were escorted from the former Cray's Warehouse shortly after.

Security footage from a nearby storage unit has since been released, now possibly placing an unidentified person at the scene. The unnamed person was caught on camera running away from the site at the time of the incident.

Havelock Police Department has put out a statement urging anyone who may have been in the quay area that evening to come forward. Any information is considered critical and key to the case.

OWEN:

Did you hear the news? Someone else there that night at Cray's. Did you see anyone there?

JESSE:

No. Did you?

OWEN:

No. Good that the heat will come off you now, huh?

JESSE:

Did you think I did it?

OWEN:

No. Did you think I did?

JESSE:

No. I thought it was Tara. Still do.

JESSE

Sunday, November 13

I wait for Donna's car to leave the driveway before I knock on Savana's door.

Barely a second passes before the door swings open and she hauls me into her room.

"Can you believe this?" she exclaims, bouncing on her toes. "Did you see the article about the CCTV footage? There was someone else there that night, Jesse!"

"Yeah," I say, dazed by her excitement. "I saw it."

She presses her hands to her face. "Someone was *running* away. That's so sketchy, right? This is great!"

"Why is it great?"

"Because someone else was there, which means we could be off the hook."

I frown. "What, just because someone else was at the port?"

She grabs my hands, threading her fingers through mine. "Someone else who *knows* they were there and hasn't come forward. Someone who's clearly hiding something."

My gaze travels over her bedroom. I catch myself, my reflection trapped in the tall mirror. My eyes look sunken, and my hair looks messy. The reflection is just another reminder, another piece of me that I don't want to see. So I bring my focus back to her. "But maybe this other person will never be found."

"Of course they'll be found! It's only a matter of time before they get caught."

I feel myself tense.

Her smile falters. "Are you okay?"

"Yeah. Yeah, I'm fine."

"Don't be nervous," she says. "This other person will be found. I'm sure of it. Maybe we could ask to see the footage. If it's someone from school, maybe we'd have a shot at identifying them."

I trap my lip between my teeth.

She reaches up and hugs me. "We could be off the hook, Jesse," she whispers. "This could all be over soon."

I take a moment. I close my eyes, feeling her heart beating fast against mine. My heart's beating fast, too, and I hope she can't tell it's because I'm scared.

SAVANA

Monday, November 14

I'm in the girls' bathroom washing my hands when Tara
walks in.

The bathroom door thumps shut behind her.

She smiles at me, but it looks strained and uncomfortable.

"Hey," I say, attempting a smile back as she lingers at the
sinks. I turn the faucet off. "Nice boots."

"Oh, thanks." She twists her leg to show me her tan thigh-
high boot. "Mrs. Arnold has been on my case, telling me how
'inappropriate'—" she makes air quotes on the word "—they
are for school. Whatever."

Another smile tugs at my lips. A genuine one this time.
"Careful," I say. "You know what Mrs. Arnold is like. She'll
make you change into shoes from Lost Property if she catches
you wearing them again."

Tara sucks in a breath and her hands flutter to her chest.
"Ew. No way. I'm not wearing someone else's gnarly old

sneakers. She can't separate me from my shoes, Savana. That's wrong on so many levels."

"Too many levels," I agree.

Her gaze wanders over me. "I like your hair today."

My nose crinkles. "No, you don't." I glance at my reflection in the mirror. My hair looks extra frizzy this morning—one major drawback of Havelock's perpetually damp, salty air.

Tara reaches out and flattens down some of my unruly strands. "Okay," she says with a quick laugh. "I was just trying to be nice. But you still look pretty, so whatever."

"Thanks, I think." I dodge to the side as she reaches for my hair again.

Her gaze moves to the mirror, landing on our reflections. She trails her fingers through her own immaculate hair before turning back to me. "I'm sorry about the fight we had the other day. I shouldn't have yelled at you about Jesse."

I shrug. "We both said some things." My thoughts wander to the anonymous text messages that have been burning a metaphorical hole into my phone. "Since we're apologizing and all, I'm sorry I accused you of sending those texts. But I had to ask."

"That's okay. I don't blame you for thinking it was me. We haven't exactly been on good terms lately." She purses her lips and lowers her gaze. "And I know I'm to blame for that."

"Well, a lot has happened over the past month."

"Yeah," she says.

There's a beat of silence, then she presses her thumbnail to her lips. "Full disclosure?" she says. "When it came out about what Raf did to you at Owen's party, I was mad. And all that anger got directed at you."

My shoulders tighten.

"I loved Raf," she murmurs. "I *still* love him, even though he's not here anymore." She takes a sharp breath and looks up to meet my eyes. "But that doesn't excuse what he did. I should have supported you right off the bat. I did believe you. I *do* believe you. I guess I was just scared of how he'd react if I went against him."

It takes me a couple of seconds to find my voice. I've waited weeks for this moment, holding out for her to say these words. That she believes me. Raf disempowered me that night, and when he and Tara accused me of lying, it twisted the knife a little harder. But now that the moment is here, the breakthrough validation I've been holding out for, it doesn't feel as good as I'd imagined. "Thanks," I whisper.

Her chin juts out. "Savana, I'm sorry he did that to you, and I'm sorry I made you feel like shit about it after. You were right to call him out on it. I would have done the exact same thing."

"Thanks." My voice sounds far away.

She combs her fingers through the ends of her hair. "With everything that's been going on, grieving for Raf, and dealing with the investigation, I just want some form of normalcy back."

"I get that."

"Can we just call a truce?" she asks. "Friends, maybe?"

"Friends is good."

"Life's too short, right?" she says. "Anyway, now that it's come out about someone else being at the port that night, it looks like the police won't be checking on us as much." She hugs her arms around herself. "Can you believe that someone else was there and we didn't even know it?"

I heave a sigh. "Well, you guys didn't see me outside, and I didn't see you inside, so I guess it's not that hard to believe."

A shudder tremors her shoulders. "It's seriously disturbing, though. If you hadn't been there to call the cops when you did, the rest of us might have been trapped in Cray's with a murderer on the loose."

I hold her stare. "So you don't think Jesse's guilty anymore?"

She shrugs. "None of *us* ran," she says. "None of *us* are hiding our identity. Because we've got nothing to hide, right?"

I breathe steadily as the unnerving text messages return to the forefront of my mind. Not only these recent texts, but also the ones I received from Jesse's phone that night, asking me to meet him at the warehouse. I'm starting to think I *should* take the anonymous messages to the police. For all I know, they're key to finding the unidentified person. But if the texter's aim is to target Jesse, this could bring the investigators' focus right back to him.

"They could have been coming for all of us," Tara adds, jolting me from my thoughts. Her fingers coil around her necklace. "Maybe we were supposed to be next. And whoever it was, they're still out there."

Her words turn my blood cold. The memory of the masked face outside my bedroom and the shadowed figures I've seen around the cove make my stomach flip in fear.

I have an awful feeling that Tara is right. This isn't over.

JESSE

Tuesday, November 15

Coach Carson pulls me out of class right before lunch. I follow him to his office and take a seat at the desk.

He sinks down onto the chair opposite me, then jumps straight in. "Tough week, huh?"

I laugh under my breath. "Yeah. You could say that, sir."

He tilts his head, deep brown eyes regarding me carefully. "How are you?"

There's something about the way Coach talks that makes everyone feel like they're important. The way he slows his words, like he has all the time in the world. I know he has a couple of kids of his own—two boys and a girl, I think. I find myself envying them sometimes, wishing I had their lives. Then I feel guilty for thinking it. But Coach Carson's patience and stability make me feel like I don't have to be the adult in the room. I like that.

"I'm all right," I answer. "I'm okay."

"How's everything at home? Your dad okay?"

I nod, numb.

"Have you…" He clears his throat. "Have you spoken to your mom since all this has happened?"

My focus strays around the sports office, focusing on anything but him. "No, sir. We don't have a number for her."

"I'm sorry to hear that." He hesitates and presses his palms together. "Jesse, I pulled you from class because I think we need to discuss where to go from here."

"What do you mean?"

"The interview you missed on Saturday, after…" His gaze dips. "After what happened to Raf."

The Saturday morning I spent in a jail cell, he means. That morning I was supposed to be at school attending an interview I had lined up with a college football scout—it was supposed to be my shot. I was waiting, ready for it. But I never made it to the interview. The dream was over in a blink.

"I've spoken to the scout," Coach Carson moves on. "I explained the extenuating circumstances for you missing the interview." He grimaces, then adds, "About what happened on that Friday, I'm sorry. To lose a friend like that…" He shakes his head, and his scalp catches the light of the bulb hanging over us.

I scratch at my palms. "Yeah."

"You know I'm here for you? If you need to talk, I'm always here."

"Thanks," I say. "I know."

"As for the interview, we can rearrange. I'm suggesting December, some time before winter break."

I fumble for words. "Uh, yeah."

"I know it's a lot to take in right now," he says, nodding. "And you're probably not in the right headspace to even have this conversation. But if you want the chance of getting scouted for college, you need to act on this opportunity."

"Yeah." I tug at my collar. "You know there's an investigation going on? I'm in it."

He holds my gaze. "I'm aware. But look, this interview is just a small step in a bigger process. Let's shoot for that interview, okay?"

The stability. The safety of his words, as though he thinks there's actually hope for me. He hasn't written me off. Better, he doesn't think I did it.

"Does that sound okay with you?" he asks.

"Yes, sir," I reply. "Thank you." And then I say it again, just in case he didn't hear it the first time. "Thank you."

Owen catches up with me in the locker room after practice.

"Hey," he says, scrubbing his hands through his damp hair. "What did Coach want to talk to you about earlier?"

"I missed my college scout interview a while back," I tell him, pulling at my laces. Owen nods like he remembers. Then he turns pale as though he's remembering *when* I missed it. And why. "He says I can reschedule," I add.

Owen's eyebrows rise.

"Do you think I should do it?"

"Yeah," he says. "Of course. You can't let what happened with Raf screw up your chances at getting scouted."

"But I'm a suspect in a murder investigation," I say quietly.

We exchange a tense look, then take a seat on the bench as the other guys start to filter out of the locker room. None of the guys have questioned us about what happened to Raf. But they still look at Owen and me with these strange, guarded expressions. They give us space, keep their distance. They're probably scared we're going to snap and start pushing them out windows, too.

I've never experienced this before. I mean, being accused of murder, obviously that's new. But the isolation that comes with it; that's new, too. When word got out about what Raf did to Savana at Owen's party, all the guys rallied. Everyone muttered about how shady it was, and how messed up Raf must be. The guys kept checking on me, asking me how Savana was, how *I* was, like it'd happened to me. They don't ask anymore. They keep away. They side-eye each other when they see me walking down the hall.

"No one thinks you did it." Owen's voice pulls me back.

I push out a tight laugh. "That's a lie." I've seen the unmarked police car lingering outside my house. I know in my gut they're trying to piece together evidence against me. The phone, the scuffs on the floor, my history with Raf, and whatever else they've got.

My heart starts slamming in my chest.

Stay calm. Savana's voice echoes through my mind: *We're all on the chopping block until we figure out who it was.*

Owen's gone quiet. We sit shoulder to shoulder in the locker room, and we stay silent, staring blankly at the lockers and tiled walls as the other guys pass us by.

Then Owen says, "Take the interview, Jesse. You've got to shoot for it."

"Yeah," I murmur. "Thanks." I bow my head and my sneaker starts tapping on the wet floor. "Have you talked to Freddie lately?"

"No. Have you?"

"I met up with him on the weekend. He says the cops are

looking closely at him because of the steroids and what happened with Raf."

Owen's eyebrows pull together. "Wait, you actually saw him? He won't even pick up my calls. Why is he avoiding me?"

I trap my lip between my teeth. The truth is on some level we're all avoiding each other, but at the same time we're the only people who understand what it was like to be there that night, to reach that room and see the smashed window and know instinctively that something was seriously wrong. We're bound by a moment that changed all our lives forever.

I glance at Owen. The guys have gone, leaving us alone in the humid room.

"Why were you there that night at Cray's?" My throat feels scratchy when I ask the question because I'm scared of what the answer will be.

He blows out a breath. "Raf told me we were all meeting so that we could figure everything out."

"But what was he expecting to happen? That we'd talk and suddenly the past would just be erased?"

He shrugs. "I don't know. I just showed up. Tara and Freddie were already there, but I didn't see Raf. Or you until you ran into the room."

"Where were Tara and Freddie?"

"They came from down the hall. We found the room together and saw the smashed window."

I frown back at him. "Freddie said he saw *you* and Tara coming from down the hall."

Owen's brow creases. "Wait, Freddie said *I* was with Tara?"

"Yeah."

"Why would he say that?"

"I don't know. None of this makes sense to me. What was Raf trying to pull with this?"

I press my knuckles to my mouth, just thinking, wondering why Raf would ambush me like that when he said it'd just be me and him. What was his motive? To set me up for his own murder?

When Owen speaks again, his voice sounds thin. "How come Freddie's meeting with you and not me? Do you think..." He hesitates, and I wait for him to ask me if I think Freddie did it. But then his hands ball, and he says, "Do you think Freddie thinks *I* did it?"

TARA:
I miss you, too. Meet at our place, after school.

                                         SAVANA:
                                              Huh?

TARA:
Miller's? Do you want to go later? Or sometime this weekend?

                                         SAVANA:
                                       Okay, sure.

TARA:
Tomorrow, 11 a.m.?

                                         SAVANA:
                                       Yeah.

TARA:
Shit. Mr. Greggory keeps looking at me. I'd better put my phone away before he confiscates it. Hate him.

SAVANA

Friday, November 18

I've sent enough accidental text messages in my life to know
when I'm on the receiving end of one. Call me cynical, but I
don't buy Tara's blasé response. That message, the *I miss you,
too. Meet at our place, after school* was meant for someone else.

Under normal circumstances, I'd let it go. It's not my business to know who Tara's meeting—who that text was *really*
intended for. But when you're caught up in a murder investigation, all bets are off. Any information could be relevant
right now, and I'm in the mood for doing some investigating of my own.

Just one catch. I don't know where *our place* is since I'm
not the person she's meeting. But I know Tara, and I have a
hunch. I have a hunch about who she's meeting, too. All I
need is to be proven right, then I'll leave them alone. For now.

I pace quickly through the port, scanning the marina for
any sign of Tara. The sun is beginning to edge lower into

the quay, making way for the faded presence of the moon. There are still people around, passing through or working in the dockyard, but there's a sense of darkness looming. It's as though the day is sinking away with one final exhale.

Cray's stands in its corner, overlooking the gray water. You'd hardly notice any changes, apart from the shattered fourth-floor window and the police tape crisscrossing the metal door. The yellow tape quivers in the ocean breeze. I can almost hear it snapping above the cacophony of tankers and their horns, and the endless slosh of water and clang of anchors and chains.

I stand still, my feet pinned to the pavement. I was right here, pretty much in this exact spot, when I saw Raf fall. Only now the sky is light, silver and streaked with clouds, and there are people wandering around. It doesn't feel intimidating or threatening. But it *was* then. In this stolen moment I feel like I'm just an echo in time. An imprint from the past. The girl who stood right here and watched Raf Lombardi fall to his death.

My breathing quickens as my mind replays it. The hazy memory of running toward him, my fingers moving fast to dial 911, like I was in some surreal dream—or nightmare.

Now, among the strangers meandering about their day, I see two people in the shadow of Cray's wall. They're almost hidden, tangled together in a private, passionate embrace. They must think they're invisible, concealed by the warehouse, but they're not.

Him—his arms sealed around his partner's waist, his head dipped to reach her for a kiss.

Her—blond hair flurried by the breeze as she rises onto her tiptoes in her tan thigh-high boots.

I stare at them, stunned for a moment. My hunch was right.

I back away from Cray's and head quickly for home.

JESSE

Saturday, November 19

I stare at my reflection in the hallway mirror. I like the person I see today because he *isn't* me. I'm pretending; I'm kidding myself and deceiving everyone around me. This rigid white shirt is my costume.

There's a button missing right around the middle, though. A telltale sign that I don't belong in this shirt. I press the empty buttonhole down flat and hope that the flaw is small enough to go unnoticed.

This is the only smart shirt I own. It's my "serious shirt," the one that gets recycled for weddings, funerals, formals, and times like now, when I need to make a good impression. When I need to look like an honorable, trustworthy guy.

I shake my hands through my hair before I leave my room.

Across the hallway, I rap my knuckles on Dad's bedroom door.

Silence.

"Dad?" I call into the closed door.

Farther down the hall, the shower stops running and the water heater clicks off. Cody emerges from the bathroom with a towel wrapped around his waist. His hair is dripping wet and stuck to his forehead.

He frowns when he sees me standing outside Dad's room.

"Is he in there?" Cody murmurs, his eyes straying to the closed door.

"He's probably still asleep." I thump on the door again. "Dad. We've gotta leave."

Cody sidles past me and twists the handle. Inside the room, the curtains are drawn. It's dark and stale, and Dad isn't in there.

My heart smacks hard in my chest.

"He didn't come home last night," Cody mutters.

I take my cell from my jeans pocket and dial Dad's number, but it goes straight to voice mail.

"I'm sure he's fine," I say, answering a question that wasn't asked.

Cody makes a sound under his breath. "Yeah. I'm sure he is, too." His voice has an edge to it, a bite. Because he's not wondering if Dad's okay. He knows as well as I do that Dad'll rock up at some point later today, looking tired and hungover. Then he'll spew out some bullshit, lying about where he was, and we'll pretend like we don't know that he's been at the bar, probably passed out somewhere.

I pull his bedroom door shut, more forcefully than I'd intended, and the slam sounds like a gunshot. "I've got to go sign in at the station," I tell Cody. I don't mention that I'm supposed to be accompanied by a parent. I don't want to remind him that we've run out of parents. So I muster an easy smile and pretend like everything's all good.

I've got everything under control.

Cody doesn't need to see that I'm drowning worse than Dad.

I hate that I have to do this.

I cross our driveway and step onto the Carusos' front lawn. The grass on their side is immaculate compared to ours. It makes me wish I'd noticed our overgrown lawn sooner. I could have mown it; I could have disguised it, just like the serious shirt disguises me.

I press my thumb to their doorbell and listen to it chime through the house.

A moment later the front door swings open. Donna's hair is scraped back, and she's wearing her beige-colored Miller's uniform.

She's instantly guarded, on edge. "Oh. Hello, Jesse."

"Hi." My voice sounds hoarse.

"I don't want Savana going out today," she says as she takes in my shirt. She thinks that's why I'm here, to take Savana out. I wish that were why I was here, at nine o'clock on a Saturday morning.

"Yeah…" I rub the nape of my neck.

She waits.

"Sorry, nothing," I stammer. "You're busy." This was a bad idea. Bad.

Donna glances at her watch. "No, go on. What is it?"

"Uh. I need to go into the station. They want me to sign in to prove I haven't skipped town. Someone needs to come with me because I'm still a minor."

She stares blankly back at me.

"My dad…" I trip over my words. "He's not doing so good. I think he's sick or something." The lie makes me grimace.

Her eyes move over me. "Right. I see. Okay, well, I can go with you." She glances at her watch again. "When?"

"Now. But it's no big deal. If you've gotta work…"

Donna shakes her head. "It won't be a problem. I'll call Miller's and tell them I'm running a little late."

She grabs her coat, and I follow her to her car. I know how this must look to her, the pitiful state of me, trying to act like I'm a good guy in my serious shirt. It stings having to ask for Donna's help. Having to ask for anyone's help, like I'm some stray dog that even the pound won't take.

I haven't heard from my mom since she left. I don't know if she's still in contact with Mike, if she ever was, or if she heard about what happened to Raf. As far as I'm aware, she's not in Havelock anymore.

I half expected her to reach out after Raf died, to call me or text me and say, *Oh, man, you lost your best friend. That must suck.*

Because the last time she saw me, Raf and I were solid.

Or even a cursory *Sorry you're a suspect in a murder investigation* would have been nice.

I climb into the front passenger seat of Donna's car, and she smiles encouragingly at me.

We drive along the suburban street in silence. I stare out the window at the rows of houses as we pass them by.

Donna's voice catches me off guard. "Jesse, there's something I've been meaning to talk to you about."

I glance at her profile, but she's staring straight ahead, her eyes trained on the road. I see the tightness in her mouth, though, and I know where this is heading.

"What we discussed on that Saturday morning after the incident, I appreciate you not sharing that with Savana." She smooths her fingers over her hair. "I'm concerned that the more she knows, the more implicated she'll become."

I lower my gaze, staring down at my hands. "Yeah. Don't worry. Like I told you, I won't say anything."

"Good. Then let's not mention it again."

UNKNOWN NUMBER:
Jesse is lying to you.

> **SAVANA:**
> Who are you?

UNKNOWN NUMBER:
Raf.

> **SAVANA:**
> You're seriously twisted.

UNKNOWN NUMBER:
What do you think I would say to you if I was still alive?

> **SAVANA:**
> I don't care. You're not Raf. He's dead.

UNKNOWN NUMBER:
Maybe I'd apologize. Raf lied about a lot of things.
Jesse's a liar, too. But you can trust me, Savana. I
know what really happened that night.

> **SAVANA:**
> Leave me alone.

UNKNOWN NUMBER:
All I want is for the truth to come out, but the consequences won't be good.

SAVANA:
Tell me who you really are.

SAVANA

Saturday, November 19

It's barely eleven o'clock on Saturday morning, and Tara is already waiting at Miller's by the time I arrive. She's seated at one of the back booths and sipping from an oversize mug.

I bypass the counter and slide into the booth seat opposite her.

Her brow knits. "Aren't you going to order anything?"

I press my hands flat to the table and hold her gaze. "I'm just going to come right out with this." I steel myself. "I saw you and Freddie together yesterday."

She hesitates for a second before relaxing into a perplexed smile. "What are you talking about?"

"I saw you and Freddie at the port, making out."

She laughs, and I hear the tension. "Huh?"

"Come on, Tara. I know it was you. I saw you."

Her lips press into a tight line. "Did you follow me?"

"Why didn't you tell me that you and Freddie had a thing going?"

She sets her coffee cup down and her eyes dart around the diner. "Savana, please," she whispers, "you can't go broadcasting this. *Shit*," she hisses. "Have you already told people?"

"No. I haven't told anyone. But it's going to get out. You two weren't exactly being subtle yesterday." I roll my eyes.

"Shit." She starts chewing on her thumbnail. "Do you think anyone else knows? It'll look so bad if this gets out so soon after Raf…" Her eyes fill with tears, and she looks down at the table.

I take a steadying breath. I know I need to tread carefully with this, to play my part as the sympathetic friend, and not let her see where my thoughts are spiraling to. If Freddie and Tara have a secret relationship, then that's motive I hadn't even considered. "How long has this been going on? You and Freddie."

"Not long," she answers quickly. "A month or two."

I suck in a breath. "A month or two? Tara, you were still with Raf then!"

She flaps her hands in an attempt to quiet me. "It only started around the time Freddie got expelled. I just…" She lets out a shattered gasp. "I don't know. I really like Freddie. I was going to end things with Raf, but then he had that huge fight with Jesse, and he got in trouble with school over what happened with you. Our whole grade turned against him. Someone had to stand by him, Savana. I loved him, even if I wasn't *in* love with him."

I rub my temples. "Wait. Rewind. You said this started around the time Freddie got expelled?"

She nods, avoiding my stare.

"Before or after he got expelled?" I press.

"I don't know. A little before, I guess."

"Oh, my God," I whisper. "This could explain why Raf set Freddie up with the drugs in his locker. Maybe Raf found out about you two."

Her eyes shoot to me. "That was *Jesse*, not Raf. Jesse set Freddie up to get him off the team."

"Tara," I breathe, raking my hands through my hair. "Seriously? It was Raf."

She tilts her chin. "Raf told me it was Jesse, and I believe it. That's why Jesse and Raf had that fight at school, because Raf told Freddie what Jesse had done—"

"No, Tara," I exclaim under my breath. "You've got this all wrong. Is that why you hate Jesse so much?"

She holds up her hands, flustered. "Savana, do we really need to dredge all this up again? Who cares what happened in the past?"

"*I* care," I say. "If it means there's a chance of getting to the bottom of what happened that night at Cray's." I glance over my shoulder into the restaurant. We're far enough away from anyone that we can't be overheard. I'm not holding back anymore—the puzzle pieces are slotting together, and I need to see Tara's reaction when I say this. "Raf and Freddie," I say, turning back to her and bracing myself. "That night... Maybe they got into a fight over you, and it was an accident."

"No." She shakes her head, blond hair tumbling. "It wasn't Freddie. He's not a fighter."

I don't miss the inflection in her tone, the insinuation that Jesse *is*.

"Anyway," she says, "there was someone else at the port that night. I thought we were on the same page about this. It had to be them."

"Okay. But what if—"

"It wasn't Freddie. I'm sure of it."

"How?" I hold her gaze. "Imagine if Raf had found out about you and Freddie. You know how jealous he was. He would have lost it!"

"Raf didn't know!" She glances across the diner, then dips her voice even lower. "He never suspected Freddie. It was always Jesse." When I frown, she elaborates. "Raf used to think I had a thing for Jesse, just because I had a tiny crush on him in sophomore year. That time you caught Raf and me arguing on the beach, that's what it was over. Jesse."

Her ghostly words from that day echo in my mind. *No. You've got this all wrong.*

"Never Freddie," she asserts. "It was always Jesse. That's why Raf used to talk about you, I think."

A chill runs down my spine. "Me? What about me?"

She starts chewing on her lip. "I don't know. Sometimes he'd joke about how maybe he should hook up with you, to show me what it's like to be second best. He made me think that the two of you had something going on."

A nauseated feeling comes over me. "You didn't actually believe that, did you?"

"Maybe," she says, her cheeks flushing. "For a minute. That's kind of why I wanted to be friends with you. Keep your enemies close and all that, right?"

A laugh escapes me—but there's no humor behind it.

"But that changed," she adds quickly. "I started to really like you! Once I got to know you, I knew Raf was just messing with me. You're not that girl."

I draw in a breath. "Look, all I'm saying is if Raf was that intense over an unfounded suspicion about you and Jesse, then it's totally plausible he could have caught on to you and

Freddie. They could have gotten into a fight that night at the warehouse."

She presses her fingertips to her eyelids. "I trust Freddie, and there's no way he could have been in that room with Raf. I saw him in the corridor. He was too far away. Between you and me…" She hesitates and takes a breath before saying the words. "Freddie's pretty sure Jesse did it."

"What? Why?"

She lets out a flustered sigh. "Just talk to Freddie." She slides her coffee cup away and stands from her seat.

"Wait, why?"

She hugs her arms around herself. "Just talk to Freddie."

SAVANA:
Hi. It's been a while. How are you?

FREDDIE:
What's up, Savana? Not great. You?

SAVANA:
Same. Can we talk? I could call you or meet you somewhere?

FREDDIE:
Yeah. I'm busy at the moment, but I'll call you sometime.

SAVANA:
Okay. Whenever you're free.

JESSE

Saturday, November 19

Owen is standing on my front porch with his hands stuffed into his jacket pockets and his head bowed away from the mist of rain that's just started.

"Hey," he says when I open the door.

"Hey." I glance past him to the quiet street. His bike is on my lawn, chained to the mailbox. I open the door wider. "Thanks for coming over."

"No problem," he says, following me into the hallway. "But I can't stay long. My parents want me home. We're going to visit Grant for the weekend."

I frown as I lead him into the living room. "Are you allowed to leave town right now? During the investigation?"

He takes a seat on the couch and starts moving the heels of his hands up and down his thighs, dragging over his jeans. "My mom cleared it with the cops. I've got to get away from here, man. This place is screwing with my head."

His words trigger alarm bells in my mind. Owen's allowed to leave town, but I've still got to sign in at the precinct twice a week?

I clear my throat, reining in my thoughts. "All right. Well, that sounds like a good idea. If you've got to get away for a while, you should go."

"I feel like I need to spend some time with Grant after everything that's happened, you know?"

"I get that." If there was ever anything that made me want to keep a close eye on Cody, it was the murder of Raf Lombardi. "I'll get to the point, then," I say. "Something's been playing on my mind, and I need you to be honest with me."

"Okay," he says, tensing.

"That night at Cray's, I went there because Raf said he had a message from my mom." There's a flash of sympathy in Owen's eyes, and he looks down at his hands. "But when I talked to Freddie," I push on, "he said that Raf set this up for all you guys to be there. He said Raf called him and convinced him that it was me who told the school about the steroids in his locker, and that's why he went along with Raf's plan. Is that true?"

Owen squeezes his eyes shut for a second. When he finally speaks, his voice cracks. "Freddie's telling the truth," he murmurs. "I'm so sorry. Just know I was never going to leave you in there. You know I wouldn't have."

And just like that, I'm holding my breath.

"What do you mean?" My voice sounds hollow.

He freezes.

"Come on, Owen." I sit forward, locking my hands. "What did you mean by that? Why were you all there that night?" My pulse is racing now because I'm figuring out fast that they weren't there to *talk*.

Owen glances at the window, his gaze lingering on the street as a car speeds by outside. "I was just…" He cringes and presses his fist to his brow. "All right. You want the truth?"

My heart starts thumping harder. "Yeah."

"Raf was a loose cannon."

The comment catches me off guard, and a sound escapes me. Not a laugh, or a sob, or a word. Just a sound.

"He had it in for you," Owen adds. "Big-time. You know that, right?"

"Yeah. I figured."

"I mean, he really had it in for you. He said you and Savana had made up this lie about him, about him making a move on her—"

"She wasn't lying," I cut him off.

"I know," he says, lifting his hands in peace. "I know. But he was stirring shit up with Freddie, talking about how it was your fault Freddie busted his shoulder because of the car accident, and how you were the one who set him up with the drugs. He was in Freddie's head. He's been in all our heads, and in those last couple of weeks it was always about you."

I struggle to find my voice. "Okay."

Owen keeps going, rubbing his palms on his jeans. "Raf wanted you to miss the interview you had lined up with the college scout on that Saturday. Because it was supposed to be his interview, right? He was supposed to be the guy moving on to bigger and better things, and you took his shot. So he got us all to Cray's on Friday night because he wanted us to…" He trails off and swallows. He won't look at me.

"What?" My voice sounds hoarse. "What were you going to do?"

"I don't know. Just lock you in there for the night, I

thought." He presses his knuckles to his eyes. "I'm so sorry, man. I don't know why I went along with it. It was supposed to be a prank, but it got out of hand."

I stare at him. Numb. "So you were setting me up? That's why you were all at Cray's?"

"I swear, it was just supposed to be a joke." He hesitates and finally looks at me straight. "But Raf was taking it too far. He was ready to come at you hard. If you had to fight back that night—"

"Come on, Owen." My voice gets louder, unleashed. "Don't go there. Don't start looking at me like I did it, like I *fought back*. I had no idea what was going on that night." I remember that Friday when my phone had buzzed with a text from Raf. He told me he had a message to pass on, something from my mom. And like the fool that I am, I believed him. Because I wanted to believe him.

I never expected this. Owen, Freddie, Tara…

I kick the edge of the coffee table in frustration. "This is my *life*. You were trying to sabotage the only shot I had?"

"I was never going to leave you in Cray's." Owen rakes his hands fast through his hair. "Freddie and Tara wouldn't have, either. It was just…"

"Raf," I finish for him. "Do the cops know about this plan you all had? Is that why they're focusing on me, because they think I *fought back*, too?"

"I don't know," he mutters. "I didn't tell the cops anything."

"Do you think Freddie or Tara would have told that Harrison Bridge guy about any of this?"

"I don't know." He sucks in his top lip. "Raf was in Freddie's ear, talking about how you needed to be taught a lesson."

I choke out an angry laugh. "Oh, right. Is this my lesson? Getting set up for murder?"

He closes his eyes. "I'm sorry."

"Did you take my phone that day?"

"No." I see the honesty in his expression when he looks me dead in the eyes. The conviction in his voice. I believe him.

"Do you know who did?"

He shakes his head.

"But it was there," I say. "Someone put my phone under the ledge."

He rubs his hands on his legs, dragging his palms over the denim in agitated motions.

"If I didn't put it there, and you say you didn't put it there, who did?" I answer my own question. "Freddie or Tara."

He holds my stare and bites his lip hard.

SAVANA

Saturday, November 19

A round of quick knocks shakes the French doors. I cross my bedroom and peel back the drapes. Jesse is standing on the deck, and dense rain clouds are looming in the distance, darkening the cove.

I twist the lock and open the door to a rush of salty air.

"Hey." He's breathing fast. "Can I come in?" His eyes look haunted, deep brown in the low light.

"Of course." I pull him into the room and close the door behind him. "What's wrong?"

He sits on the edge of my bed and musses his hair. "I just talked to Owen." He punctuates the sentence with another ragged breath.

I take a seat beside him, studying his tense expression.

His sneaker starts tapping on the floorboards. "Freddie and Tara," he says, and I almost jump in, wondering if he knows what I know, about their secret relationship. But then he says, "One of them is trying to pin this on me. It's got to be Tara, right?"

I shake my head in confusion. "Wait. Slow down. Explain."

"Owen told me that Raf and those guys were planning on locking me in Cray's that night. They wanted me to miss the college scout interview I had on Saturday." He's talking fast. His words are almost too quick for me to catch. "Then Raf died, and now one of them is setting me up to take the fall for his murder."

"What?"

"One of them is trying to pin it on me. Why else would my phone be under the ledge? Someone put it there. I've said that all along."

I close my eyes for a second. "I have to tell you something. Tara and Freddie have been hooking up. I saw them at the port yesterday, kissing."

He falters.

"I confronted Tara earlier and she admitted it," I add. "I was going to tell you tonight. It's been going on for a while."

The muscles in his jaw clench. "I knew it. I knew she was into him, but I never thought that he'd…" He swallows. "How long?"

"A couple of months." My gaze strays to the full-length mirror across the room. Our reflections are trapped inside the glass, sitting side by side on the bed. Jesse's broad shoulders are hunched forward, and his expression is torn. Pained.

Tara's cryptic statement about Freddie suspecting Jesse creeps to the forefront of my mind. Of course, it's in her interest to throw Jesse under the bus. She could be covering her own tracks, or Freddie's.

Jesse drops his head into his hands. "So they could be in on it together." He hesitates for a second. "But Freddie wouldn't do that to me, would he?"

I struggle to summon a response.

"He was going to lock me in Cray's," Jesse says, grimacing. "They all were. Owen, too. One of them killed Raf, and now they're pinning it on me." He falls back on the bed and stares up at the ceiling. "How is this real?"

I lie down beside him. His chest is rising and falling quickly, and every muscle seems tensed and strained.

"Are you okay?" I whisper.

"No," he murmurs. He inclines his head toward me, his eyes meeting mine. "This is messed up. All of it."

I fold my hand around his, and we fall silent, lost in our own private thoughts. We stay quiet, just letting our fingers interlace while our minds drift. His hand feels strong around mine, and his clothes smell faintly of sand and sports spray, familiar to my senses. I rest my head against his shoulder.

The closeness between us makes me feel safer, like we can take on anything as long as we're together. Like nothing can touch us.

"Everything will be okay," I whisper.

He almost smiles. "You think?"

I nod, managing a smile back.

And then my heart starts beating a little faster, accelerated by the sensation of being close to him. Before I can think it through, my lips have brushed his. His breathing quickens in response, and he kisses me back.

Just for a moment the world seems to pause for us. I fall into the feeling of his lips on mine, the warmth of his skin, and his touch as his arm folds around me, drawing me closer.

His heart beats fast, and I feel it. I feel everything.

When we part, he gently brushes a strand of my hair from my cheekbone. His mouth twitches with a smile—the kind of smile I've never seen on him before, intimate and private, and it makes my heart flutter all the more.

I try to find my voice. "That was…"

"Yeah," he finishes with a small laugh. "It was." Then after a pause, he murmurs, "So you think we're going to be okay, huh?"

I answer with a nod.

"I'm starting to believe you."

We fall quiet for a moment, and I rest my head in the groove of his shoulder.

"We can get through this," I say softly. "Anyway, we might be jumping to conclusions. Freddie and Tara might have nothing to do with Raf's murder. There's still the person caught on security footage. So far they're the only one unaccounted for. Clearly, they've got something to hide."

His gaze flits over the ceiling, never settling on one spot for too long. "No," he says in a distant voice. "It wasn't him."

I pause, and it takes me a second to figure out what's wrong with that sentence. I untangle myself from him and sit upright. "It wasn't him?" I echo.

I see it in the way his lips part, and how his eyes widen the smallest fraction.

"Who's *him*?"

He gropes for words, sitting up and looking anywhere but at me.

"Oh, my God." A sharp breath escapes me, and I stand from the bed. "You know who the other person is?"

He winces as he stands along with me.

"Who is it?"

He stares into my eyes, breathing slowly.

I press my hand to my racing heart. "Why aren't you answering? Who is it?"

But he doesn't respond.

"I can't believe this," I murmur, staring at him in disbelief. "You're not going to tell me." The realization makes my skin prickle. Suddenly, I feel sick to my stomach. "We're supposed to be in this together." The words limp from my lips. "We're supposed to trust each other."

When he speaks, his voice sounds weak. "I'm sorry."

I breathe out a laugh.

There's a beat of silence, a cold stillness that divides us. There's nothing comfortable about it. Nothing safe.

A painful lump forms in my throat. "I think you should leave."

I can't bring myself to look at him, but I feel a burst of icy air leak into the room as the door clicks shut behind him.

JESSE

Saturday, November 19

I step into my house through the back way. My hands are shaking.

Standing in the dark kitchen, I lean against the door and breathe slowly, wishing I could take that one slipup back. Wishing I could rewind.

Him? I rap my skull.

Footsteps thud on the staircase.

The hallway door swings open.

"Where...were...you?" Cody's words are separated by quick, shallow breaths. He's standing in the doorway beneath the dim hallway light. It looks like he's struggling to breathe, his mouth gaping as he tugs at his collar.

I take a step toward him. "Whoa. Are you okay?"

"I thought..." Another fractured breath, like he can't get the air into his lungs. "You'd...gone."

He lets out a strange, wheezing sound.

"What do you need?" I ask. "A paper bag or something?"

I start rooting through the kitchen cabinets and drawers. "Where are all the damn paper bags in this place?" I'm tearing through cupboards, knocking over cereal boxes and cans.

Cody doubles over, sucking in loud lungfuls of air.

"Dad!" I shout.

Cody sinks down to the floor and drops his head into his hands. I stumble across the kitchen to get to him.

"You're okay," I tell him, crouching before him. "Just try to breathe. Do you want me to call an ambulance?"

"I…thought…you'd gone." The words are just gasps, barely coherent. But I hear them.

I grip his shoulder hard. "I'm here," I tell him. "I'm not going anywhere."

"I thought you'd gone."

"I'm not. I won't."

He nods, breathing. Breathing. Breathing. Breathing.

"Your phone…was off." His voice is still strangled, but the words are coming out clearer now. "I thought you'd gone."

I swallow. My throat feels like it's on fire. "I'm not going anywhere. I promise you, okay?"

He pulls the collar of his T-shirt up over his face. "They know…was me." I can barely decipher his words through his choked voice and the material of his T-shirt. But I get it.

"No one knows it was you, Cody."

"You won't tell anyone?"

"Cody." I grip his shoulder tighter and press my head against his. "Come on. You're my brother. I'll never tell anyone."

He lowers his T-shirt and rubs his hands roughly over his eyes.

Here, in the weak light cast from the hallway, I stare at the dull kitchen walls and overturned cupboards. I've sat in this spot countless times before, but only when I was younger. Back when we used to build forts out of chairs and sheets, using whatever rough methods we could come up with to stop the fort from collapsing on us, because beneath the covering, we could hide out like two princes in a castle. Pretending not to hear our parents spit hate at each other. Pretending not to hear our dad stumble around upstairs. Pretending not to care about anything.

Now we're still us; it's still just the two of us. We're still pretending. But we're bigger. *I'm* bigger, and stronger. And I'm going to do whatever it takes to stop our fort from falling.

JESSE

Saturday, November 19

It's a while before Cody's voice sounds normal again. I feel like we've been here forever, sitting on the kitchen floor, stuck in the muted light. Dad isn't here—at least, I haven't heard his footsteps in the house. It's just us.

"I shouldn't have followed you to Cray's that night." Cody tugs absently at the lace on his sneaker. "But I knew you were going to meet him, and I wanted to be there."

My stare becomes lost in the dark night framed by the kitchen window.

"Were you going there to kill Raf?" he asks.

A laugh escapes me. "No, Cody. No. I was just going to talk to him."

"About what?"

I cast him a sideways glance. "Mom. He told me he had a message from her."

Cody rubs his damp eyes with his sleeve. "You think he was lying?"

"Yeah," I grunt. "I do now."

The muscles in Cody's jaw twitch. "Do you think she stayed in contact with them after she left?"

"I don't know."

"Do you think we'll ever hear from her again?"

"I don't know," I answer honestly. "Maybe someday."

A moment of silence follows my words, and it feels almost reverent, as though we're releasing a part of ourselves, because we figure we have to.

Cody takes a deep breath. "Donna might have told the police she saw me running home that night."

"No." I lock my hands. "Donna's not like that. She's a straight shooter. She'd tell us if she was going to the cops. Besides, she asked me not to tell Savana about it."

The memory still makes me cold. The flashback of showing up at the Carusos' house on that Saturday morning after. I'd spent the night in a jail cell, separated from the others and confused as hell. At first, I thought the cops had pulled us in for trespassing on private property, but when they took my fingerprints and wouldn't let me out until my dad showed up the following morning, I knew something big had gone down. I should have figured. The broken window, and no sign of Raf. When they let me out, all I could think was, I have to get to Savana.

But when I came by her house that Saturday, Donna intercepted and told me Savana wasn't home.

I knew she was lying; she didn't try too hard to disguise it. Then she told me she'd seen Cody, and suggested I let my dad know.

"Do you trust her?" Cody's voice brings me back to the present. I blink and the memory slips away. I'm back in the kitchen, sitting on the floor with my shoulder pressed against his.

"Who, Donna?" I ask. "Yeah. I trust her."

"But what if she thinks I was the one who pushed Raf?"

"She doesn't," I tell him. "She knows us better than that. She's not going to the police about the security camera stuff, and even if she does, the only evidence against you is that you were seen running home right after the incident was reported."

"The security footage *is* evidence." He scrubs his hands through his scruffy hair. "Maybe I should come forward and say it was me before I'm identified. That would look better, right?"

I rub the back of my neck. "No. Sooner or later, the truth is going to come out, and then it won't matter if you were there or not."

"And if it doesn't? If I get identified, it'll look so bad. Cops are going to think it was me. Especially after the brick thing."

"It won't come to that."

"But what if it does?" he rasps.

"Then I'll come forward and say I did it. I pushed Raf. With my phone under the ledge, and my history with Raf… even I'm starting to wonder if it was me."

"You can't do that," he argues. "I won't let you do that."

I kick his leg and grin. "You're not the boss. I'm the boss."

His eyes come to me. He isn't smiling.

"I'll figure something out." My words waver.

Cody pauses for a moment. He wants to speak, though. I can tell by the way he's tugging at his laces, pulling them tighter, then loosening them again.

"Go on," I say.

"You know what you told me about Savana," he murmurs. "About the guy that tried to…"

"Yeah."

"It's been going around school."

"I know."

"It was Raf?"

I stare at the floorboards. "Yeah."

He inhales through his teeth. "You must have really hated him for that."

"Yeah," I answer. "I did."

SAVANA

Sunday, November 20

I meet Corinne on the boardwalk. We sit on a bench and watch the tide come in, nursing warm take-out coffees from Miller's.

"So," she says, glancing at me. "Are you ever going to tell me why you're acting so weird today?"

I summon a smile. "I'm a suspect in a murder case. Isn't that enough of a reason to act weird?"

Her eyes stay on me, waiting.

I comb my fingers through my hair. The wind has tangled the strands, endlessly tossing them from side to side. "I kissed Jesse," I say at last.

She sucks in a breath.

"And then I had a huge fight with him right after. I guess it's bothering me more than I want to admit."

I can feel Corinne's gaze lingering on me as I stare out at the silver tide. There are people on the beach, a middle-aged couple walking their collie. The dog is bounding along the shore-line, leaving a snaking trail of paw prints in the damp sand.

"I'm just…" I fumble over my words. Once I tell Corinne that Jesse knows who the sixth suspect is, that's it. I'll be betraying him and whoever he's protecting. Because that's what this is—he's protecting someone he cares about. It's the only logical explanation as to why he'd keep their identity a secret. I'm pretty sure I can guess *who* he's protecting, too.

"What?" Corinne presses.

I turn to face her. "Do you think I'm delusional for defending Jesse when everyone else thinks he's guilty?"

She arches a finely shaped eyebrow. "Somewhat, yes."

"Have I been totally naive?" My question is just a murmur in the whistling wind.

"Not totally," she says, nudging my arm. "For the record, I don't *totally* think Jesse's guilty, either."

"You don't?"

She shrugs. "Well, there were four other people at Cray's that night, too. Segue, I do not trust Tara Kowalski. Never have, never will." She folds her arms. "Sorry, I know she's your new bestie and all—"

"She's not." I lean my shoulder against Corinne's. "I'm sorry if I made you feel that way. For the record, I think you're right not to trust her."

Corinne takes a small sip from her take-out cup. "I never doubted my rightness."

"But would Tara push Raf through a window? Is that even feasible? Tara's, what, five feet nothing and one hundred pounds soaking wet? Versus Raf's two hundred pounds of pure muscle? Is it even physically possible for Tara to overpower Raf enough to break a window?"

"Yeah, it's possible." Corinne blows on her coffee and the bitter steam drifts to me. "It's totally possible. If she was determined enough."

"And then there's Freddie," I say. "And Owen, and Jesse. Purely based off the biology and physics of their size and strength, they're a lot more plausible, right?"

"Or this other person," Corinne counters. "The unidentified person caught on camera."

My gaze wanders back to the shoreline, where the wind is whipping at the water. "So who's lying?"

"My guess," Corinne murmurs. "Everyone."

Farther down the beach, the collie gives way to a wailing howl.

TARA:
We need to talk. Can you meet me today?

TARA:
Please respond, Savana. You need to know the truth about Jesse.

SAVANA:
I don't want to hear this right now, Tara. My head's all over the place.

TARA:
Meet me at Miller's at four o'clock today.

SAVANA:
I can't.

TARA:
Savana. Just come. Please.

SAVANA

Sunday, November 20

The day is creeping closer and closer to four o'clock, and I still haven't decided if I'm going to meet Tara. I don't think I want to hear what she has to say.

The front doorbell chimes through the house.

From my room, I hear Mom's footsteps descending the staircase, and I freeze.

Considering everything that's gone on with Jesse and Tara this weekend, my mind is a jumble of thoughts, and I'm not ready to confront either one of them right now. I'm seconds away from barricading myself in my room when the faint sound of Mom's voice reaches me from the hallway.

"Oh." I hear the surprise in her tone. "Cody."

Cody? Of all the people I was nervously anticipating, I certainly wasn't expecting Cody.

I venture out of my room to join Mom at the door. Cody's standing on the front porch. His umber-toned hair is pushed to one side and falling over his brow.

His eyes skate over me.

"Can I talk to you both?" He's mumbling, his gaze jumping between Mom and me. "About what happened."

Mom glances at me before responding. "Okay," she says slowly. Hesitantly, *very* hesitantly, she steps aside and gestures for him to come in. "Perhaps we should sit down for this." There's a lilt to her voice, a hidden question that he seems to understand because he swallows and nods.

Raf. His name flashes through my mind. This is about Raf. My pulse starts to quicken.

Cody presses his knuckles to his mouth as Mom leads us to the kitchen. He takes a seat at the island and fans his hands over the countertop.

There's tension in Mom's expression as she takes a seat opposite Cody; her brow is pinched. I stay standing, bracing myself.

"Go ahead," Mom says to him. She glances at me again, and her mouth sets into a tight line.

"Uh…" He scratches the back of his neck, then starts tapping the countertop, drumming his fingers on the granite. "The person caught on security footage…" He pauses and fixes me with a grim stare. "It was probably me."

I take a slow breath. "Yeah. I figured."

He turns his attention to Mom. "I'm sorry I haven't come to talk to you before now. I didn't know what you were thinking."

She nods as though this all makes sense to her.

"When you saw me that night," he says, and my eyebrows shoot up. "I know I looked sketchy as hell. When Jesse found me at Cray's, he told me to run. But I didn't do anything to Raf. I didn't even know what had happened until the next day."

I hold up my palms. "Excuse me, rewind. Mom? You saw Cody that night? When?"

She gives way to a sigh. "Right after you called me from the port. I was leaving to go get you, and I saw Cody running home." She folds her hands on the countertop. "I'm not accusing you of anything, Cody," she says gently. "I know you're a good kid."

"I had nothing to do with what happened to Raf," he says.

"I never thought you did. The police, however, may think otherwise. Given the circumstances."

Cody lowers his gaze.

I stare at him, shocked into silence. My focus moves to Mom.

She clears her throat, flustered by my prying gaze. "We don't need to say any more about it," she says, standing. "As far as I'm concerned, I didn't see anything." She glances meaningfully at me. "This conversation never happened. Did it, Savana?"

They both turn to me, waiting for my answer.

"What conversation?"

Cody drags his hands through his messy hair. "Thank you," he says softly.

"Thank you for coming over here," Mom adds. "I appreciate this wasn't easy for you."

He purses his lips and says nothing.

"One more thing while you're here…" Mom crosses the kitchen and roots around in one of the drawers. She returns to the island and discreetly hands Cody a slip of paper. It looks like a pamphlet, and I catch the *AA* logo branded on the front page. *Alcoholics Anonymous.* "If you need support for your dad." Her voice is hushed, and I take that as my cue to avert my gaze. "Remember, I'm only next door."

Cody takes the pamphlet and stuffs it into his jacket pocket. "Thanks," he says, standing from his seat. His face looks flushed.

Mom nods.

He heads for the hallway, and I trail behind him, frankly stunned from his visit. We leave Mom in the kitchen as we begin for the front door.

Without Mom around, Cody lowers his voice to address only me. "I'm sorry about what happened to you, Savana," he says. "What Raf did."

I muster a smile, but I imagine it looks more like a grimace. "Yeah. Thanks."

"Sorry it wasn't me who pushed him." His mouth quirks at the corner.

"Raf didn't deserve what happened to him," I answer quietly.

He shrugs and hovers in the open doorway with his hand resting on the frame. "You know Jesse only lied to you because I begged him to. He cares about you a lot."

I draw in a deep breath. "I care about him, too." A knot tightens in my stomach when I think about Tara's messages, and her suggestive remarks about how Jesse can't be trusted. Whatever she's got to say, I don't want to hear it. I can make up my own mind on who I can and can't trust.

"He never wanted to lie to you." Cody's voice brings me back.

"I understand," I tell him. "You two look out for each other."

"Yeah." Cody presses his fist to his heart. "Always. He's my brother."

As the door closes behind him, I stand in the hallway for a minute, contemplating the silence.

Four o'clock keeps edging closer.

But I don't want to hear it. I don't want to hear any more lies.

Savana. Just come.

Just come.

A fractured breath escapes me.

"Oh, my God," I whisper into the empty hallway.

SAVANA

Sunday, November 20

I run along the boardwalk, racing to get to Miller's for four o'clock. A harsh wind skims the ocean and steals the breath from my lungs.

Buried way down in my text messages, there's a thread from Jesse's old number. Right at the top of the thread is the conversation I had with him on the night of Raf's murder. Only, it wasn't him I was talking to. It was someone who wanted me to *think* it was him.

Just come.

That's what they'd said. But they're not Jesse's words, they're *hers*.

I slow my pace as I round the corner to Miller's. Tara's already there. I can see her through the window, seated at her usual booth. There's a half-full latte on the table, and her gaze is dipped as she taps on her phone. My heart is galloping in fear of who she is and what she might be capable of, but we're in broad daylight, in a public place, and I need answers.

I pause at the window, catching my breath. My own image is faintly reflected in the tall windowpane. The breeze whips strands of hair across my face.

I know I have to do this. I have to go in there and confront her. And I'm going to have to lie if I want the truth.

Miller's door thumps shut behind me.

My heart feels like it's beating right out of my chest as I cross the diner.

"Hey," Tara says without looking up from her phone. "I'm so glad you came." She raises a manicured finger, as if to say *hold on*.

So I do. I wait, breathing steadily.

When she finally glances up, her face falls. "Wow. You look…"

I lock eyes with her. "Why did you text me from Jesse's phone on the night Raf died, asking me to come to Cray's?"

Suddenly, she's rigid, bolts upright. Her phone slips from her hand and hits the table with a clatter.

"What?" She lowers her voice. "I didn't." Her pale blue eyes dart across the restaurant, moving quickly from left to right.

If only her expression didn't look so guilty, I might have actually believed her. Almost.

"I know it was you. The location." I try not to stammer when I say it because I don't want her to see that I'm bluffing.

"Location?" Her sugary voice sounds raspy, and she grips the edge of the table. "What do you mean?"

"I installed an app on my phone that shows where texts and calls were made from, and those messages were sent from your house. And I know for a fact that Jesse wasn't at your house that night." I breathe evenly, just praying she can't hear the lie in my voice.

Her lips part.

I keep going. "You stole Jesse's phone and you texted me pretending to be him, asking me to come to Cray's on the night Raf was killed."

"Shh," she hisses. "Savana, *please*. There are people here."

I don't look around to see if anyone's watching. I only look at her. I need her to say it, to prove that my theory is right.

"Why did you send me that message, Tara?"

She clutches her chest. "Oh, my God, do the police know?" Her words are shrill with fear. Genuine fear. "Did the police get the location, too?"

"It was you, wasn't it?" I take a step back from her. "You pushed Raf?"

Tears begin to stream down her cheeks, leaving charcoal mascara tracks in their wake. "No." She chokes out a sob. "I swear, I didn't."

"But you texted me?"

She swipes at her tears. "Yes, okay. But I didn't..." She presses her fingers to her mouth and her eyes stray across the diner. "I didn't push Raf."

"I don't believe you," I challenge, and I turn to leave. A couple of twentysomethings seated at a table near us quickly avert their stares.

"Savana, wait!" Tara springs to her feet, fumbling to get out from the booth. "This isn't how it looks."

She follows me outside and suddenly we're on the cold street, striding toward the coastline.

"Raf told me to take Jesse's phone on Friday." She rakes a hand through her long hair as the wind flurries the strands. "He made me do it!"

I stop walking and spin around to face her. "Oh, Raf *made* you text me to come to Cray's to watch him die."

She grabs my arms, tugging at my sleeves. "No. Listen to me. Raf told me to take Jesse's phone during their football practice on Friday. We were going to lock Jesse in Cray's, and Raf didn't want him to be able to call for help."

I shake myself free from her.

"Can we just talk, please? Privately." She nods toward the beach below, a sandbank sloping away from the people meandering along the boardwalk. "I'll explain everything, I promise. Please."

We venture down to the beach, heading for the arcs of the pier structure. The sand is damp from where the tide has spilled over the shoreline, and our footprints leave a trail.

A shiver moves over me when I realize that she's leading me to the spot where I overheard her hushed argument with Raf. I remember the sound of the gulls shrieking above them as he gripped her arm and hissed into her ear.

I halt in the shadow of the pier. "This is far enough. Talk." We might be out of earshot, but we're not out of sight of the busy pier. That's good; I need that security.

"Okay," she says in an unsteady voice. "Raf wanted to lock Jesse in Cray's on Friday night." She catches her hair as the wind spirals it. "He tricked Jesse into showing up."

My stomach turns and I hug my arms around myself.

"It was just supposed to level things out," she adds quickly. "Payback for everything Jesse did. The car accident, getting Freddie busted with drugs, humiliating Raf—"

"Unbelievable," I snap. "You guys are warped."

"I didn't want to do it! Which is why I texted you that evening, pretending to be Jesse. I'd already taken his phone.

I thought if you showed up later, then you could let him out and get help if he was really hurt. I didn't know how far Raf was going to take this. I was trying to do the right thing, Savana. Surely, you see that?"

I shake my head in disbelief. "You could have just let him out yourself! You could have given him his phone back!"

"How?" she cries. "Do you honestly think Raf would have let me get away with something like that? He was seeing red with this."

"So then what? After Raf fell, you planted Jesse's phone at the window to make it look like he killed Raf? Or did you drop it when you killed him yourself?"

Her pale eyes glisten and fresh tears roll down her face. "I didn't kill Raf. Yeah, I tossed Jesse's phone when I realized Raf had fallen through the window. But I only did that because I was scared. I was so scared."

"*You* were scared?" My voice rises. "You think I wasn't scared being hounded by anonymous messages after Raf died?"

She reaches out to catch my hand. "No," she says. "The other messages you've been getting, I promise they're not from me. I only sent the messages from Jesse's phone on that Friday night, asking you to come to Cray's. That's it, I promise." She looks down, avoiding my gaze.

I slip my hand free from her cold grasp. There's more. I know there's more; I can feel it.

My eyes wander over the stilts of the pier, where the echoes of their argument still linger.

No. You've got this all wrong...

That was the night someone showed up at my house wearing

a mask. She thought I had something going on with Raf. *Keep your friends close, and your enemies closer.* Those were her words.

"Oh, my God," I murmur. "You came to my house in a mask."

She draws in a shaky breath. "It was just a dare," she says, stumbling over her words. "Raf dared me to do it. Just as a joke."

"It was a *sick* joke. I was terrified."

She claps her hand to her mouth. "I'm sorry. I didn't mean anything by it."

"Did you come back to my house again after that?" My thoughts jump to the hooded figure I caught staring into my bedroom. I'm still haunted by the memory. I still triple-check the lock on my door at night, just in case.

"Only once or twice," she admits quietly. "I didn't mean to scare you. Just when Raf wasn't picking up my calls or texts, I wanted to make sure he wasn't with you."

"You're unbelievable."

She throws up her hands. "I was a mess, Savana. Because of what I told you, about how he used to talk about you sometimes."

I grit my teeth at the thought. "Were you spying on Jesse's house, too? On the night of the charity football game, I saw someone looking in through his window."

She pauses and frowns. "No." She takes a small breath. "But Raf… They went to Cray's that night, and Raf didn't invite me. When I started to get close to the guys, Raf stopped inviting me to hang out. Freddie and I figured out what he was doing. Raf would tell me that the guys didn't want me there, and he'd tell them that I was busy with Maddie and Anaya, but I wasn't. I only went to Jesse's house that night to see if they were there, but then I saw Mike and Jesse's mom together through the window, so I left."

"Wait, so you knew about the affair?"

"I knew about Raf's dad and Jesse's mom," she says. "It had been going on for ages. Raf knew way before it came out."

"Of course he did," I mutter. My pulse is racing, but I gather myself and stare into her glassy eyes. "What happened that night at Cray's, Tara?"

She lets out a shattered cry. "It wasn't me. That's why I wanted to meet today. You need to hear the truth. And now that I've told you everything, I hope you'll trust that I'm being honest about this, too." She stands taller in the shadow of the pier. When she speaks again, her words come out calmly. Unnervingly calmly. "I know who killed Raf."

A wave breaks on the shore and sweeps across the sand. The grains collapse beneath our feet and we sink into the damp ground.

I stare into her eyes, breathing fast.

"It was Jesse," she says. "I saw him do it."

SAVANA

Sunday, November 20

I leave Tara alone on the beach and run the whole way home—my heart feels as though it's about to burst from my chest by the time I reach the cove. I climb onto the Melos' back porch and bang on their kitchen door.

The door rattles open.

I let out a breath at the sight of Jesse. I don't know what I would have done if it was his dad or Cody standing before me. A ripple of wind moves through his hair, stirring the short strands.

"Hey," he murmurs. "I'm glad you came over. I'm so sorry about last night."

The fight we had in my room last night feels like some distant memory. It feels like something that happened a lifetime ago, and it doesn't matter anymore, because in this lifetime everything just got a whole lot worse.

His eyes turn coppery in the weak winter sunlight. He sighs

and his breath fogs the air. "There was so much I wanted to tell you, but Cody—"

"Tara was the one who texted me from your phone that night." My words sound shaky, and I can tell by the change in his breathing that this has caught him off guard. "You were right. She's trying to set you up."

He links his hands behind his head and closes his eyes.

"She's saying you did it," I carry on. "She's saying she saw you push Raf."

His focus jumps to me. "No," he says. "No. That's not true. She's lying." He's breathing fast. Panting. "You don't believe her, do you?"

"No," I whisper. I almost did, for a second. But her words were too controlled, too rehearsed. Besides, I know Jesse better than that. The police might not, but I do.

I pull him closer and press my lips to his. I don't know if it's because I'm scared, or he's scared, or because I just want him to know that I trust him.

He hesitates, falters. But then he kisses me back.

My heart beats fast against his and my head spins from the rush of closeness. His lips on mine, and the intimacy between us as his arms lock around me.

"You're not taking the fall for this," I murmur.

He doesn't respond. He kisses me again, and just for a moment we can believe that everything is okay. Everything will be okay.

Because we're in it together.

JESSE

Sunday, November 20

I lean against the kitchen counter with my cell pressed to my ear, listening to the dull ringing. Savana is seated at the table, her eyes following me as she nervously twists her bracelet.

"Hey." Owen answers.

"Tara's saying I killed Raf." I jump straight in. "She's saying she saw me do it."

I hear him exhale down the line.

I drum my fist on the edge of the counter. "Why?" The word comes out in a rasp. "She's lying. Does she really hate me that much?"

"I... Because of this... Freddie?"

I press my hand over my other ear, trying to sew together his fractured words as the signal starts to waver.

"You think Freddie knows?" Something twists in my gut. Freddie is my friend; he wouldn't let her do this to me. He wouldn't let her lie like this.

"I don't know...for... Freddie...like he has to rescue her?"

The line breaks, splintering his voice. I push through the kitchen door and move outside onto the deck. Cold air envelops me as I lean on the railing, looking out over the gray ocean.

Savana steps up behind me and rests her hand on my arm as I try to catch the fragmented pieces of Owen's sentences.

"...in their heads, maybe... You and Savana lying about Raf—"

"Raf was the liar." I can't hold back the bite in my voice; I don't even try to. "He *did* make a move on Savana, and she had to fight him off."

Her fingers tighten on my arm. I glance at her, reassuring her with a look. A nod. Just something to let her know that I'm here with her.

"I know Raf was lying," Owen says across the line. "He admitted it."

My brow furrows. "He admitted it?"

"Yeah, right before he died." The signal cracks and a long stretch of silence follows. The line breaks and the call ends.

My screen fades to black. Owen's gone. All I can hear now is the howl of wind and the *shh-shh* of the tide.

I stare out at the ocean as whitecaps rear and shatter on the sand.

JESSE:

Do you know what Tara is saying about me?

                                          FREDDIE:

Yeah. She says she saw you.

JESSE:

She's lying.

                                          FREDDIE:

I don't know. I'm sorry.

JESSE:

What does that mean? Do you believe her or me?

                                          FREDDIE:

Your phone was under the window ledge.

JESSE:

Because Tara took it and put it there.

                                          FREDDIE:

She says she saw you push Raf.

JESSE:
She's lying. You don't have to save her anymore, Freddie. Raf's gone.

                              FREDDIE:
                              I'm sorry.

JESSE

Sunday, November 20

Savana and I are in my kitchen when we hear the doorbell ring.

My heart sinks. Don't ask me how I know who's waiting on the stoop; it's just a gut feeling. Instinct.

I think Savana knows, too. She takes a breath and reaches across the table. Her hand locks with mine.

We fall quiet, listening to my dad's footsteps coming down the stairs. I was right, of course—he was fine. He always turns back up. Then we hear the mumbled voices drifting from the front porch.

My dad. Another guy. A woman.

"I'd better go," I murmur to Savana.

My chair scrapes as I stand.

She stands, too, and she hugs me.

So I kiss her. Once. Twice.

"I'm going to run," I declare.

She's shaking, but she nods.

I kiss her again. "Tell Cody I'm sorry." And then I leave.

Beyond the back door, night has fallen, and the streetlamps are lit. At the front of the house there's a cop car parked along the curb.

Then a voice, a woman's voice, drifting out into the night from the front stoop. She's talking to my dad, and she says my name. Her words sound woolly, like I'm underwater and nothing can reach me. But hidden in the shadows, I hear it: *We're arresting your son under suspicion of the murder of Rafael Lombardi.*

SAVANA

Sunday, November 20

My heart's pounding as I flip open my laptop and start a new Google search.

This can't be happening. I won't let this happen.

My hands are trembling as I type fast on the keyboard.

I keep thinking over Cody's words when he stood on my doorstep with his hand pressed to his heart. *He's my brother.*

And Owen's words, broken by the patchy phone call. *I know Raf was lying.*

There's a court case I want to look into, a memory that has been lost in the furthest corners of my mind.

The search results spill down the page and my eyes rove over the summary text.

I recognize the people in the pictures—a guy and a girl. I recognize them from school, but they look older in these images. It's been a while since I last saw either of them.

He has a beard now, and his fair hair is longer than I remember it. She looks pretty much the same, but her dark brown curls have been highlighted and makeup accentuates her high cheekbones and full lips.

The court case was supposed to be over nothing; it was just *lies. Lying, as usual.* That's what I was told.

But this wasn't nothing.

My eyes move fast over the text, poring over the detailed write-up documenting the court trial.

The accusation.

The evidence.

The verdict.

SAVANA:
You and I need to talk.

UNKNOWN NUMBER:
I'm listening.

SAVANA:
I know about the abuse case. Meet me.

UNKNOWN NUMBER:
Cray's. Alone. Half an hour.

SAVANA

Sunday, November 20

It's late. Too late. It's already too dark to be at the port.

My pulse is racing with every step I take.

I could have called the police, and maybe I should have. But if I did and he saw them, then he'd never talk. He'd sit back and let Jesse take the fall, just like he's been doing all along.

But I've figured him out; I know I have. I just need him to trust me enough to give me proof.

I head for Cray's, a looming silhouette in the darkness. Beyond the seawall, the moonlight reflects off the thick black ocean, and an agitated breeze ripples the water.

I duck beneath the police tape and the iron door closes behind me with a resounding thud.

My skin prickles as I forge a path through the dark building and up the metal steps, because I know where he'll be.

My breath hitches when I see him standing at the shattered window, staring out into the night.

"Hi, Owen."

He turns slowly, and a chill runs down my spine.

Run, I tell myself. *Run.* This is all the proof I need—he's here, so I know he's the person behind the anonymous messages. Maybe that's enough to convince the police of his involvement.

But my legs won't budge.

"You wanted to talk." His attention returns to the night sky.

I stand, frozen, trying to get a handle on my racing thoughts.

"Come on," he says. "You brought me here to talk, so let's talk already."

I swallow my fear. "Police came to Jesse's house to arrest him."

"Sucks that he did it."

"He didn't do it. You did."

Owen stares into the darkness. I can hear the tide slapping at the seawall below as I edge farther into the room. He's close—too close. But I can't back out now.

His jacket rustles as he shifts, and his eyes glide over me.

I summon my voice. "What were all those messages about, Owen? What, you wanted to get caught?"

He laughs faintly.

"Why the burner phone?" I press.

"I've been using it for a while," he supplies. "It's the only way my parents can't keep track of me. They didn't like me talking to Raf. Our families don't get on so good anymore."

Countless questions race through my mind as I face him. "You said Jesse was a murderer." My voice haunts the cavernous room.

"No, I didn't. I just said he'd get locked up for it. And he will."

"You said he was a liar. But he isn't."

"Jesse *did* lie. He lied to you about Cody being there that night," Owen says, turning suddenly to face me. "Do you know about that? I saw Cody at Cray's."

"Yes," I whisper. "I know about Cody. I know about your brother, too." When he doesn't respond, I add, "I read about the details of his case. It sounds awful. I'm sure that was really hard for you and your family."

The wind groans, and he inhales sharply through his teeth.

I shrink back, half expecting him to lunge at me. My eyes aren't working fast enough in the darkness. The desolation of the port aches with loneliness, and we're invisible here, swallowed by the warehouse. Back where it all began, with shards of glass still covering the floor.

This is the spot where Owen pushed Raf, and Raf fell violently, tragically, to his death.

Run.

"I didn't believe Grant," Owen murmurs, his voice lost somewhere.

I take a small breath. "You believe him now, though, right? He won the court case against Lisa. No matter what's gone down, if there was ever anything that made me want to keep a close eye on Cody..."

"Yeah." His thumbs move, twitching. "He won the case. Still didn't believe him, though. Even though the judge called it *incontestable evidence*." His eyes meet mine and the wind sails through the open window, hissing around us, whispering. "Did you see her picture? Lisa's?"

I nod, catching my spiraling hair and holding it tightly.

"Did you see the pictures the court used as evidence, too?" he asks. "They're online. All these marks on Grant's back, like burns?"

My voice catches. "I saw."

"She did all that, and she used to threaten she'd kill herself or come after my parents and me if he ever left her. Messed up, right?" He coughs, then wipes his eyes with his sleeve.

A painful lump forms in my throat. "I'm sorry, Owen."

"She's so pretty," he says in a strained voice. "Lisa Lombardi. Do you remember her from school? When my brother first started dating her, Freddie and I used to think she was straight-up fire." He grimaces, and the fringing shadows distort his features.

"I remember her," I tell him. Lisa was pretty, and popular, and commanded every room in the same way her brother, Raf, did.

"Grant and Lisa moved to Boston together right out of high school, and we didn't hear much from them for a while. Then when all this came out, all this stuff that went down between them, I just thought—no way." Owen shakes his head. "No way. Lisa's all petite and cute, and Grant's a big guy." His gaze wanders beyond the window, to the moorings where fishing boats are docked in the harbor, rocking and clunking with the tide. "I didn't believe Grant. I thought he was a liar. Told him so, too. Told him I don't have time for liars."

He echoes the words he used when I asked him about Grant's court case at Jesse's house. *Lying, as usual. I don't have time for that shit.*

The memory makes me shiver.

"I felt like I owed Raf," he says. "I owed him because my brother made up all this twisted shit about his sister. I mean, she's serving time over this."

I stare out at the black water. It's hard to tell where the ocean ends and the night sky begins. "Do the others know? Jesse never mentioned it."

He works his lip between his teeth. "They knew some stuff, but we all thought that it was Grant. That it was Grant who did this stuff to Lisa, poor Lisa. Because that was her story, and we believed it. The guys didn't push it, and Raf and I kept it between us, just played it down." He laughs grimly. "It was his hold over me."

"What happened in Cray's that night?" I whisper, catching his gaze.

He licks his lips. "Truth? I think Raf was going to kill Jesse that night. He'd been texting me on my burner a couple of days before, talking about payback, some plan he had to get even with Jesse. He was just supposed to mess with him, lock him in Cray's so he'd miss his interview. Settle the score for everything Jesse did."

I press my cold fingers into my palms. "What did Jesse ever do to you?"

"Nothing," he says, running his hands over his face. "But Raf had this over me. Grant's court case put our families through hell, and Raf never let me forget it. My brother's *lies* ruined their lives. *Their* lives." He barks out a strange laugh.

I shiver and hug my arms around myself. "Is this what you and Raf fought about that night at Cray's?"

"No." His eyebrows pull together. "We were just upstairs waiting for the others to arrive. Raf started getting really worked up, talking about what he was going to do to Jesse. Real twisted shit, you know? He had a knife in his pocket. I saw it." My stomach flips, and Owen drops his head into his hands as he relives the memory. "We said some things, Raf and me. He fired off about how Jesse had betrayed him, siding with you after what happened at my party. He said you wanted it that night. You were begging for it."

Something between humiliation and anger tightens my chest.

Owen lowers his hands and sucks in a breath. "When he said that, I realized that all the time Raf said you were lying, and that you came on to him, you *weren't* lying. He *did* make a pass at you."

"Yeah. He did." My thoughts stray to Owen's ambiguous text message from the burner phone. *I know the truth.*

"I saw him follow you upstairs that night," he says. "I saw, and I didn't do anything."

"It's okay," I murmur. We'd passed on the stairs on my way to the bathroom. We'd talked, laughed. Everything was fine.

"I saw what he was like with Tara, too, and I let it slide. The way he intimidated people, and..."

"He was hard to stand up to," I finish.

"When Raf admitted it," he says, "about what happened with you that night at my party, I went right back there, right back to the time Grant opened up to me. I was the only person he'd told about Lisa back then, before he went to the police. He confided in me, my brother. He opened up to me and I called him a liar. I told him to man up." He raps his fist on his skull as though he's trying to knock the memory from his mind.

"It's okay, Owen," I whisper.

His frustration keeps building as he slaps his head. I glance at the opaque sky and my heart goes into overdrive. We're too close to the broken window. We're too close to each other.

A strangled sob escapes him. "And then Raf said, *Don't be a little bitch like your brother. Man up.*" Owen's shoulders start to shake. "All I could think of was Grant, and his trial, and those evidence pictures. His face when I called him a liar. I just..."

"Pushed Raf." The wind steals my words.

Owen chokes out a broken sound.

"You know Tara's changed her story. She's saying she saw Jesse do it, and Freddie is backing her. He believes her. She's already gone to the police. But Tara didn't see anything, did she?"

He presses the heels of his hands to his eyes. "When Raf fell, I ran. Then I came back in when I heard everyone else coming. Tara and Freddie came from opposite directions, and Jesse came from downstairs." He glances at me and inhales the bitter cold air. "You know, she won't say it, but I think Tara thinks it was Freddie who pushed Raf, and I figure Freddie thinks it was her. Freddie shut me out when I tried to convince him it was Tara. He got really weird with me after that. They're covering for each other, and I'm just going along with it. Letting them each believe that it was the other one."

"Because that motivates them to set up Jesse?"

"The cops know about Grant and Lisa's case. That gives *me* motive. But Jesse has motive, too. He has a ton stacked against him. The fight he had with Raf in school, the stuff that went down with you, his mom's affair. And his phone was under the ledge—"

"But he didn't do it!" I snap. "Don't let Jesse take the fall for something he didn't do. For something *you* did."

Owen starts rocking back and forth in jerky motions. "It's murder. I'll be locked up for life."

"Not necessarily," I say quickly. "It was an accident."

He turns away from me, and I know I'm losing him. "You say you feel guilty about how you handled things with Grant. Can you imagine the burden of letting Jesse rot in a jail cell because you're too scared to admit the truth and face the consequences? Jesse's your friend."

He knots his fingers through his hair.

"You're a good person, Owen," I whisper urgently.

"No, I'm not, Savana." There's a catch in his voice. "But thanks for saying it."

We're silent for a moment as his words sink in—for both of us.

"And what if I go to the police?" I challenge. "What if I tell them everything you just told me?"

"It's too late. Tara's already given her statement, and there's enough evidence against Jesse to tie this up." He meets my eyes in the darkness. "No one's going to believe you because it'll seem like you're just looking out for your boy. Anyway, with college around the corner, would you really risk lying to the police about me? You know how this shit works. You could get locked up, too."

For the first time since I stepped into the room, I let my gaze stray away from him, back toward the door. "I texted them, Owen. They're here."

There's a beat of silence. One by one, Tara, Freddie, and Jesse walk into the room.

In the moonlight, I see Owen's face fall. His whole body seems to sag.

The trio is silent; silhouettes standing side by side.

It hits me, then. We're all here, together for the first time since that night. Only, I'm right here with them now. And I'm just hoping, praying, that Tara and Freddie have heard enough that will convince them to do the right thing.

JESSE

Saturday, December 17

Even weeks on, I still get flashbacks, remembering the way Owen's mouth fell open when we walked into the room, Tara, Freddie, and me. That haunted look on his face. *I'm sorry*, he kept saying. *I'm so sorry.*

I wasn't surprised to hear his admission from outside the room, with my back pressed to the cold wall. Something stood out during our last phone call, when Owen said he knew Savana hadn't been lying because Raf told him right before he died.

Right before he died. *Right before.*

But I stayed quiet. If Owen hadn't intervened with Raf when he did, I'd probably be dead by now.

Owen's trial starts next month, but his lawyer thinks he might be able to get a reduced sentence because of the circumstances of self-defense with Raf concealing a weapon.

Tara could be charged with obstruction of justice, but she's got a good lawyer. They're spinning it that she saw *someone* push Raf, and mistakenly thought it was me.

She was protecting Freddie; I get that.

I don't blame Freddie for protecting her, either. I see it now; Tara wasn't as strong as I thought she was. In so many ways she needed us to back her, to speak up, and we didn't. We didn't see it. Freddie did, though.

I know how it feels to want to defend the people you love. How that instinct burns through everything else. That fierce, innate instinct to move heaven and earth to protect them.

I did it for Cody.

I'd do it for Savana, too.

I see her now, hurrying across the school parking lot. "You're late," I tell her, but I'm smiling. A nervous, jittery smile.

"I know." She throws her arms around me, and her breath brushes my neck in the best way. "I'm sorry. I couldn't find my car keys. When do you have to go in?"

"Now."

It's Saturday, and the lot is nearly empty. Savana's car is parked next to my dad's truck, but he's gone into the school already to have a debrief with Coach Carson.

Dad's been doing well lately. Things have been better since Donna's stepped in; he listens to her. She's a sound voice in all our lives. Dad's been sober for three weeks now.

Savana's doing well, too. Grant Keaton decided to share his story, about what he went through with Lisa. He wants to bring awareness to any guys—or girls—out there who are going through stuff. He wants them to know that they can get help, that it gets better. Savana is writing his story, and Grant thinks she should use the piece for her college application. She wanted to write about personas and perceptions, and Grant's story is one that I never saw coming.

I think she should use the piece, too. His story should be read, and so should hers.

"Good luck." Savana's voice pulls me back, reminding me that I need to move. Her lips warm mine in the December air.

"Thanks," I murmur. "I need all the luck I can get."

"No, you don't." She smiles, then takes a step back to inspect me. She nods in approval.

I brush out a crease in my serious shirt. "Am I good?"

"You're good," she tells me.

"All right. I'd better go."

"I'll be waiting right here." She gives me one last kiss before I leave.

I walk toward the main entrance. My serious shoes crunch over the frost that glistens the path.

Inside, the corridor is quiet. My footsteps rebound off the wall of lockers as I make my way to the sports office.

I think of Raf, as I often do when I walk these halls. We spent a lot of time here, back when we were good. *I'm sorry,* I think, speaking to the echoes of him that still linger. *I'm sorry I hurt you, and I'm sorry you hurt other people.*

A man in a polo shirt is standing in the hallway, holding the office door open for me.

"I'm here for my interview," I tell him.

"Jesse Melo." He says my name in a way that makes me feel like I'm something. Someone. Then he smiles, shakes my hand, and says, "I've heard great things about you."

★ ★ ★ ★ ★

ACKNOWLEDGMENTS

The Last One to Fall will always have a special place in my heart as my companion during a global pandemic lockdown! As we all muddled through the strange new reality that we found ourselves in, I immersed myself in these characters and their world, and I daydreamed my way through. And that's how this book began...

When I think about what it took to get to the point of publication, there are so many people to thank.

My wonderful agent, Whitney Ross, who read the early drafts and helped me shape this idea into a fully grown book, advising me and cheering me on through every step.

Huge thanks to my editor at Inkyard Press, Connolly Bottum, for selecting this concept to be our second project together and guiding me with editorial magic to bring out the best in these characters. Two years on from our very first phone call, I still can't believe my luck that I get to be here, doing this!

To the fantastic Melissa Frain, who edited this book with such incredible insight and advice. I'm beyond grateful for your clever input and words of wisdom!

To the Inkyard/HarperCollins team, Bess, Brittany, Justine, Kathleen, and all the lovely people who worked on this book, thank you so much.

Thanks, always, to my incredible parents, Angela and Elio, who taught me what "true grit" is with kindness, patience, and unwavering support. I began this book when I was living in England and ended it back home in Wales. On to our next adventure!

Thanks to my husband, James, for always listening to my early-draft dilemmas and encouraging me to keep chipping away. And to my sweet daughter, Sophia, who graciously takes long enough naps to allow me to write this entire book while she dreams.

Thanks to my sister, Natalie, and brother-in-law, Rhodri, who have been boldly reading books way out of their genre and discussing whodunit!

Thanks to my family and friends for your constant support over the years: Lepores, Nelsons, Shirley, Team Carter, Roger, Trisha, Sue, Chimbwandas, Nan, Nikki, Louis, Becky, Lorna, Maureen, and Janet and the Marlows.

And, of course, big thanks to *you*, for choosing *The Last One to Fall*. I'm so glad you decided to take this book home with you, and I hope it kept you guessing!